WE SEE EVERYTHING

WILLIAM SUTCLIFFE

By the Same Author

WE SEE EVERYTHING

WILLIAM SUTCLIFFE

BLOOMSBURY

LONDON OXFORD NEW YORK NEW DELHI SYDNEY

BLOOMSBURY YA
Bloomsbury Publishing Plc
50 Bedford Square, London, WC1B 3DP, UK

BLOOMSBURY, BLOOMSBURY YA and the Diana logo
are trademarks of Bloomsbury Publishing Plc

First published in Great Britain in 2017 by Bloomsbury Publishing Plc
This paperback edition first published in Great Britain in 2018 by
Bloomsbury Publishing Plc

A catalogue record for this book is available from the British Library

ISBN: HB: 978-1-4088-9019-6; PB: 978-1-4088-9018-9;
TPB: 978-1-4088-9598-6; eBook: 978-1-4088-9017-2

2 4 6 8 10 9 7 5 3 1

Cover design by Levente Szabo, 2017
Typeset by RefineCatch Limited, Bungay, Suffolk

Printed and bound in Great Britain by CPI Group (UK) Ltd, Croydon CR0 4YY

MIX
Paper from
responsible sources
FSC® C020471

To find out more about our authors and books visit www.bloomsbury.com
and sign up for our newsletters

For Maggie

How can you sleep through this? How can you even think of sleeping? And yet, sleep deprivation will drive you mad in the end: the flares in the sky, the symphony of explosions, the roar of mortars, the whir of drones ... all this chaos will beat you, if you let it.

Atef Abu Saif, *The Drone Eats with Me: Diaries from a City Under Fire* (2015)

The City

I don't know if I can go through with it.

Pressed against a shrapnel-pitted wall, I stare out over the expanse of collapsed brick, crumpled tarmac, crushed concrete and twisted steel at the blackberry bush I spotted yesterday, a short distance into the exclusion zone.

I could run there in a few seconds. Anywhere else it would be so easy. But anywhere else, the berries would be gone.

A woman with grey-streaked hair, wearing a thick winter coat despite the bright September warmth, emerges from the apartment block behind me. She eyes me warily before shuffling away.

You don't see many people on the streets round here, at the outer edge of London. That's why I come, to look out at the exclusion zone and feel briefly alone, away from the noise and crowds of the city. I don't do it often – it's an eerie

1

place – but there's nowhere else to catch a breath of wind or look at anything further away than the other side of the street.

All night I've been turning over whether I dare risk going out into this lethal, barren area between me and the fence, wavering one way then the other, but even now, having returned with bags to collect the berries, I still can't decide.

Is it really likely that someone is watching this desolate space all the time, alert enough to spot one teenager breaking cover for a few seconds? If they did see me, would they really shoot?

I look beyond the wasteland towards the nearest watch-tower, attempting to gauge the distance, scanning for a flicker of movement or a flash of reflected sunlight, but the concrete and tinted glass give nothing away.

When my eyes fall back to the bush, picking out the glisten of dark, ripe berries, my mouth begins to water, and all the dire warnings I've heard about entering the exclusion zone evaporate from my mind. After a whole night of anxious wavering, my legs rather than my brain seem to make the final decision.

I crouch low and sprint, scurrying like a cockroach out into the troughs and hillocks of rubble, my knees almost knocking my chin with each step. As soon as I'm in motion the distance to the bush seems to stretch. I barely breathe, feeling utterly exposed, braced for the impact of a bullet I wouldn't even hear until it had ripped through my flesh.

While every cell of my body drives me on over the angular, dusty surface, a disembodied voice drifts through my skull, asking, *Why are you doing this? When did you get so dumb? Why would you risk your life for something so small?*

I fling myself to the ground in the shelter of the bush, cutting my knee on a jut of broken concrete, but I feel only a dull echo of pain, even as blood pearls through my jeans. I can barely believe I have come out here, into this vast flattened rectangle of land that surrounds what's left of London.

I lie still under the spiky foliage, willing the sickening judder of my heart to slow down, waiting for my mind to settle, then slowly raise my torso from the earth and look around. I don't know anyone else who has dared set foot in this forbidden place, but under cover, shielded from the border fence, I feel strangely detached from the reality of where I am, as if the boy who is out here, under this bush, cannot actually be me. Even though I know I could be killed, a vague sensation of immunity, almost of immortality, closes over me. This feeling, of being present but absent, in the moment but outside it, of being someone other than myself, reminds me of being lost in a video game.

In this city, death seems to perpetually hover nearby, like a needy bully requiring constant appeasement, but for all his vicious unpredictability, sometimes you get the feeling he's forgotten you.

I can't remember the last time I had a single minute away from the claustrophobic press of the city. To have emptiness stretching around me, low curves of soil and rubble in every direction, feels bizarre and delicious. Most exquisite of all is the silence.

Or near-silence. I can hear only my own breath, a distant rumble of traffic, and the usual incessant buzz from the skies.

Each lungful of air feels like a small, weightless parcel of time, held and then released. It's a sensation that makes me want to stay for the rest of the afternoon, hidden away from all the noise, the crowds, the stress, the cramped, struggling millions.

I know I should stand and pick, should get out of here fast, but the thrill of being alone, quiet and unseen, seeps through me. I roll on my back and look up. Instead of fighting on through the day, I could just lie here and let the hours wash over me.

It's a long time since I saw this much sky. Only in the largest bomb sites or out here can you see anything that resembles a horizon, or feel the sky to be more than narrow corridors of air hanging over each street.

The clouds are high today, distant pale streaks against which the drones are easier to see than ever, giant locusts with digital bug eyes which circle over London day and night, watching everything we do.

The closest one banks directly above me, changing pitch slightly as it turns back towards the city.

Sunshine prickles deliciously against the skin of my face. Beads of sweat begin to form on my forehead and upper lip, and I fight the instinct to wipe them away, thinking of how they will evaporate, then float away out of this prison-city: a tiny part of me staging an invisible escape.

On the underside of a leaf, I notice a ladybird. I haven't seen one for years. Reaching out an index finger, I coax the insect on to the back of my hand. It ambles towards my wrist, its feet giving such a light tickle that I can't be sure I've actually felt anything at all.

I squeeze my cuff closed so it can't walk up my sleeve and the ladybird butts a few times against the obstruction, then turns back and walks up my thumb. At the tip, it runs out of ideas, waves its antennae in mid-air, suddenly seems to wonder where it's going.

This is probably how I look to whoever is in that drone. Though of course, nobody is in a drone. Somebody somewhere is watching, but wherever they are, it isn't in the sky above me.

My limbs are heavy now, enjoying this moment of laziness too much, but I need to get the blackberry-picking done and leave. I rise to a squat, pull two plastic bags from my pocket and spread them into basket shapes on the ground. The first few berries go straight into my mouth, and I feel my eyes prickle with tears, partly from the sweet sharpness nipping my tongue, partly from a surge of hot, tangled emotion. Among all the chaos – the bombs, the death, the grief and strife – this simple act of finding a berry and eating it feels like a miracle, and that something so small can seem miraculous feels unutterably sad.

But I can't waste time on self-pity, and I can't eat too many. These berries aren't for me. They'll fetch a good price, and I need the money.

I pluck from branch after branch, working my hands between the thorny stalks to pick the bush clean. My fingers are soon streaked with cuts and stained dark red. How much is juice and how much is blood I can't tell, but it hardly matters as I pick and pick, gradually filling my bags with the dense, black fruit.

I have no idea how long it takes. Everything beyond the bush seems to disappear as I work, until I hear a voice calling my name, shouting frantically.

'LEX! LEX! What are you doing? What the *hell* are you doing?'

I look up. There, at the corner where I was standing only a short while ago, is my father. His face is red with fury, his arm jabbing at the air between us.

I can think of nothing to say. The sight of the terror and rage on his face snaps me out of myself, dizzying me with the sudden awareness that I have no explanation for why I am picking berries in a military exclusion zone.

'LEX! LEX!'

It's like he thinks I'm drowning – as if I'm being swept out by a receding tide and he's calling to see if I can be rescued.

'I … I'm coming,' I say.

'No! Don't! They'll shoot!'

'Stay there. I'm coming,' I repeat.

'NO! DON'T MOVE!' he shouts.

He springs into motion, bent double, running out across the uneven ground towards me.

He's on me in seconds. Still crouching, he grabs me by the shoulders and pulls me down towards him.

'WHAT ARE YOU DOING?' he screams. 'HOW COULD YOU BE SO STUPID?'

He raises his arm, and even though there can only be one reason for this movement, I still cannot believe that he is about to hit me, because this is something he has never done. So I am not even flinching when his open palm whacks against my face, snapping my neck to one side, bringing an instant, roaring burn to the flesh of my cheek.

I topple from my crouch and fall to the ground. He pulls me up, then hauls me into him, under cover of the bush, squeezing me so hard to his chest that the buttons of his jacket dig painfully into my ribs.

'Lex! Lex! Lex!' He's saying my name over and over, high and thin, like some strange, stuck song, his voice wavering as if on the brink of tears. 'Why would you do this? You want to be killed?' he says.

I don't know what to say. I have no explanation beyond a useless, inexpressible idea that sometimes you just have to do something – anything – to break loose.

Eventually he goes quiet and slackens his grip, but still doesn't let go of me. He squeezes my shoulders and turns his face aside as if he is trying simultaneously to hold me and hide from me.

'*Why?*' he says again.

I shrug, a swelling prickle of tears beginning to fight its way upwards from my throat. I feel suddenly, hopelessly, lost, swamped by a helplessness that seems for a moment to be reflected right back at me in the infinitely weary expression on my father's face. In this ocean of rubble, we are two despairing castaways.

Dad waits and waits for an answer, but I have none.

'How did you know I was here?' I ask eventually.

With a croaking, thin voice he says, 'A friend,' and points vaguely towards an apartment block at the perimeter of the city. 'He saw you. He called me. He was worried.'

'It's fine. I'm safe.'

A renewed flash of anger crosses his face.

'Don't be an idiot! You're smarter than that. Don't insult me by trying to tell me this is safe. Now let's get out of here. We'll talk at home.'

He tentatively peers through the foliage, towards the border fence. Above, I see a drone again, lower now, making a tighter circle than before. Its buzz is louder, higher, insect-like.

Dad grabs my arm and takes off at a sprint. I only have time to reach for one of the bags, snatching it clumsily by a single handle and gathering it up as we run for cover.

Again, I brace myself for gunshots from the border fence, but there is no sound, no attack.

Even when we escape the buffer zone Dad doesn't slow

down. We hurry past the city's outermost apartment block, round the first corner and continue at top speed down Camden Road, past a long row of identical old brick houses, most of them still standing. Just one block in from London's stark perimeter the claustrophobic press of the city returns. Choking traffic fills the streets, lines of rusty and dilapidated cars fighting for every inch of tarmac against bicycles, scooters, motorbikes and traders pulling handcarts, but even as we dissolve into the crowds Dad continues to run, dragging me with him.

A gaggle of students is hovering in front of the City and Islington College sign, clutching books and notepads, tussling and flirting under the flapping grey tarpaulin facade. Dad hauls me across the road and we weave towards a gateway which leads us behind the building, into a dim alleyway loomed over on all sides by grey brick and boarded-up windows. Next to an overflowing dumpster, in heavy silence, he finally releases me from his grip.

It takes my eyes a while to adjust to the murky air, which is thick with a stench of rot. As I listen to his fast, wheezing breath, his face slowly reveals itself: cold, exhausted and angry.

He takes off the black wire-framed glasses that usually seem like part of his face and wipes the bridge of his nose. The skin under his eyes is puffed and shiny, stippled with tiny pockmarks. He looks momentarily frail and helpless, but when he replaces the glasses and fixes me with a chilling stare, an anxious jolt pulses through me. I take a step back, away from him. He's never hit me before today, nor have I ever seen him so close to tears. It's almost as if I can see a man who is not my father bubbling through those familiar features. He has always seemed, above all else, predictable. Steady. But at this moment, I have no idea what he will do next.

'I'm sorry I hit you,' he says after a long silence.

I nod, raising a hand to my cheek, which feels hot under my fingertips.

'But you deserved it,' he adds.

I shrug.

'Why did you go there?'

I shrug.

'Tell me. You think you're special? Some kind of super-hero who can bounce bullets off his skin?'

I look down, my eyes falling on a disc of sky reflected in a greasy puddle.

'You know how long it takes to get shot? A split second. You think they care who you are? You think they only shoot adults?'

I shake my head.

'How could you be so *stupid*?' he spits.

A surge of suppressed rage zips through me. Suddenly, I feel as if everything is his fault, as if this imprisoned, constrained, terrified life has been designed by my father to torture me. For this I want to strangle him. Only by closing

10

my hands around his neck and squeezing could I show him what it's like to be me.

But I say nothing.

He steps forward, closing the gap between us, and speaks in a slow, menacing voice that seems to be hauled up from his guts. 'I understand that you have to be your own person. I know what it's like to be sixteen. You're not going to do everything you're told. But don't defy me on this. Do not ever go out there again. If you get killed, it's not just you that dies. You'd be killing the whole family. Do you understand?'

I nod, but I haven't yet given up on the bag of berries that was left behind.

'If you want to be selfish, be selfish, but not about this. The warnings are clear. They'll shoot on sight.'

I nod again, turning away.

'SPEAK TO ME!' he snaps, jostling my shoulder.

'What do you want me to say?'

'Tell me you won't go there again.'

'I won't.'

'Tell me properly.' He places a rough thumb against my chin and lifts my head, forcing me to look at him. I can feel my eyes betraying me, but I meet his stare.

'I won't.'

He doesn't let go. I sense him struggling to read me, knowing he can't.

He gasps, exasperated, and spins away, kicking out a spray of gravel.

'Take those home to your mother,' he says, pointing at the bag of berries. My heart plummets. All that effort and risk, for nothing.

'I was going to sell them.'

'No. You can't.'

'Why not? They'll get good money.'

'Exactly. Then you'll want to do it again.'

'I won't.'

'Why should I believe you?'

'*I won't.*'

'Give them to Mum. Tell her what you did.'

'If I tell her, she'll only worry.'

'You want to lie to her?'

'I don't know …'

'You want *me* to lie to her?'

'It might be better.'

'Take the berries home. Tell her the truth. We'll talk later.'

'You're not coming?'

'I have to go. I'm late.'

'For what?'

'A meeting.'

It's the end of the day and he's changed out of his work clothes. Since when does a car mechanic finish work then go to a meeting?

He walks away, out of the alley; I hurry to catch up.

'What kind of meeting?'

'It's nothing. Just a get-together.'

As soon as we reach the pavement, he looks up. I follow his gaze and see two high, circling drones. I half register the strangeness of seeing a pair of them so close together, but when I look down again Dad has already headed off at speed, and by the time I catch up with him, the drones have slipped from my mind.

'Where are you going?' I ask.

'IT'S NOTHING!' he snaps. 'Just forget it! You need to get home.'

Near the shattered bulk of Holloway Prison, he pauses, looks around, and glances skywards again. A middle-aged man in a scruffy suit, with a dark baseball cap pulled low over his face, crosses the road in front of us, and I notice him catch my father's eye, then look away sharply. Their contact is fleeting, but I sense something pass between them. They know one another, and know not to acknowledge it in front of me.

Motionless at the kerb, Dad watches him enter the nearest building, a run-down corner pub whose sign, a cracked painting of an old castle, is dangling precariously, swaying above the entrance. He then looks back at me, his forehead knotted as if he's making a complex private calculation.

'I'll walk you some of the way home,' he says, setting off at speed down Camden Road.

'What's the hurry?' I ask.

'Will you stop this?'

'Stop what?'

'The endless questions! Just get yourself home.'

'I only asked why it's such a rush.'

He walks on, faster than ever, keeping himself a couple of steps ahead of me. We pass the gnarled, spidery mess of a bombed construction site, scaffolding twisted and fallen in on itself like giant spaghetti, and continue walking in silence. As we get further from the edge of London, the pavement becomes thicker with pedestrians: teenagers roaming in jostling packs; dirt-streaked children dragging carts of all kinds, scavenging in bins and bomb sites; occasional mad people bundled in stinking clothes, muttering furiously to themselves; and streams of sour-faced Londoners clutching tatty bags of whatever food they've cobbled together that day.

At the next corner, he stops, looks at his watch, the street, the sky. 'Go home,' he says. 'I have to go this way. I'll see you later.'

With a quick nod of farewell, he scurries away down a side street lined with the stumps of trees long since cut down for firewood. I see him glance up, but not back towards me.

He turns left again, doubling back on our route. This is when I decide to follow him. He's concealing something. I don't know much about his past, but I know enough to guess where he might be going, who he might be meeting.

I break into a run, past an apartment block, the top few floors of which are windowless and smeared with soot, and pick my way along a makeshift platform of old pallets which have been laid across a stagnant pool of rank, greenish-brown water.

Rounding the corner I spot him again, still speed-walking, too far ahead to be aware of me. I match his pace, weaving through a stream of lumbering, weary pedestrians along a narrow street lined with laundry-draped balconies.

At the next junction he takes another left, completing his circuit of the block. I keep my distance now, hiding myself among the parked cars. Within a couple of minutes, he's back where we encountered the man in the baseball cap.

He pauses, looks up yet again, glances at his watch, then turns towards me. Before ducking out of sight, I glimpse his face. He looks closed in on himself, locked into a thought so intense he doesn't entirely know where he is. I have a feeling I could step out of my hiding place and he wouldn't even recognise me.

In this instant, it occurs to me that perhaps he didn't just hit me to punish me for straying into the buffer zone, or even because he was afraid for my safety. Something else has happened to him.

I peep out between the cars, just in time to see him cross the road and enter the corner pub we walked past only a few minutes earlier.

My father is not a drinker. I've seen him have the occasional beer with friends, but he's not a pub man, not a boozer. He must be meeting the guy in the suit and baseball cap who we saw enter this same building a short while ago.

I have only an instant to register my suspicion of who this might be, to contemplate who else could be at this meeting, but that is enough to make a difference. Even though it's the worst shock of my life, I immediately understand what happens next. Part of me is less surprised than it ought to be. The streak of light across the sky, so quick I can't even be sure I've seen it; the white flash an instant before the ear-splitting boom; the suck and whoosh of air; a breath of heat across my face; the mushrooming crawl of an approaching dust cloud which wraps me in filth as I pointlessly, too late, throw myself to the ground.

When I stand, my ears are squealing so loudly I can hear nothing at all, not even the screams from wide-mouthed people all around me. It is hard, at first, to balance. The ground seems to be tipping. I use a parked van to steady myself. I look down at my chest, arms, legs, feet. There's no blood; nothing is missing. I am intact. I raise my head and stare through the dissipating dust cloud, which slowly, agonisingly reveals that there is no longer a pub at the corner of this street, only a charred, flaming mound of rubble.

The Base

Nobody ever thought I'd amount to anything. Teachers wrote me off from the start, always accused me of goofing off and not trying, of dozing through school because I'd been up half the night gaming. Mum was the same. I remember endless, boring lectures on how I had to focus on the real world instead of wasting all my attention on games, constant nagging pressure to spend time with 'real people', as if the online friends I played with were somehow a figment of my imagination.

Dinosaurs, the whole lot of them, lost in the past, stuck with the idea that there's 'real' and there's 'virtual' and one is somehow realer than the other.

When I got into the national semis, with thousands of hits from all over the world on YouTube videos of my gaming, none of those idiots knew what it meant. They all still thought I was wasting my time, when in certain circles I was almost a celebrity.

Even after a military recruitment team came and grabbed a whole bunch of us for the drone programme, including guys I'd slaughtered in the quarters and the pool, Mum still thought I was a loser, but I knew where I was going. I was as good as anyone they'd scooped up, and it was obvious to me that as long as I kept focused, I'd make it through.

After weeks of tests and whittling down, followed by a mind-numbingly methodical and slow training programme, then months on end of grunt work, monitoring and logging screen after screen of nothing, eventually there's this. The day that makes it all worthwhile. My first mission as a qualified pilot, with my own work station, controlling a drone operating over London, and my own target: subject #K622.

These people are cunning and they know they're being watched, so you have to look out for narrow alleys and multiple exits, but that's all in the training. We have methods for dealing with almost anything.

The first time I walked into the flight room, it blew my mind. Billions have been spent to shift the parameters of the possible, and a near miracle has been pulled off. The aspiration of every army throughout history has been to see your enemy without being seen, to attack before your opponent can defend or hide, and our technology takes that as far is it can go: we've achieved near invisibility for us, total transparency for them.

We see everything and we can kill anyone. We have absolute power without a single boot on the ground. They crawl to and fro across our screens, thinking they're in charge of their destinies, behaving as if their resistance has some effect, but we can squash whoever we like, whenever we like.

We won't of course. We're the most disciplined army in the world. There are rules and protocols. But we could.

People slave their whole lives, hustling to win scraps of power over others, toiling for every little advantage, but look what's happened to me. Twenty-one years old, and already here I am. Me and #K622. When I try to grasp the power I have over him it makes my head spin. If he knew who I was, he'd be in awe of me. He'd do anything to win my favour. He'd go on his knees and beg me to show mercy. And how many people can say that? How many 'losers' can say that?

Mum has changed her tune since I got this job. She doesn't act like she feels sorry for me any more. She seems to have stopped worrying I'll never amount to anything or make a living. Instead, there's a suspicion, a wariness, a resigned disappointment, as if I've let her down.

There's no point trying to please her, no point imagining I'll ever become the kind of son she would have wanted. As soon as I've saved enough money, I'm going to move out. That's all I'm focused on right now: getting enough cash to move away from her for good, away from those judgemental, hangdog eyes that trail me around the house, silently wishing I wasn't me.

My colleagues couldn't be more different. Such a great bunch of guys. There's a real camaraderie. Most of what we do is secret, so it's only here, at work, we can really be ourselves. With anyone outside the base there are too many things you can't say.

The pilots and sensor operators are all gamers, all high-skill, sharp, good people. Only a few of us from the big recruitment sweep got through training. Everyone there had the manual skills, but in the programme we were like rats in some psychological maze, being watched and examined for every choice, every flicker of emotion, every moment of weakness or fear. The stoners didn't last more than a couple of days.

They've picked out only the strongest minds – guys whose hands get steadier as pressure mounts – men with laser brains. We've been tested and tested, and every one of us has the steel to do what needs to be done when the time comes.

Walking into the base this morning, in uniform for my first day of operational service, I glimpsed my reflection in a window and had to stop. I couldn't move on without pausing to take in the reality of what has happened to me. It seemed hard to credit that the uniformed pilot smirking back from the glass was really me.

And I'm being paid! Earning a good wage for becoming a member of the club I always wanted to join but never even knew existed.

I was told that even on active duty with a specific subject to monitor I should expect weeks on end of nothing more interesting than observation, logging and pattern-forming. But that's not how it turned out. Day one itself was simply incredible.

You don't get told much about your subject. I've been informed that #K622 is a mechanic of some kind, but that's just about all. I guess I'll know every detail of his life soon enough, but what you never find out – other than what you can deduce from your own observations – is why they're being watched, and if there's an endgame. My job is just to gather the pictures. My stream goes to analysts I'll never meet, and gets turned into data I'll never know. Me and the other guys here, we're just technical operatives. We do what we're told. We press the buttons we've been trained to press and don't ask any questions.

Although I'm buzzing to be in my new job, the bulk of the first day is so routine you could almost call it boring. I watch #K622 walk from home to work. He doesn't stop or talk to anyone. There's no further visible movement until lunch time, when he takes a short stroll, eating something out of a small bag. I can't yet make out anything of his age, appearance or personality. My afternoon is spent gazing at the roof of his workplace.

Just when I'm beginning to wonder if this may not, after all, be the job of my dreams, #K622 unexpectedly emerges, running. My body tenses, rising upright in my chair as I watch him jostle eastwards over London's crowded pavements, his gait gradually slowing to a heavy stumble. When he gets to the edge of the city, he stops and stares out at the buffer zone as if he's never seen the place before, as if he didn't even know there was a border. Then I notice he seems to be cupping his hands over his mouth and shouting. Shouting out into empty space like a madman.

Though I know exactly what I should do, at first I'm hesitant. I don't want to overreact or draw attention to myself on the first day, but there is a procedure for the current situation.

My mouth is dry, my finger quivering slightly as I action a raised threat level, triggering a feed alert to the analyst team.

I zoom in and sharpen to maximum resolution, just as he does something extraordinary, something unimaginably dangerous. He starts running, directly towards the fence. I lose him on screen for a second, then zoom out and get a clear view of his awkward, stumbling sprint across the rubble wasteland. I instantly hit a top level alert. An orange square appears top-left of my screen.

The buffer zone is one hundred per cent sterile. Nobody sets foot in the buffer zone. No warnings are given, no tear gas or rubber bullets are used. If you go in there, you face combat ammunition, shoot to kill.

Could this be a suicide attack on the fence or a watchtower? If so, that's unprecedented and insane, because he stands no chance of getting close to either target.

He's barely a third of the way across the buffer zone when he dives at a mound of soil covered by a large bush. That's

22

when I notice the boy, who's already at the same spot. #K622 grabs him and pulls him into what looks like it might be a hug, then hits him across the face. The boy topples to the ground.

They both crouch, clinging together, probably fighting – it's hard to tell – but without much movement. It looks like they're trying not to break into the sight lines from the fence, which is pointless since this feed is going straight to the nearest watchtower.

They're so close together that the two silhouettes blur into one. I can't see what they are doing. For a while, there's no further movement. The orange square in the corner of my screen goes red, just as they morph back into two forms, sprinting back out of the buffer zone, the man seeming to drag the boy, who might be injured. The boy is carrying a white package.

I signal the lowered threat of their retreat from the buffer zone, but the icon in the corner of my screen stays red.

My heart is beating fast now. I never got this sensation during training. Whatever they put you through, even the most lurid exercise, you know it's not real. This is real. I am watching two people flee for their lives, knowing they are seconds from death, a death that will be played out in real time on a screen inches from my face.

I go in tight on the white package. It's unidentifiable, but I put a marker on it.

They keep running, back through the city, then dart into

an enclosed alley. I find a sight line, but the light isn't good. It's just layers of shadow now, so I mark up the likely positions of the man and boy for anyone coming to the feed without context.

Nothing happens for a while, but the square stays red, and my heart keeps hammering. My drone is unarmed, but someone somewhere is on the brink of calling in a strike. A jet has probably already been scrambled.

I lean back slightly in my chair and lower my shoulders, reminding myself to keep a blank expression. I want to appear alert but relaxed. The thudding in my chest must remain a secret. I can't even tell if I'm thrilled or terrified, but I know my job is to be neither. My place is to observe and act, not to think or feel.

I've lost all sense of time passing now. I'm just zoned in on those shadows, focused entirely on watching for any movement. If someone other than #K622 leaves the alley, identification will be tricky. I have not much more than a silhouette to go on.

The next movement is two figures – man and boy – boy still holding the white package. It could be a switch, a trick, but I have to go with the most likely scenario and assume this is still #K622.

They walk together for a while, at speed but not running, then seem to part, the man diverting to the south, away from his expected route towards home. I stay on him, noticing after a few seconds that the boy appears to follow him.

The man turns left at the next corner, then left again. An alert window pops up on my screen: *Confirm #K622 entry to target zone.*

I zoom out a short way, quickly spotting the corner building a short distance ahead of the man, which is target zoned.

I OK the command.

That's when I notice the thickened atmosphere in the room, a thrum of tension which seems to almost crackle in the air. I unlock my eyes from the console for a moment and notice that a few other screens in the room have a red square. Several have the target zone. I've spent many months in this room as a trainee, but I've never seen anything like this, or felt such a buzz of anticipation.

I can't afford more than a glance away from my monitor, because I mustn't lose #K622. He is walking ever closer to the target zone. He glances up, momentarily seeming to look straight out at me through the screen, then accelerates. I stay tight on him, too close to see if the boy is still following.

I'm not sure why, but I find myself willing him towards the target. I want to be part of this. I want to play a role in whatever is happening around me. I mustn't be the team member who drops the ball. That's the person I've left behind, not who I am here, in the base. I haven't proved myself yet, and it takes time to win respect in the flight room, but I will. All it takes is to put in the hours and not slip up.

In school, people you hardly know can turn on you for reasons you barely understand, for wearing trousers you have no idea are too tight or too baggy, for having the wrong hair-cut or schoolbag or facial expression. You can be crushed and humiliated at the whim of a complete stranger. You never know what's going to happen next. Here, it's simple. I just have to do my job.

He's less than twenty metres from the target now.

My right hand is on the drone control joystick, left hand poised to click the target zone confirmation.

He crosses the street.

He pauses, looking left and right, then enters the building. I confirm.

Armed assets must already be in position, because the effect is almost instantaneous. A streak of light flashes downwards and the screen flares white. After that, flames and a plume of dust obscure the target.

In the flight room, nobody speaks or moves.

The dust begins to clear. A few people are staggering away from the blast site. The corner building no longer exists.

Here, silence. Until a whoop rises up from one of the other desks, then more whoops, and suddenly everyone is on their feet, high-fiving and hugging. I notice for the first time that a cluster of top brass is in the room, not hugging or high-fiving, but quietly smiling to one another and shaking hands.

We're not supposed to leave our stations, but everyone else is doing it, so I stand and copy the others, eyes wide as I stumble round the room joining the celebrations. Three guys

I've never even spoken to – a few years older than me – pull me into an embrace like I'm some long-lost brother. I've never had any siblings. Until now.

It is forbidden to celebrate publicly. We're not allowed to mention any operation outside the base. So after that massive high, at the end of the shift we all just have to drift home as if nothing has happened. We're not even allowed to tell our own families that we wiped out a bunch of terrorists today, and saved God knows how many lives.

People have no idea what is keeping them safe, who the real heroes are.

I walk with two other pilots to the car park, guys I barely knew this morning, but now we feel close and tight. We shake hands, the bone-crushing military way (I'm going to have to get one of those grip-trainer gadgets), and part. I get into Mum's clapped-out Nissan and my eyes drift out of focus. I don't put the key in the ignition, and I don't reach for my seat belt. I just sit there, behind the stippled plastic steering wheel, feeling the sensation of standing at the brink of a worm-hole between one world and another.

My body is still tingling with adrenalin, brimming with relief at having shown competence under extreme pressure, with sheer joy at having established myself in this world of men. I can't go home feeling like this, forbidden from saying anything about what just happened, from even trying to communicate the thrill of my day. I can't just drive back to that house where I'm still made to feel like a kid.

I ought to be saving my salary for a deposit to move out of home, but there's something I've been planning for a while, a little treat for myself, and I decide that today's the day. I need to mark what has happened to me. I need to show everyone what I have become.

I google the address of the showroom and dock my phone on the dashboard to direct me there. I can afford it now. It'll set my savings back down to zero and max out my credit card, but there's regular money coming in, so I'll manage. I simply can't let myself be mocked for driving around in a granny-car any longer. And besides, I just want it. The Kawasaki Z750R. 750cc. Black. The bike of my dreams. I've been tracking the listing, and I know it's there. Second-hand. Low mileage. Perfect condition.

This could be the last time I ever drive my mum's stupid, effeminate little car. Even if it delays moving out, buying that bike will change everything. At a stroke, I'll be free.

I turn the key, and the Nissan's tinny splutter pierces the bubble of my thoughts. After flying a drone, this car feels like a donkey cart.

As I pass security and drive out through the last ring of razor wire, my body seems light but heavy, as if I am waking from a dream of weightlessness.

Seven months later

The City

I saved my father's life.

Fetching me from the buffer zone made him late for his meeting. If he'd arrived just a few seconds earlier and had made it up the stairs he would have been killed like all the others, but when the missile hit he was still in the stairwell.

It was the middle of the night by the time they dug him out of the bomb site, unconscious, barely alive, and he was immediately taken into surgery for an operation to save his right leg.

The entire leadership of The Corps was wiped out that day. The rage at their joint funeral was like nothing I've seen before – thousands on the streets shouting, marching, chanting – banners swearing revenge – swarms of people clambering over one another to touch the coffins as if they were holy relics that could transmit courage. I watched the

31

whole thing on a TV bolted to the wall of my dad's hospital ward.

I was half deaf for almost a week, with a headache that felt as if my brain was scraping against the inside of my skull, but I still went back for the bag of berries I'd left behind in the buffer zone. There was nobody to stop me now, and I needed the money more than ever.

I waited till twilight, since I was only collecting a bag, not picking any fruit, and was in and out in less than a minute. Some of the berries had softened to a dark goo, others had grown a delicate white fluff, but most were still saleable. After wrapping handfuls of the good ones in paper, I found an out-of-the-way corner and began to sell, watching out all the time for the gangs who control street hawking, ready to run.

Working discreetly so as not to risk being spotted, it took a while to offload all the berries, but as soon as they were gone I hurried to Jake's house and poured the cash into his hands, figuring this would make it harder for him to say no. He invited me in and we counted the coins out on his kitchen table, sliding them into eight one-pound stacks, plus a spray of small change.

'I'm selling it for ten,' he said, unimpressed.

'It's old,' I replied, trying not to look disappointed that my weighty handful of money had added up to so little.

'That's why it's only ten.'

Jake's rich. He always has new-looking clothes and his

family even have a Merc. It's rusty and belches thick grey fumes, but it's still a Merc.

'I'll owe you the rest,' I said.

'Where are you going to get it?'

I shrugged, feigning indifference to the outcome of our negotiation, but I wanted that game as much as I'd ever wanted anything. It's a mission-based hyper-real war game, with graphics so sharp it looks almost like a movie, and every boy at school is obsessed with it. If you don't play, you're nobody.

I wanted to tell him I'd risked my life to get those eight pounds, but I sensed that wouldn't help. The more desperate I seemed, the more likely he was to hold firm. He's that kind of guy. His dad probably is too. You don't get rich round here with a soft heart.

It's against all my principles to beg, but after an awkward silence, I heard myself say, 'Come on, man. That's almost the whole amount. Please.'

He rocked his chair back, putting both arms behind his neck and tilting his head so he could look down at me.

'Maybe I should be nice,' he said, spinning out the moment.

A fantasy of hooking my feet around his chair legs and sending him flat on to his back flashed through my mind, but I just shrugged and kept my face blank.

'This is everything you've got?' he asked.

'Forget it then,' I said, cupping a hand and beginning to scoop coins off the edge of the table.

Jake rocked his chair back to the ground and put his hands over the remaining piles of money. 'All right, all right. I'll give you two weeks to get me the rest.'

'Fine,' I said, knowing I had as little chance of finding the money as Jake did of getting his game back from me.

We shook on it and he handed over the disc.

The next few weeks Mum was half-crazed with worry, not knowing if the doctors had saved Dad's leg, not knowing when he'd work again and how we'd survive if he couldn't go back. The twins reacted by becoming even more wild, noisy and annoying than usual. It was the game that got me through.

The power never works for more than a few hours each day, but whenever it was on, I was at my console. It sucks you in, pulls you away from reality, transports you to a place where everything is OK, which is strange, because the new game is set in the only place I can imagine worse than where I actually live. Most of the gameplay is in a bombed-out city, with barely a civilian in sight, and consists of house-to-house fighting, full-on armed combat with your buddies dying all around you non-stop. The mission scenarios are worked out in amazing detail to put you under maximum pressure. If you relax for a second you'll be killed, which might not sound like fun, but the truth is I feel more alive when I'm gaming than when I'm walking real streets, or at school, or talking to my family. The adrenalin of it wakes you up, pulses through you, brings you more into the moment than any-thing else.

You wouldn't think a game like that would be popular here, but it is. Every boy at school plays it when the power's on and daydreams about it when the power's off. Gaming is a trapdoor we can jump through at any time, taking us out of here, to another world. And in this other place, it's us with the guns.

Dad came out of hospital after two months, and though he never complains about the pain, he winces whenever he sits or stands and moves with a heavy wooden shuffle. His skin is sallow, his eyes sunken and hooded. There's something distant and menacing in his face now, as if even when he's right there, talking to you, part of his mind is elsewhere, fighting something back.

The smallest things make him lose his temper, but worse than that is the hovering sense that even when he isn't angry, he is. The threat of it is always right there, like with a guard dog.

He lost his cousin that day and I don't know how many friends. He's never said why he was at that meeting. The Corps is never mentioned openly in my house, but long before his injury I remember often lying in bed at night, overhearing my parents arguing about it, straining to catch words I knew I wasn't supposed to hear. This is how I learned he was once a fighter, but stepped down after I was born, and that they repeatedly tried to recruit him again, but Mum always insisted he stay away. I've heard endless, muffled variations of this argument for as long as I can remember, so often it's a sound that almost helps me get to sleep.

Maybe he was at the meeting to turn them down, maybe to accept the call, or maybe he'd been with them secretly for a while. I'll never know what his role was, or would have been without that missile strike, but it's obvious what has happened now.

Dad still goes to work, same as before, in the same blue overalls, but now his hands are clean when he comes home, his clothes never stained with a single spot of oil. He's even been given the garage manager's desk. The man who is supposedly his boss now has to run the place from an old, rickety table in the corner.

The Corps can do that. If they tell you to make way, you make way. His boss can't do anything about it. I don't know if he still pays Dad, or if The Corps is taking care of that, but I know we have more money now. Dad brings home food you can't find in the shops, sometimes even flowers for Mum, who behaves as if she doesn't really want them, though you can tell she does.

It's clear that Dad's taken the post of one of the dead men, and that my mother accepts his decision. I'm not sure why, but the strike must have changed her mind about The Corps.

He's an important man now, and you can feel the difference everywhere. It's strange, because his stiff, slow walk makes him seem older and weaker, but now people make way for him, usher him to the front of queues, sometimes refuse payment in shops and cafes, and not from pity. You

36

can see it in their eyes. This is something else, either respect or fear, I can't tell which. Or perhaps you can't have one without the other.

He still says nothing at home about The Corps, and there's never a single phone call or even text message. The only sign of his new work is that every day teenage boys come to the door and deliver notes by hand. Dad always reads them immediately, standing up in the hallway, and scribbles an answer to be sent back on foot.

Even after weeks of guys exactly my age turning up at the door with scraps of paper, I'm amazed when Dad summons me to the living room one evening, after the twins are in bed, and asks me if I'd like to be trained as a messenger. He doesn't spell out what kind of messages he means, or who they'll be for, but he doesn't have to.

Straight away, my heart surges as if I've broken into a sprint. I look across to Mum, who is standing at Dad's shoulder with her arms folded, and she gives a small nod. This has been discussed and agreed between them. They're inviting me to step up and take my place in the struggle.

Without giving any thought to what this really means, I respond with an immediate yes.

'Are you sure?' he asks, scrutinising my face.

The room seems to spin around the axis of his stare as I nod in reply. This brief, simple conversation has somehow, already, changed everything.

His gaze softens, his mouth breaks into the faintest hint of a smile, and he ushers me to the dining table with an open hand, as if I were some kind of invited guest. Mum slips away.

As I sit, he turns to the corner shelves and slides out a dog-eared book with the word *London* on the cover, above a large red *A* and a blue *Z*. Ten pages are loose from the binding, the paper thin and crinkled from use. He lays them out on the table, five by two, sliding the sheets together to make one long, thin rectangular map. This is what's left of London, a seething spine of overcrowded land shaped like a sticking plaster, cut off from the rest of the world, these days often just called The Strip.

Leaning closer to the carefully tessellated sheets, I realise this shows The Strip as it used to be. Countless landmarks and buildings on these pages are now ruins, but it is the expanses of parkland that jump out at me first. In the city I know, there is no green: every inch of open space is crammed with the tents of families whose homes have been bombed. It's almost impossible to get a permit to leave London, so for every house that gets hit, a new cranny of unclaimed space is colonised. It always seems like there's no space left, but somehow, after each assault, we squash in closer together.

Four lines of marker pen, neatly ruled, cutting across a tangle of streets that no longer exist, mark out the perimeter. A thin rectangle of land inside the fence has been shaded out with dense cross-hatched pencil to indicate the buffer zone.

I've often seen the layout of London as it is now on screen, but nothing like this, showing how the edge of my universe is just a line on a map, slashed through a city that once sprawled out, unfenced, into the free world.

I stare, mesmerised, until my eye is drawn by the rest of the *A–Z* perched at the edge of the table, closed, containing page after page of maps. A vanished metropolis. I never set foot in that London, but Mum and Dad were children there, living in those lost streets, unable to conceive the destruction that was to come. I have no idea how many of those houses are still standing, out beyond the fence, or who is living in them.

Right up until he died, my grandfather's most treasured possession was a key. To a home out there somewhere. We still have it, but the house must now belong to someone else.

A sudden yearning sweeps through me. I would give anything to see that place, just for one day. But it's a pointless fantasy. I must comfort myself with the idea that maybe life here is easier for me than for my parents, because The Strip is all I've ever known. The world before and beyond is simply unimaginable.

Dad pulls up a chair beside me and sits.

'You've never seen this, have you?' he asks, eyeing me with grave interest. 'How things were.'

As he speaks, his voice soft and low, I'm struck by the force of his presence. Or, rather, his attention, which these days rarely seems to be directed at me.

'I marked it up myself,' he says. 'You see the border? The buffer zone?'

I nod, distracted by the smell of him, a reassuring waft of a particular kind of pine-fragranced soap mingled with an ever present undertone of motor oil. This scent, more than anything else, is the very essence of my father, unchanged since my earliest childhood.

'Yes,' I say, tracing the four lines of the city's edge with a finger, then looking back at him, and noticing for the first time that his stubble is grey. A heartbeat-long flicker of the notion that my father is mortal, more mortal now than ever before, flashes through me.

As if reading my mind, or being struck by the same thought in reverse, Dad says, 'You don't have to do this. It's your decision.'

'I know,' I say. 'I want to.'

'It's dangerous.'

'I know.'

'And when things are urgent, they're urgent. You always have to be ready.'

'I will be.'

'You're going to be busy. There's still school, and there's still homework. Those things don't stop. They're just as important.'

'Unless there's a message.'

'I'm saying you have to do both. And you can't just drop in and out as you fancy. If you're in, you're in.'

'Then I'm in,' I say.

'You need to think about this properly. It's a big decision.'

'I'm in.'

He eyes me steadily, piercingly, before saying in a low voice, 'Good.'

That word reverberates softly in my chest, as if two grinding cogs have slipped together and fallen into synch. For several years we have grated against one another, nipped and scrapped over endless details of daily life. Whatever he said, I found myself wanting to disagree. But something in his tone, and in the way he's looking at me now, makes me feel as if at this moment we are breaking through towards a truce.

'There are some ground rules,' he says. 'No phones. Not for messages, not for maps, not for anything. They're insecure, and phone signals guide missiles.'

I nod.

'And no addresses. It all stays in here.'

He jabs my temple, harder than is comfortable, making a point. This is not a game.

'There used to be a protocol for how to destroy a message if you encountered a patrol. Now there are no more patrols, only drones, but you need to know that nothing on paper can ever fall into the hands of the enemy. That is of utmost importance.'

A weird desire to smile creeps up on me. It's that word, 'utmost'. Who says 'utmost'?

I strain to keep a straight face. Sometimes it feels as if the more serious an atmosphere becomes, the harder it is not to laugh.

'Why are you smirking?' he snaps.

'I'm not.'

'Focus,' he says, hammering the table with a fingertip. I see a flash of doubt flicker across his eyes. He's not sure I'm ready.

'You never dispose of anything casually,' he continues. 'You give it to me for burning. OK?'

'OK.'

He stares at me for a moment, assessing me, then waves an open palm over the map. 'Where are we?' he asks.

For a moment, I think this is some strange, vague question asking me to account for myself, or somehow prove I'm serious enough to do what he's asking, then I realise he simply wants me to find our location on the map. I look down at the garish tangle of lines and words which, under the pressure of my father's scrutiny, now swim confusingly before my eyes.

I'm desperate not to fail, but my mind seems determined to whirr with futile noise, nagging at itself to concentrate instead of actually looking for an answer to the question.

'Faster, faster. Where are we?'

I wrench a moment of clarity from my zipping brain, and touch a finger on our street, near the top of the map, just behind a struck-through red circle which marks the remains of a tube station. It's a strange thought that millions of people used to criss-cross this city every day, invisible, underground, re-emerging into daylight at these little circles which pepper the map.

He nods, then points at a street on the next page across.

'You're going here. Number 16A,' he says, levering himself up from his chair and stepping towards the kitchen. 'I'll give you five minutes to learn your route,' he adds, turning back at the doorway.

I quickly work out a simple route, following it with my finger three times, then close my eyes, and rehearse it twice more in my head.

Dad reappears, clutching two steaming mugs of tea and a half-finished packet of biscuits.

'Tell me,' he says, sitting at the table and passing me a digestive.

I take a bite and look down.

'No map. No map,' he says gently. 'Just tell me.'

I reel off a list of left and rights. He looks straight at me, following the route in his own head.

'That's decent,' he says. 'But look again. Think again. You never know when you're being watched. Drones can log movement between key addresses. After this, you might go on a watch list. You want to disguise your route. Narrow streets and alleys are useful to obscure sight lines.' He lifts a page from the table and leans towards me so we can both see, pointing at the map with the tip of a teaspoon handle. 'There are shops here and here with a front and a rear exit. There's an overhang around this car park which is useful. You think you can plan again?'

I nod.

'Five minutes,' he says, passing me the loose page, then returning to the kitchen.

I rethink: a twisting, circuitous route this time, and struggle to commit it to memory.

He returns and immediately tests me, but interrupts after the first few turns. 'No no no. You're lost. Overcomplicated. You can't use all those elements. Find something simpler.'

We go through five routes, and all the biscuits, before he is satisfied. He tests me several times, then he pulls from his shirt pocket a small piece of paper, folded in two, taped shut, and hands it to me.

'You never read them,' he says. 'Don't be tempted. Every single thing you learn about The Corps is an additional danger. The less you know, the safer you are. The more you know, the closer you are to being a dead man.'

I nod, rising from my chair to slip the paper into my jeans pocket, again fighting that strange urge to smile. Dead man. Not boy.

He stands, grunting as he lifts himself from the chair, and places a hand on my shoulder. It occurs to me that the last time he touched me was months ago, in the buffer zone, slapping me across the face. That seems like two quite different people.

'You don't walk fast, you don't dawdle,' he says. 'Try not to look as if you have a destination. Just walk. You are simply out walking. Natural.'

'OK.'

44

'You wait for an answer, but not longer than five minutes. You come back by a different route. Complicated is fine – you won't get lost on the way home – but don't take too long about it or I'll worry. Now are you sure you want to do this?'

I feel as if I am both utterly sure and entirely unconvinced at the same moment. I know this is something I need to do, and I also know the consequences are incalculable. I swallow, run a finger along the perforated edge of the note inside my pocket and nod.

'It's up to you,' he says.

'I know. I want to do it.'

'Good. Now hand me your phone and go.'

'Now?' It's late, the time of day they usually start nagging me to go to bed.

'Now,' he says, palm outstretched.

As usual, I have no credit. My phone is more or less useless, but I still feel strange handing it over.

He takes the mobile and places it on the dining table, alongside the map. As we walk to the front door, across the living room, I have the sensation that the house seems somehow smaller than usual: the ceiling lower, walls huddled more closely together.

Just as I'm about to walk out, Mum appears, her face rigid and tense. She pulls me into a tight embrace, but doesn't speak. I'm thinking about the route I've memorised, clinging to the details which I can feel slipping away, so I wriggle free instead of returning her hug.

45

The moment I'm out in the cool night air I regret it. As I hurry away, I ache with the urge to have given her one last hug, but it's too late. I'm on my way.

The Base

I've never met my father, but he must be out there somewhere, and if he knew what I was doing he'd be proud of me.
I'm fighting for my country, and what man wouldn't want his
son to do that?

All Mum will tell me about him is that he was a musician,
it was a short affair, and he disappeared as soon as he learned
she was pregnant. She once told me he was good-looking,
but made it sound like an insult, as if this was his only quality.
Mum is useless with computers and couldn't play even the
simplest video game to save her life, so I must have inherited
my gaming talent and my vocation from him. Flying a drone
is all about timing and dexterity, turning a machine into an
extension of my body, which, if you think about it, is a similar
task to being a musician.

My parents have never been in contact since the day he

walked out. He can't have forgotten I exist, so I imagine I'm like some ghost floating silently in the background of his life, never appearing but never disappearing, a presence that is mostly an absence. He must wonder sometimes where I am and who I have become.

I can't understand how two decades could go by and you would never once want to meet your child, see what they look like, find out if you have a son or a daughter. He's probably had other children, half-siblings I'll never meet, who could walk right past me on the street without either of us knowing.

When I was younger, I used to think of my missing father as not so much a person out there in the world, who I'd never find, but as a presence inside me. Sometimes this presence felt benign: a man with my genes, an imaginary adult who would understand me. Other times even the most fleeting thought of him felt like a shard of glass stuck in my throat, cutting me with every breath and swallow.

I have taught myself that if you are strong – if you have enough self-control – you can choose what to feel. When you sense yourself slipping towards painful thoughts, there are ways to lock them down, step away and move on before they suck you under. I can't avoid sometimes thinking about my father, but when I do, I have trained myself to feel nothing. My guess is that he has done the same for me.

I often think my feet don't touch the ground as firmly as they should – as if I'm not exactly hovering, but not quite rooted either. There's some essential ballast everyone else seems to have, which I've learned to live without.

When I watch people in bars or at parties, chatting and laughing, it always looks effortless. I've taught myself how to behave the same way, but it feels like a struggle, like acting. Which isn't to say I'm unhappy. I'm happier now than I've ever been. In fact, I'm in love. With my bike. If everyone had one I swear there would be world peace, because there is no faster route to bliss than wrapping your legs round one of these beauties, revving her up and hitting the road.

After a couple of corners, you forget that you're driving. She becomes part of your body. She becomes your super-power. You're faster than a car, as nimble as a cheetah, with acceleration so raw and perfect it's as close as you can get to flying.

When I'm on the bike, every worry, every problem, every thought disappears. It's just me and the tarmac. Total focus. I have no past, no future, no body, I am just pure movement. The only thing that ties me to reality is the faint tingle of risk, the thought brushing past at each touch of the controls that an error could be fatal.

That's the drug. There is no way to feel more alive than stretching out your hand and giving death a tickle under the chin.

I was made for this bike and she was made for me. The world can seem a spiky and confusing place, but when I'm

49

on my Kawasaki I know for certain who I am, and that everything I do is just fine. The rest of the time, I'm not so sure.

I'm building up that deposit to move out, but it's taking a while. Money seems to come in and go out again faster than I always think it will. Half the time I don't even know where it's gone. I keep trying to remind myself to be more disciplined, to stay focused on the goal of finding my own place to live, but I often go out with the guys after work, and once you're there you have to keep up.

I always thought Mum still wanted me at home, even though we argue and don't have much to say to each other, because without me she'd be all alone, so it's a shock when she summons me to the dining room one day after work and tells me it's time to start paying rent.

'Fine. I was about to suggest it myself,' I say. I'd toyed with the idea of offering, which would have looked better, but it's too late for that now.

'And what stopped you?' she asks, pulling her ancient maroon cardigan tight around herself, as if my arrival in the room is a cold wind.

I catch a glimpse of us in the mahogany mirror that has hung above this dining table for as long as I can remember: a young man in full military uniform and a grey-haired woman in ratty old knitwear, and it seems bizarre that we have anything to do with one another.

When I meet her steely, critical blue-eyed stare I feel my spine stiffen, and remind myself not to be cowed by her.

'I ... I was *about to*. I just said,' I snap, willing this to be the day she learns she can no longer talk down to me.

'OK. But there's a problem. Sit down.'

She pulls out a chair and sits.

'It's fine,' I say. 'I'd like to.'

'Sit,' she says, in a voice that demands compliance, using a particular tone I have never been able to defy.

As I slump into a chair at the far end of the table, Mum looks at her hands. There's a strange pause. The atmosphere suddenly feels less like a mother and son talking in their home, more like a job interview.

'It's not fine,' she says. 'Because it's time you started contributing towards your upkeep. You're an adult and you're getting a wage. But I can't take money you've earned at the base. Doing what you're doing.'

For a moment, I can't even understand what she's saying. I just stare at her.

'That money's tainted,' she says, her voice flat, the dry, pale slot of her mouth entirely expressionless. 'It's blood money. I don't want anything to do with it.'

Her meaning slowly sinks in. I can sense my cheeks reddening, burning with outrage. My jaw opens and closes stupidly.

'What?' I say. 'My money's not good enough for you?' I'm aware as the words come out that I'm spouting a feeble cliché, but my brain is fuzzy and off-kilter. Her accusation is so contemptible, so disloyal, such an insult that I'm too shocked to summon up a response.

'You know how I feel about your job. I don't think it's right.'

She has done this to me all my life, and still it surprises me. I know instinctively and viscerally that whatever I do will in my mother's eyes be wrong, yet for some reason I cannot fathom, every time she gives voice to her scorn it cuts me.

I square my shoulders and stare her down, struggling to keep my voice low and steady, fighting back the shrill clench gripping my windpipe. 'I'm protecting this country from our enemy,' I say. 'From terrorists who want to destroy us! You have no idea what I'm doing!'

'I have enough of an idea. It's in the news.'

'You don't have a clue!'

'You're flying drones. That's all I need to know. I don't want tainted money in my hands, but I don't want you lounging around here frittering away your wages with no sense of how to look after yourself like a proper adult. So I thought we could choose a charity.'

I know this makes no sense, I know she has zero grasp of military strategy or of counterterrorism, but I can never find the words to defend myself against my mother. I keep thinking that one day I will stand up and assert myself over her, but I have no idea how to make this happen.

'There are organisations that collect for people in The Strip,' she continues. 'The blockade keeps them very low on medical supplies. We can help with that. Or we could find a charity for orphans there. That might be more fitting. Given what you've been doing.'

Ripostes, arguments, howls of outrage, screams of unadulterated anger flit across my brain, but nothing gets as far as my mouth.

'If I was in your shoes I wouldn't want to hear the truth either,' she says. 'But if nobody else is going to mention it to you then I suppose it's my job.'

'I'm good at what I do!' I bark, willing my legs to carry me from the room, to release me from her presence, but for some reason I do not move.

'That makes it worse. I don't want to hear any more.'

'Why can't you respect me? You always act like I'm a failure, but I have a career! I get paid! I have colleagues who recognise me for who I am and you … my mother … you think you can endlessly judge me and criticise me …'

'A career?'

Blood is pounding in my ears, and I realise that I am on my feet, with a chair toppled on to its back behind me. My mouth is open, gulping in air for another tirade, when I notice that her eyes are glistening with tears. She's dead still, hands folded neatly in front of her on the tabletop, grey ponytail pointing limply down her stiff, straight back.

My hand closes into a fist, which I pound down on to the table.

'YES! A career.'

A silver candlestick clatters on to its side, the candle rolling across the tabletop in a lazy arc. I walk away, then find myself hovering, hands pressed against the door frame, head bowed.

The rattle of the candle rolling back towards the centre of the table fills the room.

'So we'll go for that medical charity then,' she says.

I turn back to face her. She doesn't look up.

'The other guys at the base … to their families, they're heroes.'

She shakes her head, still not looking up. 'I don't understand. Why can't you see what you're doing?' she says. It looks as if she's talking to her hands.

'You can give the money to whatever bunch of do-gooding idiots you want. I don't care. I'll be out of here as soon as I can. I can't take this any more. I don't have to listen to you!'

'Of course you don't,' she says, with a falling intonation which makes this sound like another accusation.

I'm on the brink of asking her why she hates me, but I can't let myself say something that would sound so weak and needy. However I put the question, it would seem like I was begging her for something, and I'm not going to beg.

I look down at her frail, bony form, ankles tucked neatly together under the dark wooden dining chair. She looks so small, so vulnerable, yet I know she is immoveable. Nothing I can say will change her opinion of my work, or of me.

If I want to be my own man, I have to stop caring what she thinks. While she can wound me with her disapproval, I am still a child, still somehow encircled and enslaved by her personality. The time has come to throw her off. I have waited far too long. I must leave home, leave her behind, grow up.

I walk out, turn for my bedroom, then spin on my heel and head for the front door. Even though it is late and dark, I need to get back on my bike. It doesn't matter where I go, I just need to ride.

The City

There's only a message or two each day, which Dad usually hands me as soon as I get home from school, but I'm always thinking about it now: planning routes; noticing short cuts, overhangs and alleyways; building up my own bespoke messenger's map of London. Dad says my movements are data the enemy wants, and the more intelligently I navigate, the less they get from me.

He wasn't expecting me to pick things up so fast, but all the video games I've played have trained and prepared me. Navigating through hostile territory, concealing myself from the enemy, stealth: I've been practising this since I was old enough to operate a joystick. Though at the moment, I'm hardly playing. My days are too full, and also, for the first time in my life, gaming has begun to feel unreal, slightly pointless. I seem to have lost the knack of jumping into another skin and losing myself in an imaginary world.

In those games, the enemy was always visible, right there, leaping out from behind a wall to either shoot you or take a bullet himself. Our struggle here is different. There's no invader on the ground, but as Dad often says, if a hostile army rules your skies and borders, if you can't leave or return, cannot export or import without the permission of outsiders, then you're under occupation.

Everyone knows that fighting back is futile, but a wasp in a jar only stops battering itself against the glass when it is ready to die. My city has become an enormous jar, filled with wasps.

Besides, The Corps rules London, and it's becoming clear to me that joining up connects you to the only network powerful enough to lift you above the desperate, miserable throng who are simply scrabbling to survive.

I don't get paid for delivering messages, not officially, but Dad now gives me pocket money, which I've never had before. It's only a small amount, but getting anything at all sets me apart from my friends.

It takes me a while to realise that even though I don't tell anyone I'm working for The Corps, people somehow figure it out. This is a city where everyone watches everyone else, alert for any scrap of information that might find you extra food, lead you to a source of work or confer a shred of power.

Our lives are sucked up into the lenses that perpetually circle above us, but on the ground too, secrets leach away.

Informers are everywhere, so we all watch each other warily, never sure who to trust. Nothing in this city can remain private. The only people here who aren't paranoid are the ones who've gone insane.

I noticed quickly how friends and strangers began to defer to my dad when he took up his new role in The Corps, but it's weeks before I perceive something different in how people talk to me. Then, from other teenagers, from neighbours and shopkeepers, from friends' parents, I begin to hear a new kind of a courtesy, a respect in their tone and vocabulary. Even my teachers seem slightly different, hesitant to criticise or discipline me. If I'm short of time and hand in rushed or unfinished homework, nothing, however sketchy, seems to get any mark below a B minus.

When I offer Jake the money I owe him for the video game he sold me, months later than promised, he tells me not to worry about it, and won't accept.

It takes me a while to realise what my change in status means. I don't understand, at first, that it's a resource which can be tapped.

One of the other messengers gives me the idea. After clocking each other on deliveries several times, it's obvious to both of us that we're doing the same work, but at first we follow the protocol and ignore one another. Then, one evening, waiting for a reply in the draughty stairwell of a block of flats near Mornington Crescent, he offers me a cigarette. He holds out the pack with an awkward grip, ensuring I can see

58

this isn't a cheap local brand but a foreign import, smuggled in, the type of cigarette used more often as currency than as something you might actually smoke. Lighting one of these is like burning money.

I decline – I couldn't possibly afford to smoke, even if I wanted to – but I can't resist asking him where he got them.

He gives a knowing smile as he pulls out an ornately engraved lighter, flicks open the lid and sparks up.

'Easy,' he says, 'if you know the right people.'

He leans back against the wall and blows a funnel of smoke towards the ceiling.

'And if you don't?' I say.

'But you do,' he replies. 'You know me.'

At that moment the apartment door opens, a message is passed out to him, and he leaves at speed, wordlessly, without a backward glance. Just before descending the stairs, he turns and gives me a wink.

I see him a couple more times after that, once at the door of my own place when he comes with a note for Dad, once coming out of a crowded lift that I'm about to enter, but we greet each other with nothing more than a nod, and make no attempt at conversation.

When we eventually find ourselves in private again, I ask him immediately about the cigarettes.

'You thinking of running a little sideline then?' he says with a smirk.

I shrug. I don't really have any idea what he's talking

about, but don't want to look naive.

He toys with me a little longer, then tells me everything: where to go (a particular newsagent on Caledonian Road), what to say to get the product, and how to sell it on. Something in the detail of his instructions makes me think he must be getting a kickback from the supplier. He reinforces several times that I have to say I'm 'a trusted associate of Phoenix'. I know better than to ask his real name.

Sensing my uncertainty, he tells me 'everyone does it', which it is clear means not every kid, but every messenger. 'We're protected,' he says. 'If you're in The Corps, you're bulletproof. That's our wage.'

'Is it?' I say.

He breaks into a laugh and claps me on the arm. 'You'll see,' he says. 'Or you could walk around in those shitty trainers for the rest of your life and see where that gets you.'

As I'm examining his immaculate clothes, elaborately gelled hair and pristine shoes, the door opens and we swivel away from one another, pretending we weren't talking. A message comes out. He takes it and hurries off, throwing me a knowing smirk as he goes.

As soon as I have a free afternoon, I head for the Caledonian Road newsagent, where I tell a specific man with a grey side parting and two missing fingers on his left hand that my 'trusted associate', Phoenix, has told me this is a place where foreign cigarettes can be bought.

He looks me up and down, and without a word withdraws from view through a bead curtain, which rattles back into place behind him.

Anything worth buying has usually been smuggled in through the Brixton Tunnels. Only the bare minimum to keep us alive enters London above ground, through the check-points. The Corps dig and control the tunnels, and the more I learn about how the organisation's tentacles spread through-out the city, the more it seems as if the only way to carve out a comfortable life for yourself in The Strip is to find a way to tap into this black market.

The cramped, dimly lit newsagent, smelling of sugar, news-print and old sweat, seems to close in on me as I wait in tense silence for the return of the shopkeeper, looking up at the jars of ancient-looking sweets which line the walls.

A distant conversation wafts through the bead curtain.

I'm beginning to wonder if I have the wrong place, and should run for it – if this is some kind of trap – when he even-tually returns with a red and white packet, which he sells to me without uttering a syllable. It costs more or less every penny I have earned delivering messages.

I've never held one of these in my life. To my surprise, the packet weighs almost nothing. As I stuff the glossy rectangle into my back pocket, it occurs to me that never before have I spent so much on so little. If I can't resell these cigarettes, this will be a heartbreaking mistake.

I feel light with nervous anticipation as I head south,

skimming through the ravaged streets, barely noticing that I'm walking until south of the canal, when the atmosphere suddenly changes. Without warning, I find myself struggling against a current of people who throng towards me, knocking me off the pavement. I hear snatches of conversation about an aid delivery, a distribution centre, talk of blankets and bread. A few people are running, some so old their run isn't much faster than my walk. I'm tempted, briefly, to follow the horde, but resist the urge. Nothing good ever happens in crowds.

The swarm has died down by the time I reach the crumbled hulk of King's Cross Station, one vast fire-scorched arch still standing as a gateway to nothing. Every inch of the plaza is covered in the close-packed maggot-like lumps of the blanketed street dwellers who are always here, always seemingly asleep.

A heavily made-up woman with a tangle of grey hair falling down the back of a torn, jewel-encrusted dress is standing on a marble plinth, warbling an operatic lament. As I pass her, a flurry of sprinting boys dart at a diagonal across Euston Road. A few shouts rise above the background rumble of engines, there's a loud bang, what sounds like it might be a scream, then the boys are gone.

I don't turn back, don't look to see what has happened, but press on, past a gaunt man yelling into a loudhailer about Judgement Day, to my destination: a prime corner, in front of where St Pancras Station used to be, traffic always backed up in four directions, gangs of boys weaving between cars, selling cigarettes, newspapers, flowers, gum, sweets, vegetables, toys, balloons, shoes – anything.

I lift the silky cigarette packet out of my jeans and weigh it in my hand, looking out at this helter-skelter street market, which looks like chaos, but isn't. Everybody's kicking something back to the men who own the corner, and if you're not, you'll be beaten up in minutes.

'Phoenix' has told me that I'm exempt. I just have to go out there and sell, and when I'm challenged, let them know who I am. According to him, it's that easy.

I stand beside the crawling chain of stalled traffic, buffeted by a relentless stream of pedestrians, sliding the cigarette packet nervously from hand to hand as I scrutinise the junction.

Teenagers are stationed at every branch, working the cars, vans and trucks, tapping on windows with outstretched palms and pleading gestures, selling their goods in a way that feels not entirely different from begging as they hustle from vehicle to vehicle.

Four roads makes eight lanes of traffic. There seem to be three or four kids working each lane, with territory earmarked and agreed upon. Each seller appears to cover the same patch at every change of the lights. Between them, there's no arguing and little conversation, just the weary efficiency of a nimble, well organised workforce.

What strikes me most isn't the show they put on to sell their wares, it's the way they go limp when the lights change to green and just stand there among the traffic, dead-eyed, resting on the spot, not even bothering to walk to the kerb.

I zero in on the lanes heading back towards King's Cross, which I decide have the smallest, least intimidating hawkers. There's a kid in ripped jeans and a sagging grey T-shirt who dances fast between the cars, selling combs and hair clips. He has a smiling, shrugging routine that he performs over and over again to try and get people to open their windows. He's selling a performance of youthful charm as much as he's selling his pointless combs. There's a bigger guy in a pale blue anorak zipped right up to his neck washing windscreens. He doesn't give people much choice about whether he's going to do it, then leaves it up to their conscience if they pay him or not. Some people get angry, waving and shouting at him, or put on windscreen wipers to shoo him away. Others resignedly pay up, knowing they've been scammed. A few let him finish cleaning their windscreen then stare straight ahead, refusing to acknowledge what he's done or to pay him.

He never reacts. Just waits, and if there's no payment after a minute or so, silently walks away. It's the not looking at him that seems worst – the pretence that despite his work, he doesn't even exist. If anything riles him, it must be that, though his face shows no emotion.

There's one other guy, dwarfed by a huge red hoodie, who's turned his fist into a dandelion of lollipops, lurid orange and yellow sticks sprouting from his hand in every direction. He's quicker than the others, darting between cars with balletic skill, less persistent, but covering more customers.

I once had a paratrooper game which began with a sequence where you walk to the hatch of a transport plane, then launch yourself into mid-air. That's how I feel as I slide the cellophane off the cigarette packet, flip the lid and head in.

I've always been a nobody, a nobody living in a whole city of nobodies, and if my status has risen I have to capitalise on it. Mine is not a life where any opportunity can be squandered. If I really am protected from above, I need to know, and I have to make use of it.

Within a few seconds of stepping out into the choking fumes of the junction, the windscreen-cleaner boy is inches from my face. Up close I can see he's dirty, wet and cold. He's half a head shorter than me and at least a year younger, with bloodshot eyes and pallid, shiny skin, but I can tell immediately that he knows how to fight and isn't afraid of me.

'What are you doing?' he barks.

My instinct is to walk away, but I know this is the moment of truth. I've started an experiment, and I have to see it through. The sponge in his hand drips water and suds into a puddle next to his scuffed, falling-apart trainers as he waits for an answer. I can feel a coil of suppressed violence in him twisting ever tighter.

'What do you think I'm doing?' I say, fighting the urge to take a step back.

'This isn't your corner.'

I snap back fast, 'Says who?'

'Are you an idiot or what?' he demands.

'You're the idiot,' I reply, which is hardly very witty, but seems to shock him. Everyone knows how things work. For a moment, he's lost for words.

The lollipop seller arrives and it's only up close, seeing inside her hood, that I realise this is a teenage girl, with pale, almost translucent skin and coal black hair cut into a fringe that partially overhangs her green eyes.

'What's going on?' she asks.

'This guy …' says windscreen boy. 'He thinks he's …'

She turns to me, wilting my determination with the power of that clear green gaze, and says, 'What's your problem?' Her voice is authoritative, slightly husky, surprisingly low for a girl so slender.

'There's no problem,' I say. 'I'm selling here now. Just for today. And if either of you touch me, you'll regret it.' I say this lightly, as if it were a neutral statement of fact, rather than a threat.

'Why's that?' the guy snarls, unimpressed, his right hand tightening into a fist.

'Whoever it is that runs this corner,' I say, 'who do you think runs him?'

I jut my chin at them, a tough-guy posture I must have picked up from some movie. I've never thrown a punch in my life, have previously run away from any fight that seemed to be brewing, so this is all an act, almost a game, but a deadly serious one, with bloody consequences if it goes wrong.

Windscreen boy and hoodie girl step into the central reservation and form a huddle, watching me as they mutter to one another. With each passing van they flash in and out of view. He pulls a phone from his pocket and writes a text.

I could start selling while I'm waiting for them to decide what to do, but that might be too provocative. The goal here is to find out how much of The Corps' power has trickled down to me, without getting beaten up in the process. So I wait, a rock within the gushing stream of traffic, sensing the fumes begin to rasp at my throat and eyeballs.

Through the crowds of ambling scavengers, desultory strollers and hurried commuters, I see a man approach at speed. I sense immediately who he is. He's only a few years older than me, but seems like another species, with gym-honed muscles stretching the fabric of his T-shirt and a clenched streetwise face. He steps off the kerb and walks in my direction so fast he's almost running, staring me down as he comes, seeming to navigate through the stream of cars by blind instinct. A van jams on its brakes centimetres from his shins and blasts out a volley of hoots but he doesn't break stride or even glance in the direction of the angry driver. He just zones in on me, approaching with a menace in his eyes that makes me think he might be intending to punch me out without even a moment's discussion.

I have to wring every drop of courage from deep within to stay put. An inner voice screams at me to run, to save myself, but I somehow override it and stand my ground.

His pace gets no slower as he approaches until he stops dead, toe to toe, so close I can feel the warmth of his meaty breath. His eyes are such a pale blue that his pupils seem almost white. He has a small upturned nose and sunken cheeks cratered with acne scars.

'What are you doing?' he says, his voice menacingly quiet.

'Selling cigarettes,' I reply, struggling to meet his wolf-like stare.

'Get out,' he says. 'Now.'

I sense, as clear and unnerving as the drop in air pressure before a thunderstorm, that I have only a few seconds before he punches me. 'You don't know who I am, do you?' I say.

A muscle under his left eyeball twitches. His whole body pulsates with the tension of a pit bull straining at the leash.

'I told you to get out. I don't usually have to say that twice.'

I tell him my name, adding pointedly my father's name. 'Do you know who that is?' I add.

He breaks eye contact for the first time, looks up, sniffs and wipes a thumb along the rim of one nostril. The electricity that had been crackling between us since his approach begins to dissipate. He takes a quarter-step back. His shoulders fall and he interlaces his fingers, swiftly cracking the knuckles of one hand then the other.

Above the roar of traffic, a silence stretches between us.

'Are you going to make a habit of this?' he asks eventually.

I shrug, fighting to keep my face blank as I hold back the twin urges to collapse on the ground with relief and dance a jig through the traffic.

He spits on the tarmac and walks away to the two hawkers. I don't want to look as if I'm waiting for his permission, so I turn away and begin to sell cigarettes, though my thigh muscles suddenly seem barely strong enough to hold me upright.

A bearded man in a battered yellow Ford immediately buys two, but my trembling fingers struggle to pull them from the packet. Within the next few minutes, as the adrenalin seeps from my bloodstream and my coordination returns, I sell almost half the packet.

I double the price, and still sell out within half an hour, hauling in a bigger profit than I had ever imagined.

As I walk to the kerb I scan all four roads of the junction. It looks like the boss has disappeared. I'm about to head home, but when I take a last glance back at hoodie girl, I see that she's staring at me.

Riding a wave of newfound confidence, I walk towards her through the stream of cars, attempting a casual stride. She turns away, seemingly embarrassed to have been spotted looking at me, but she must sense my approach because she turns back just as I reach her.

Her eyebrows are pinched together in a look of curiosity and puzzlement. I sense that she wants to know who I am and why I wasn't kicked off her corner. Until now, no one has ever wondered who I am because the answer was obvious: nobody.

'How much?' I say, nodding towards her lollipop fist.

She names her price, holding eye contact with an intensity that brings a flutter to my chest.

'That's a rip-off,' I say.

She shrugs, a hint of a smirk playing at the corner of her lips.

'I'll take two,' I say, handing her a coin from my jangling pocket. The nervousness and uncertainty that normally overtake me in a situation like this have, for some reason, taken flight. I feel as if I'm on stage, playing the part of a tougher, older, cooler version of myself.

She gives me two lollipops. I unwrap them both and hand one right back to her. 'That's a thank you. For letting me share your corner,' I say.

She smiles reluctantly.

'Don't you ever take a break?' I ask.

She looks around, scanning for her boss, then follows me to the kerb, where we sit with our feet in the gutter, sucking our lollipops.

A broken hubcap is on the tarmac between us, which she spins with a flick of her shoe. As the lollipop dissolves on my tongue, I concentrate on trying not to look as if I'm straining every brain cell in search of something to say.

'So you're protected?' she asks eventually.

I nod.

'By who?'

'Who do you think?'

She rolls her lollipop from one side of her mouth to the other.

'And that means you can do whatever you want?' she asks.

'I wouldn't say that.'

'Lucky guy,' she says, with an edge of sarcasm, popping the lolly from her mouth and scrutinising its lurid, shiny surface.

The idea drips into my head that I might be coming across as arrogant and aloof. This silent, cryptic, macho thing isn't who I am at all, and I can see it's not the way to impress her.

'What's your name?' I ask.

'Zoe.'

'You here every day?'

'Most days.'

'What about school?'

She shrugs. 'I don't have a choice.'

Her green eyes flash towards me, and I sense her catching the intensity with which I'm staring at her mouth. We briefly examine one another, in a silence that teeters on the brink of weirdness. There's a *how dare you* thing that girls usually do if they see you look at them this way, and she isn't doing it. She's looking right back at me, inscrutably, but without hostility.

'So what's it like to be lucky?' she says, in a voice that sounds half joking, half not.

I waft a hand towards the bombed-out railway terminus, taking in the clogged, potholed streets, the hordes of ragged pedestrians, the teams of underfed hawkers battling through a tide of scrappy, rusted vehicles. 'You think anyone here is lucky?' I say.

'Yes,' she replies, looking down towards the hubcap, which she flicks into another spin. 'I was lucky. Then I wasn't.'

It's rare to hear anyone open up the armour you have to wear in this cold, hard city; astonishing from someone you've only known a few minutes. This tiny, enigmatic admission feels like a confession, a testament of unexpected trust.

'What happened?' I say.

She looks at me. For a moment, she seems to stop breathing. Her eyes moisten. Then a distant noise resolves itself into a repeated word, shouted from across the street. 'ZOE! ZOE!'

It's the boss. Zoe swears under her breath, drops her half-finished lollipop into the gutter, leaps to her feet and darts through the traffic towards him. With an angry hand gesture, he sends her back to work.

As I stand, I find myself looking momentarily into his predator's eyes. I can sense him sizing me up, scoping out my weaknesses, straining again at that leash which, for now, holds him back from harming me.

I turn away and begin the long walk home, oblivious to the crowds and fumes and cratered pavements and blocked roads, barely feeling the ground under my feet.

So now I know for sure that Dad's position in The Corps is a shield which extends over the whole family. I'm protected. But even this amazing discovery feels insignificant compared to what I think has passed between me and Zoe. Even though we've barely spoken, I have the sensation of a key slipping into a lock, of a tantalising secret poised to reveal itself.

The Base

I haven't spoken to my mother since our argument. She never said how much rent she wanted me to pay so I've cooked up a figure on my own, deliberately too much in the hope that it makes her feel guilty. I leave it on the kitchen table every Sunday evening, fanned out like a poker hand.

I'm only half living there now. I eat breakfast at home, timing it so she won't be in the kitchen, lunch at the base and dinner in a cafe with other pilots. On days off, I head out on my bike and don't come back till late. I no longer touch her leftovers in the fridge. I buy my own bread and milk.

Time has a strange effect on anger, like sunlight on a photograph. The sharpness is dissolving, colours fading.

It's not like I never see her – it's a small house – but we don't speak, and by not looking at her, it's almost as if I can make her disappear, though it probably seems to Mum as if I'm the one who has disappeared.

At the time of day when I get home, she's usually in the sitting room. From the hallway I can see the flickering TV, hear the blare of newsreader bluster or maybe a bark of canned laughter, but where she sits is out of sight.

Sometimes I stand there for a while, watching the screen. I could easily go in and sit next to her on the sofa. I wouldn't have to say anything. I'm sure she'd be pleased, and wouldn't make me speak. But I prefer not to.

Whenever I'm awake around midnight, I hear her footsteps as she shuffles to the toilet, then the flush, which is directly through the wall from my pillow, then her slow walk back to bed.

I sometimes wonder what she hears of me. My showers? The revving of my bike? A clatter through the walls when I remember to empty the dishwasher?

It's a curious kind of intimacy this: sharing a home, hovering around one another, kept apart by a hostility that has made us ghosts in one another's lives.

Our house feels as if it has filled with the sour, musty smell of loneliness. I sometimes worry that guys on the base will catch a whiff of it on my clothes, or glimpse it in my eyes. It seems somehow shameful to live like this, but I can't think how to change course.

When I'm riding home from work, my brain seems to empty. It's as if my mind loses itself in the task of operating the bike, pulling me entirely into the moment, while somehow freeing an inward eye to float idly through my deepest thoughts, probing and sifting. It's strange how often Mum pops into my head.

As I arrive, shunting my bike into the narrow gap of paving between Mum's purple Nissan and the neighbour's rickety fence, the same idea often sits heavy in my chest. My drifting thoughts, as I ride, often seem to come down to this. I have spent my whole life trying, and failing, to be loved by her. She is a kind and generous woman, who has refused me very little, given me every comfort a son could want, except for this, the most fundamental essence at the heart of it all. She has always been there, by my side, helpful and diligent, but the innermost door is closed.

So as I walk in, and glance at the same TV she is watching, I often feel this position says everything about who we are. Even when we're looking in the same direction we can't see one another, and we've got so used to the barrier between us that I can no longer tell whether my invisibility is a source of comfort or pain.

Of course I also have another ghost family, with whom I share most of my waking hours. They too know I'm with them but cannot see me. They have no idea who I am, but they're in no doubt they are being watched.

Maybe all of us, everywhere, are in some way both more alone and less alone than we'd like to be.

For half a year I have followed every move made by #K622.

I know his daily routine, where he eats, who he talks to, when he gets up, when he goes to bed, how he walks, where he shops, how much he plays with his children, everything. I may know more about him than his wife.

His security profile has changed recently. Someone must have informed on him, because he's now on the highest level, and that hasn't come from anything I've observed. What I see could hardly be less interesting. He gets up. He goes to work. He goes home. He visits friends. He sits in cafes, chatting. He goes to bed.

The most suspicious thing is that he never does anything suspicious. He behaves like a man who knows he's being observed. Nobody would be that cautious unless they had something to hide.

He wouldn't be on this security profile if he wasn't a top guy in The Corps, maybe even one of the organisers. Which means he's a marked man. He might as well have a bullseye painted on his head.

What I can't tell is if the people he meets in the evening are other marked men. I'm only told what I need to know for my own work, so beyond #K622 I have no idea who is who. It could be that the guy sitting right behind me in the flight room spends every day following one of #K622's friends (or accomplices), but I'll never know.

My suspicion is that The Corps have understood our capabilities, and the terrorists come together as infrequently as possible. They've realised how much we can see, and everything has gone underground. Anyone #K622 meets in public is probably blameless. Not that anyone in The Strip can really be above suspicion. They all want revenge, every last one of them, which is why they can be given no leeway and shown no mercy.

His younger kids, who must be twins because they're the same size and are always together, seem to spend half their time in their tiny garden, which is usually crammed with toys, balls and scooters. #K622 never joins them, but the mum is always in and out, hanging washing, resolving disputes, playing with the children, or weeding. She never sits down.

The only time he goes into the garden is at night, after the kids are in bed. He knows we could wipe out his whole house at any time, but he must think he's more vulnerable when he's outside, visible from above. He often stands out there after dark, having a cigarette last thing before bed. Maybe he thinks this is safer, but even in the dark I can see it's him. We have his heat signature. Day or night, it makes little difference.

He never smokes at the back door. He always walks to the far end of the garden, away from the house. There are no trees for cover, so he's not hiding. He must know that every cigarette entails the risk of a missile appearing out of the night sky and obliterating him. My suspicion is that he's decided this is a risk worth taking, but he doesn't want his family to be in the blast zone.

Some of our bombs can take out a whole city block, so he's not really keeping them safe, he's just rejigging the odds to make them marginally less unsafe, but maybe that's the best you can hope for in The Strip.

He often sits just inside the back door, probably thinking he's out of view, talking to the kids while they play in the back garden, but if I lower my position and find the right angle he's as exposed there as he would be anywhere else.

If he really cared about their safety, he'd get out of The Corps. That's what I have to remind myself if I ever begin to feel sorry for him or his children. He may seem ordinary, but he isn't. He's a terrorist. He works for an organisation that launches missiles out of The Strip, towards innocent people, and offing him, when his time comes, will make the world a safer place.

It's the son I feel bad for. I remember being his age, mid-teens, feeling half the time there's nothing to do, even though, looking back, I had every luxury a kid could want. Young people in The Strip have nowhere to go, no open space to kick a ball or mess around. Even from thousands of feet above I can feel the boredom and frustration coming off them. This boy never seems to loiter aimlessly on street corners like other teenagers though. More and more, I've noticed that he seems to spend his free time taking long, solitary walks.

At first I didn't think much of it, but #K622's habits are so predictable and uninteresting that I began to keep track of the boy out of simple curiosity. After a while I flagged his activity with an analyst, raising the possibility that he was making deliveries for his father, pointing out suspicious movement patterns and seeking permission to include him in my observation remit. Within an hour I had the OK.

I cover the boy and his father now. When I feed a database of the boy's destinations upstairs, I can tell the analysts are pleased. They react fast and tell me to keep on it. I'm guessing the addresses correlate with ground intelligence for Corps members.

My first thought, when I'm messaged to report to my commanding officer, is that it must be something to do with my work on this boy. I know they're interested in what I've found, so I can't help hoping they might reward me with a promotion.

I hand over to a stand-in and hurry to the meeting, forcing myself to slow down so I don't arrive out of breath. I mustn't look too keen. Nor can I look unkeen. There's a demeanour of flat but alert obedience, without any glimmer of personality or emotion, that is expected during all contact with a superior.

Flight Lieutenant Wilkinson, sitting behind his vast metal-framed desk, has not one word of encouragement or congratulation for me, or any preamble at all, before informing me that #K622 might be upgraded on to a kill list, and since all my operational flight hours so far have been on observation drones, I'll soon be seconded away from the flight room for a refresher training programme on an armed MQ-9.

'It's a pass/fail,' he tells me without eye contact, shuffling papers as if our meeting is already over.

'I'm confident I'll pass, sir.'

'We'll see. There's plenty of others if you don't,' he says, in a tone of voice that makes it clear I should already have left. Wilkinson has a habit of making you feel you've overstayed your welcome as soon as you enter his office.

'Thank you, sir,' I reply and walk out.

I spend the rest of the afternoon just watching #K622's workplace, waiting for him to emerge. When he does, at his regular time, he does nothing more than follow his usual route home, yet despite the utterly humdrum nature of this activity, I find my heartbeat accelerating at the first glimpse of him.

How long before I'm watching him do this exact same walk from an armed drone? How long before I'm given the order to strike?

He probably knows he's a marked man, but he can have no idea how close he now is. I watch his casual progress home – buying a bag of fruit, pausing to chat with a neighbour – riveted by the exact same acts which for the last few weeks have come to seem crushingly dull.

The connection between us feels transformed. I am no longer a mere observer. I have been chosen as the agent of his destruction.

When I think of the godlike power I hold over this man quietly going about his daily tasks, it is dizzying.

Every soldier knows the time will come to kill. We are trained and prepared for this task above all else. But for few others can killing seem so hauntingly intimate.

The City

I never read Dad's messages or the replies I carry back to him, but the volume of communication is revealing, and I have a sense that some kind of action is brewing. I now have at least two every day.

At the same time as overloading me with errands, Dad has become stricter about attending school, insisting it's an exam year and that I need to make something of my life. It might seem pointless to study, trapped in a city where there's no future and little hope of a job, but on the other hand why would you stop? However much you poke an anthill, ants don't stop behaving like ants. They keep going, because there's no alternative. We're the same, though sometimes I find it hard to see the point. If my parents knew the truth about how often I've bunked school, they'd kill me.

Whenever there's a free hour or a delivery run that takes

me near St Pancras, I head for Zoe's corner. I keep a stock of imported cigarettes in a hidden pocket of my schoolbag. Selling them is easy, and the profit is good, but that's not why I keep going back. The pull – the reason why I think about this place nearly all the time – is that whenever I go, Zoe is there.

We always say hi, sometimes with a wave, sometimes with a quick chat, but we never seem to talk for long.

I try not to stare at her too much. I can't repeat the lollipop-buying trick, because that would seem as if I was trying to buy her attention, but there doesn't seem to be any other way to approach her for a conversation.

I know the theory. I know a guy is supposed to just chat up a girl and ask her out. That's how things happen in movies. That's what my friends seem capable of doing. But the reality of it never feels remotely straightforward.

Eventually, having thought through and rejected endless plans for somewhere I could suggest taking her, I decide on a strategy. The next sunny day, I set off in the morning carrying my homework and school lunch, but change course at the first corner, heading for the newsagent on Caledonian Road to stock up. By reinvesting all my profits I now have enough cash for five packs, but the shop assistant still addresses me with nothing more than a grunt.

A sharp spring shower spits out of the sky as I set off again. The pavements, always filled with ambling hordes of ragged Londoners, suddenly empty as people rush for cover. I raise the collar of my jacket and break into a run, dodging the jets which pound down from broken gutters, hopping between huge puddles and the rivulets of stinking water which bubble out of drains and manholes whenever it rains, happy to be moving fast, indifferent to the weather, fizzing with anticipation as I sense the distance between me and Zoe shrinking.

By the time I get to St Pancras a bright low sun is back in the sky. Cars, buses, motorbikes, handcarts and lorries are criss-crossing in every direction over the wet, glistening tarmac, pedestrians weaving through traffic wherever there's a gap. Scores of street hawkers dot the junction, swarming around every stationary car.

I pick Zoe out from within the chaos in an instant. It's as if she's emitting light on our own private wavelength. Her presence amid the grime blazes out at me. I feel like I could find her with my eyes shut.

I'm not sure if she sees me as quickly as I see her, and I don't want her to think I'm stalking her, so without saying anything I start work. As I go from car to car with the cigarettes, preparing myself to approach her, I begin to have the dispiriting feeling of my excitement knotting itself into something else.

I've spent days refining my plan, but I can sense the confidence to put it into place draining out of me. Just finding the right moment to make eye contact and say hello feels like a conundrum I can't solve. The more I fret about where to start, the more my brain begins to cloud, and soon I find myself with no idea where to look, what to do with my mouth or how to stand. As for what I might actually say to her, I can think of nothing. My mind can summon up not one single comment, observation or greeting.

The word 'hello' is vaguely swimming around somewhere in my consciousness as a possible opening. After that I have no idea what I could say other than blurting out the invitation which is my ultimate goal. But I know that's not how things work. You have to chat. Work up to it. Be relaxed and charming and funny.

This whole area – the girl thing – is not my strong point.

'I SAID HOW MUCH!'

A bald man in a tattered T-shirt is shouting at me out of a van window. He wants cigarettes.

I make the sale and step out of the road on to the central reservation, thinking the only way not to humiliate myself is to give up and head to school, but suddenly she's right there, darting into my path from behind a bus.

She comes to a stop in front of me, her two feet neatly together on a single paving stone, and smiles but doesn't speak. One hand is holding a hedgehog fistful of lollipops, the other is resting lightly on a twisted traffic bollard.

The green of her eyes and the black of her hair fling themselves dizzyingly at me. It strikes me for the first time that her fringe is cut at an angle: above her brow on the left, slanting down into her eyelash on the right.

Instead of speaking or smiling, I find myself just staring at her, wondering if she cut her hair into a slope on purpose. Then I realise I have no idea how much time has passed without me remembering to say hello.

'It's deliberate,' she says.

'Oh! I wasn't … I mean …'

'It's OK. You can stare. If I didn't want people to look I would have done it straight, wouldn't I? Like everyone else.'

'I suppose so. I like it.'

'Do you?' she says.

A lorry brushes past so close that the slipstream ruffles her fringe, but she doesn't move, just looks at me, waiting for an answer. She genuinely wants to know if I like her lopsided hairstyle, which makes me realise I only told her I liked it out of politeness, automatically, but now I look properly, I decide I actually do like it.

'Yes,' I say. 'It's classy.'

With her non-lollipop-holding hand, she lifts her hair and shows me a thin diagonal slash across her skin, running along her forehead at the same angle as the fringe, just hidden from view by her haircut. It is the dark purple of a healed wound, not yet the white of an old scar. It cuts a narrow slit through her right eyebrow.

'Shrapnel,' she says.

The roar of traffic around us seems to fade away. The pitted, crumbling facades of nearby buildings somehow retreat, as if to make space for a surge of desire which rips through me, telling me to move closer, to hold her. My life, for a moment, feels poised, balanced on a fingertip. Then the sound of the city returns again, buildings slide back into position, and time restarts.

She lets her hair fall back into place, a blush of self-reproach passing across her cheeks. 'I don't know why I did that,' she says. 'Sorry. It's a weird kind of showing off. I'm so stupid.'

'No!' I say. 'Don't be sorry. It's beautiful.'

'The scar?' A wrinkle of annoyance puckers the skin between her eyes. She thinks I might be mocking her.

'Everything.'

As soon as that single word passes my lips I know I've said too much, given away what I should have concealed, and embarrassed myself.

She looks down at her feet. I can see her eyelashes and cheekbones, but can't make out her expression.

An accelerating bus belches a cloud of grey diesel between us. I notice several sirens wailing in the distance, rising and falling against one another in clashing waves.

It shouldn't be this difficult to converse with another human being. How did something so straightforward become such a treacherous obstacle course?

I can't retreat now, can't take back what I've given away. My only option is to press on and go for broke. 'I've been … I mean … I've made some money working here, and I've been saving up for a … I hope this doesn't sound weird but I'm about to buy a mountain bike. A guy on my street is selling one, and … you know … it's hard to get anywhere but I was thinking of going on a trip this weekend. It's got a carrier on the back so it's not comfortable or anything, but if you don't mind a backie maybe we could do something. I haven't been up Parliament Hill for ages. We might need to walk the last bit. I mean it's probably a stupid idea, but if you want to come …'

That wasn't the speech I planned and rehearsed, but I decide to stop talking. I've stumbled through the gist of the idea. The more I go on, the dumber I'll sound.

She lifts her chin, tucks a strand of hair behind an ear, looks away for a moment, then stares back at me. Those eyes! When they meet mine, I almost forget to breathe.

'Are you serious?' she says.

'Yeah. I mean … you're probably busy, but –'

'I'd love to.'

'Really?'

'Yes! I haven't been on a bike for years. I used to have one when I was about ten. It was purple and I loved it, but … anyway. When do you want to go?'

'Er …'

'Saturday?'

'OK.'

'Meet here? Ten?'

'You don't hang around, do you?' I say, not really knowing what I even mean, but she laughs, tossing her head back, revealing for a moment the soft, pale skin of her neck.

'Don't be late,' she says, raising one eyebrow, before swiftly turning away, hopping down from the central reservation and returning to work.

I stand there, watching her dart left and right through the torrent of steel and glass, like a fish driven by some elemental survival urge swimming tirelessly upstream. I can feel an astonishing energy and verve coming off her, an electricity to her restless, never-still limbs, but watching her work, I sense that if she stopped struggling for one moment, her frail, lithe body would be swept away. I saw something new in those eyes today, something mournful, a knowledge of pain that makes me feel for her even more deeply than before.

Who else was taken in the blast that scarred her forehead? I can feel that she's lost someone. Or perhaps her whole family. Why else would she be out here every day, battling for pennies?

Everywhere in The Strip, people are fighting simply to stay alive. Just to have parents and a home and a family income is to be one of the privileged. Some of us can afford to help grandparents, uncles, aunts, cousins. Beyond that, there's nothing you can do. Desperation is everywhere. To let yourself care about strangers would be like grieving for every falling leaf in a forest.

If I reach out for this girl who is battling to survive, I'm stepping into a lethal current that could sweep me away.

But I have already reached out. I'm already with her. It's done.

The Base

I spot her across the mess hall immediately.

Every day, whatever shift I'm on, I have lunch in the same corner with the same bunch of guys, but when I step away from the service hatch and see this new girl, eating alone, I stop, turn, and stroll casually towards her to take a look.

She has a small, pointed nose and a narrow, faintly severe mouth which moves with an odd circular motion as she chews, but is still kind of attractive. She's eating fast, with her head down, showing no sign of wanting the empty seats that surround her to be taken up.

I watch her for a few seconds, considering my options, trying to summon up the confidence that always eludes me in this situation. New pilots, sensor operators and analysts appear all the time, but women are a rarity, and they don't go short of attention. Any minute now, someone will take one of those chairs.

I've never done well with girls. You could say I haven't really tried, but when you know in advance you're going to fail at something, it's hard not to be stymied by caution and anxiety.

I was never part of the cool crowd at school, or anywhere else for that matter. I'm happier in the background. And what I've discovered about girls is that if you don't push yourself forward and make something happen, then nothing happens.

I often observe how confident people talk, how they stand, the kind of things they say. I've been studying it in the way you'd revise for an exam. I know the theory, I've memorised the training manual, now I need to find the guts to take it out into the field.

During my pilot training, there was lots of talk about transferring skills into the 'theatre of war'. This is what I have to remind myself. Everything is theatre. Life is a performance. There's no way of knowing what is genuine, because nothing divides the real from the unreal. Who we are, what we do, how we behave: it's all an act. Which means you can choose the part you want to play.

Watching this girl a few tables away across the dining room, clutching the rim of my tray, fighting the urge to slink away and sit with the usual people, I silently give myself the motivational pep talk that has gone round my head hundreds of times before. I tell myself that life isn't defined by some averaging out of good or bad behaviour, of niceness or nastiness, but by how you act at a small number of crucial moments. It's when these crossroads come that you have to be who you want to be. A few instances of success or failure, under pressure, are what send your future in one direction or another. This is when you have to man up and perform.

I take three deep breaths and, feeling like I'm going into action, walk over to the girl.

'Is this seat free?' I say.

With the sweep of an open palm she gestures that it is.

'First day?' I ask as I sit, raising my voice over the echoey hubbub of a hundred conversations, scraping chair legs, the clang and clatter from the kitchen.

She nods, chews, swallows.

A comforting waft of beef and custard drifts up from the table as I cut into my food, struggling to affect a relaxed demeanour. I can feel the eyes of the lads on my usual table burning into the back of my neck.

'What department are you?' I ask.

Somebody drops a plate, which shatters on the tile floor. A desultory cheer rises up from a distant corner. My collar feels suddenly tight and too high.

'Software.'

'Software?' I say, my tone of voice more surprised than I intended, which is strange, because I'm actually not surprised at all.

'Just a trainee,' she adds.

'So you're a coder?'

'Mostly patches and updates. You?'

'Pilot.'

'Pilot?' Her clear, brown eyes look at me properly for the first time. She has a fast blink and guardedly penetrating eyes, which are reluctant to meet mine for more than an instant. Her face seems to be without make-up, but her eyebrows have been plucked to two narrow, arched slivers, which give her an air of permanent surprise.

'Stick monkey,' I say. I can afford to be self-deprecating now I've got her attention. This is a standard joke in the base, but since it's her first day she might not have heard the term before. One of the things I've analysed is how there's a line you have to tread between showing off and making light of yourself. To impress a woman you have to balance one with the other. The goal is to demonstrate how great you are without it looking like you are attempting to do this, which is a crazy paradox, but that's what you have to pull off.

The girl cuts a green bean in half and slots it between two crowded rows of teeth.

'Mainly Watchkeeper day to day,' I say, in a humble-sounding voice, 'just surveillance and reconnaissance, but I'm Reaper trained, so that's only a matter of time.'

'You like it?'

This is a weird question, one I've never been asked before. I can't say no, can't pretend I don't like my job, but if I say yes, that makes me sound bloodthirsty.

I take a mouthful of beef and chew slowly, playing for time. An old formula drifts into my head, a line I must have heard from some other soldier, and I tell her I like defending my country.

She smirks and turns her attention back to her steak, cutting off a neat square, which she smears with a dab of mashed potato.

'What?' I ask.

She looks back at me steadily, through narrowed eyes. 'Well, it looks like you're in the right job.'

'Why's that?'

'You do all the calculations before you make a move. By the book.'

'What do you mean?'

'Just – that was a very careful answer.'

'Is that bad?'

Our conversation is finally beginning to flow, but I'm not sure if she's making fun of me. I can feel my confidence ebbing.

'No!' she says, perhaps noticing that she's giving offence. 'It's fine. It's good.'

'You can't be careless in my job,' I say, with a tone I immediately realise is snippier than I wanted it to be. 'I mean, it's a hard habit to break. The training gets into your system.'

'Or maybe you have to be like that in the first place.'

I still can't tell if she's mocking me, and I begin to feel that

95

familiar tidal drag at my ankles, like standing in a retreating wave – the sinking pull of failure.

Beyond her left shoulder, I glimpse a group of my guys on their way out of the mess room, waving and pointing, making stupid hand gestures and doing disgusting mimes. I don't look, don't acknowledge them, keep a straight face.

This somehow helps me focus, ready for one last attempt. I decide to manoeuvre the topic under discussion towards her.

'So are *you* in the right job?' I ask.

'Definitely.'

'Why's that?'

'I'm good at it.' The way she says this somehow sounds objective rather than arrogant.

'Do you like working here?' I ask.

'Just started, but … it's an exciting place. I mean, this is the future, isn't it?'

'Absolutely. We're at the forefront.'

'Nobody out there knows what's possible.'

'Exactly. We can do almost anything.'

'It's awesome,' she says, looking directly at me for the first time. I don't want to be the first to break eye contact, but the moment seems to stretch and intensify, until I lose my nerve and glance down.

As I slice through a knotty chunk of gristle, I sense that we've somehow run aground again. I can feel an awkward silence seep towards us through the cacophony of the mess hall like a falling winter mist. I rifle my brain for conversational topics, but can come up with nothing better than asking her who she works with.

She lists a few names. I ask what she makes of them. She tells me, and suddenly, miraculously, this whole thing doesn't feel so hard. This is how to talk to women. You ask questions, followed by more questions. You concentrate, listen, and bounce the ball back at them.

Talking to guys is like boxing; talking to girls is like a sedate game of lawn tennis.

I feel my fear slip away, sense my body loosening with the slow realisation that I'm doing OK. We are patting words to and fro in the way you're supposed to. I'm not making a fool of myself.

'What are you doing after work? Do you want to go out?' I ask, a little too suddenly and without adequate preparation. As soon as I've spoken, I know it's a mistake. From her expression I sense I may have cut across a sentence. Worse than that, I've skipped a few stages. I've jumped ahead too fast, but once the words are out, there's no way to backtrack.

She raises one of those thin eyebrows and scrutinises me thoughtfully, a loaded fork poised halfway between plate and mouth.

'Can't today,' she says, biting down on her food.

After a few chews, she adds, 'Maybe Friday.'

A lot hangs on that 'maybe'.

Sometimes you have to be cocky. In films it works all the

time. The push and pull is all part of the procedure, and it's the man who has to do the pushing. So I decide to ignore the 'maybe'.

'Friday then,' I say. Not a question. A statement. It comes out just right, assertive with only a faint whiff of arrogance.

She shrugs, and mutters, 'OK.'

Amazing!

Slam dunk.

I don't want to mess things up or give her a chance to change her mind, so as soon as we've arranged a time and place I tell her I'm late for my shift, finish lunch as fast as I can and head back to the flight room, lofted on a magic carpet of triumph and relief.

For an hour or two the screen isn't much more than a blur in front of my eyes. I stare towards the images, but my brain won't focus on what they mean.

Mid-afternoon, I just about register #K622's son buying a bike. I don't see the transaction, but I notice him appear with it down the street. The bike must be a wreck, because he doesn't ride, just pushes it along the pavement and into the house.

A few minutes later the bike reappears through the back door, with the boy and his father. It's one of the only times I've seen #K622 in the garden during daylight. They turn the bike upside down, and the two of them get to work. They take off both wheels and put in new inner tubes. There isn't enough resolution to be sure, but it looks like they strip off all the cogs and the chain, put them in a bucket and scrub them piece by piece. Then there's more fiddling, maybe new brake cables, I can't tell, followed by a long session with the boy getting on and off, and the dad getting the saddle and handlebars to exactly the right height and angle.

#K622 seems to be in charge, telling his son what to do, handing him tools, but mostly it looks like he's just talking and guiding, getting the boy to do it all for himself, teaching him how to care for his new purchase.

It feels strange that my job is to watch this. They have no idea when or how closely I'm observing them – all they see is a drone thousands of feet up in the sky – but for the first time, I have a creeping, uncomfortable sensation that I am intruding. It doesn't feel right that I see this man and his son spend those private hours together, yet I can't take my eyes off them.

After a while I realise that a bubble of self-pity, perhaps even of envy, is swelling in my chest.

It makes no sense for me to look down on these people living their dismal, trapped lives in a brutal hellhole of a city and feel envious, but watching this, it's impossible not to wonder how my life might have been if I'd had a father.

Who would I have become? How would it feel? I have no idea.

Every day of my life I collide with this overwhelming absence, usually just a passing graze, sometimes a dizzying headlong impact.

A pang arrows into my heart as it occurs to me that the reason #K622 is taking such care to make sure his son knows how to repair the bike is because he knows he's being watched, and he knows his days are numbered. I am invisible to them, yet also very present. Me, here, watching them now, might be the reason why they are doing what they're doing. The boy must be taught what to do, before it's too late.

People like #K622 are neutralised all the time. It's clear to me now that he's preparing his family for life without him. The son, too, probably knows he is being readied for life without a father.

As soon as the bike is fully adjusted, the boy takes off through the streets. I call him a boy, but I have the feeling he's at least sixteen. There's something about the way he moves, a weight to him, a breadth to his shoulders. I'm sure the analysts know, but they haven't told me. We're supposed to see everything and understand nothing, just fly and point the lens and, if ordered, launch a missile. The thinking happens elsewhere.

I can't see facial expressions from up here, but I can feel the joy as he zooms around the city, speeding down through Camden, swerving ever faster between the clogged lines of traffic, across the heart of the city and down to the river. In all the time I've been watching him he's never gone this far from his house.

Only at the waterside does he dismount, laying his bike on its side and climbing the rubble of an embankment wall to look out at the water. He sits and takes in the view, motionless.

As I watch him, the queasy thought prickles through me that #K622 may not be alone when I am told to attack. He could be at work, he could be on a walk, or he could be at home with his family. Collateral damage is always assessed, but in time-sensitive operations it isn't a primary consideration.

Just when I am most in need of distance, of indifference, I feel as if a membrane between me and this boy is somehow dissolving. As he looks out at the Thames, relaxed and still, I see not just the son of a terrorist resting after a cycle ride, but a young man enjoying the buzz of subsiding adrenalin, bathing in relief at bursting free from a claustrophobic home, relishing that pure solitude when nobody knows where you are.

I push myself sharply upright and glance around the room. I must not let my mind wander to this place. I cannot allow myself to imagine that I know these people. If my professional detachment cracks, I'm lost.

Every face in the flight room is turned towards a screen. A thick, dead hush fills the air, underpinned by the whirr of hard drives, the hum of air conditioning, a faint buzz from the fluorescent tubes. There are no windows. You have to look at a watch to know if it is day or night.

I take off my headphones, stand, lift my water bottle and drink deeply. The cool liquid passing through my mouth and throat wakes me up, brings me back to my own body, though the flight room is such a strange, otherworldly place that turning away from my screen sometimes feels like rising from a dream only to surface in another dream.

I sit, crushing my empty water bottle, the crunch of plastic in my hand a minuscule reaffirmation of who and where I am. As soon as I'm back at the controls, I redirect my drone to #K622's house.

Nothing will be happening there, but I no longer feel comfortable watching the son. If I zone back on to the home I can sink into contented boredom and let my mind drift back to the girl from the mess hall, to that mysterious, enticing creature whose name I now realise I forgot to ask.

The City

I remember learning to ride when I was small, and I've had occasional turns on other people's bikes, but I had no idea that a couple of wheels and a metal frame could set you free like this.

I'm a little wobbly at first, but the knack quickly returns. Last time I had one I was younger than the twins, and forbidden from straying beyond the end of the street. Now, with this simple machine, I can go anywhere. I can explore the whole city.

Most of the time I can cycle faster than the most expensive car. All those frustrated, boxed-in adults sit there, locked into stalled, angry lines, and I can just weave through, leaving them in my wake. On a bike, you're above every rule. When the jams are tight, you can hop up on to a pavement, dart out into gaps in the oncoming lane, cut corners, anything. As I float through rows of sluggish, stuck drivers, it feels like the closest I'll ever get to flying.

You have to stay alert, as concentrated and vigilant as when you're gaming, but that's part of the excitement. The challenge is to never be stationary, never wait in line like all the fools spouting fumes from their expensive steel boxes.

The first few days I have the bike, Dad slims my workload down to only one message each evening, which he insists I do on foot, but as soon as that's done I strike out through the city, hunting for places I've never seen before, trying to lose and then find myself in London's vast, ancient web of streets.

With every trip, I feel my mental map of the city growing, spreading outwards from the familiar patch around my home: north as far as the encampments on Hampstead Heath, eastwards along the length of the fence, westwards to the other border, and south through the clogged, busy heart of the city as far as the river. There's more to see beyond the Thames, more to see everywhere, and this sense of there suddenly being new places to discover, unseen things to find, feels like a jailbreak.

It's a jailbreak within a jail, of course, since The Strip is fenced-in, blockaded, a giant mantrap, but to be able to explore the entire place, alone and unseen, powered purely by the strength of my own legs, feels like freedom. It would take years to see every street, take in every building and bomb site, fully soak up the whole metropolis.

When you've lived in a city your whole life, finding the true shape of the place feels like finding yourself. With each evening on my bike I sense that I'm learning a little more of where I am, and also, somehow, of who I am.

By Saturday I'm as comfortable on the bike as on two feet, confident that I can take Zoe anywhere she wants to go in the northern half of The Strip without getting lost. I arrive at our meeting place dead on time and spot her straight away, even though she isn't where I'm expecting to find her and is only intermittently visible through the crowds of pedestrians clogging the junction. She's standing in a shaft of dusty sunlight opposite the corner where she usually works, staring down Euston Road, an anxious crease separating her eyebrows as she peers through the waves of traffic. Her head is turned aside, raising a diagonal tendon across her long, smooth neck.

There's a moment when I'm looking at her and she hasn't seen me yet. I don't do anything. I just watch. Her weight is on one leg; the other is bent, with the heel of her trainer resting against an ankle bone. She's wearing tight jeans and a fitted T-shirt, without one of her usual oversize hoodies, and for the first time I can see the curves of her body, take in the full force of her explosive beauty.

I don't wave. I don't even smile. Not yet. I just stand there, wanting her, getting used to the look of her, trying to slow down my heart rate. I find it hard to believe this girl can really be watching hundreds of people stream past, sifting through the onrushing crowds for a glimpse of one person: me. Just that thought on its own feels like an extraordinary gift.

Our eyes meet, she smiles and waves, then darts out through the traffic, weaving towards me. Before I've even thought how to greet her, she plants a kiss on my cheek.

'Sorry,' she says.

'What for?'

She licks her thumb and wipes it against my cheek. I notice that she's wearing lipstick, and has a thin black line drawn along the rim of her eyelids, which extends a few millimetres beyond the corner of each eye, ending in a neat point.

'That's better,' she says, examining my face, standing deliciously close.

I nod, struck dumb, mesmerised by her presence, her physicality, right here in front of me for no other reason than because I have invited her. I feel as if I am at a cliff edge, readying myself for a swallow dive into the rest of my life.

I almost tell her she's looking beautiful, but worry it might sound lecherous or corny. As I try to puzzle out other ways of expressing this thought, which is so powerful it's blotting out all other mental activity, a silence sways between us.

'So this is your new bike?' she says eventually.

'Yeah. Well, it's second-hand.'

'That's why you've been selling cigarettes?'

'Mainly. You like it?'

'Looks good. Not as good as the little purple one I had when I was a kid, but you can't have everything.'

'I'll repaint it if you want,' I say.

She laughs, a wheezy, throaty ripple more enchanting than any music. 'It's OK. But thanks.'

'Whatever colour you want.'

'It's fine,' she says, reaching out for the handlebars. 'So how do we do this?'

'You sit on there, side-saddle, and cross your ankles to keep your feet off the ground. When your legs get tired we'll stop, or we can swap over. You have to hold on to my waist. Are you ready?'

'Totally. Let's go for it.'

I brace the bike. She sits on the carrier above the back wheel. When she's balanced, we set off. Out of the corner of my eye I spot the guy who runs Zoe's corner watching us, his face impassive, thick arms crossed over his meaty torso, the only still body in a swirling crowd.

She squeals with surprise as the wheels begin to turn. Her body sways, making the bike wobble dangerously. A cascade of laughter continues as we head up Midland Road, between the two mountains of tumbled red brick that used to be St Pancras Station and the British Library. It's a one-way street in the opposite direction, so I keep tight to the kerb, ignoring the occasional hoots of disapproving drivers and a cat whistle from a row of guys in a dust-caked white van.

We soon find an equilibrium, and though it seems more than twice as hard as cycling on my own, having Zoe as my passenger is a dizzying thrill. The sensation of her hands pressing against me rockets through my body, setting every nerve alight.

'Parliament Hill?' I say.

'Why not? Are you sure you can manage?'

'We can walk when it gets steep.'

For now, this is perfect: being together, going somewhere, without having to talk. I want to know everything about her, I want to solve the mystery of who she is, whether she has a family, why she has to work as a street hawker instead of going to school, but it feels too early for those questions. I don't yet know how to say what needs to be said, or ask what needs to be asked.

We continue through Camden, up the high street with its vacant block along one side, just mounds and craters of scorched brick. A scatter of children is swarming over the rubble, either playing or scavenging or both.

Where the broken road narrows to one lane, traffic thickens to an angry, hooting clump. Zoe dismounts and we pick through on foot, fighting for gaps between cars with the throng of pedestrians that has turned this junction into an almost impenetrable anthill of humanity.

We don't talk or look at one another as we battle our way forwards, somehow cooperating in the pretence this isn't really happening, because it's impossible to look good while elbowing your way through a crowd, but when a man jostles heavily against my shoulder, pushing me and the bike off balance, Zoe reaches for my hand and pulls me upright. Even though it's much harder to steer the bike with one arm, I don't let go of her.

Only as we emerge from the worst of it do I catch her eye, and a look passes between us that seems to say everything and nothing: *Thank God that's over,* and also *We live in hell, but we are young and alive and together.* In that instant, holding hands with this girl at the edge of a brutal crush of pedestrians, I feel myself grasping as never before the dizzyingly intertwined magnificence and awfulness of life.

After a while she slips her hand from mine, her touch brushing the full length of my palm and fingers.

'You OK?' she asks.

Instead of confessing to her that I am woozy with lust, I nod and ask if she wants to get back on.

She smiles enigmatically, as if she somehow knows what I'm thinking, and mounts the luggage carrier. We set off again northwards. Zoe holds herself closer than before, with both arms around me, and her hands pressed against my chest. These few touches have changed everything. The pull between us already bears no resemblance to a mere friendship.

As we cross the canal I have to brake suddenly when a bearded man with snakes of grey hair streaking down his back steps off the pavement into our path. Before I can shout at him, he grabs me by the forearm and says with desperate intensity, '*I knew you'd come back! I knew you'd come back! I knew you'd come back!*'

I recognise the look of crazed grief in his eye, and let him yell his awful mantra round and round a few times, but it soon seems he will never stop. The sweet, rancid stench of stale urine drills into my nostrils.

'That's not me,' I say. 'You're thinking of someone else.'

He doesn't respond, just rants on and on, still clutching at me with his feeble claw-like fingers.

'Let's go,' says Zoe.

I twist my arm through the air, breaking his grip, and cycle away. His chant continues behind us, neither rising or falling in response to my flight.

Even though Camden Market isn't much more than a few old women selling crates of gnarled home-grown vegetables, and endless tables of hungry-looking people flogging whatever bric-a-brac they have left in their homes, it's still thick with shoppers who block the street as they flood in and out. After that the road begins to clear and I pick up speed.

Beyond the remnants of Chalk Farm tube station the gradient steepens, and when my pace slows to a crawl, Zoe slides off. The attacks must have been sparse around here, towards the northern perimeter of The Strip. Apart from crosses of tape on every window and the occasional bomb site, the streets show few signs of war.

I push the bike and she walks beside me, hopping over the tree stumps that jut periodically from the pavement, as we wind through the backstreets towards Parliament Hill.

'So do you have a slot on my corner or not?' she asks

lightly, but in a way that implies this has been puzzling her for a while.

'Sometimes,' I say.

'That's not how it works,' she replies.

'What do you mean?'

'You haven't bought it?'

'Bought what?'

'Everyone else paid for theirs. Plus the percentage you have to kick up. It's a job, not a hobby.'

'Well, maybe I'm different.'

'Because your dad's in The Corps?'

I shrug.

'Do other people ever just turn up without buying a slot?' I ask.

Zoe lets out a cackle. 'They wouldn't last five minutes.'

'What does he do? Your boss.'

'Craig? He just speaks to them. That's always been enough.'

'He doesn't beat them up?'

'Doesn't have to.'

'What about you and the other sellers? What does he do to you?'

'Nothing much.'

'But you have to do what he says?'

'Yeah.'

'Or what?'

'You just do. Unless your dad has magic powers and you can drift in and out whenever you fancy.'

There's something delicately hostile in her tone, which plunges a sudden heaviness into the air between us.

'Anyway, we need him there,' she adds. 'For protection. He looks after us.'

'Do you like him?'

Zoe stops walking and looks at me with weary, disappointed eyes.

'What do *you* think?' she asks.

'I don't know.'

She gives a single sharp out-breath.

'Not even slightly. He's a thug.'

'Good.'

'Good that he's a thug?'

'No. Good that you don't like him.'

She walks on, seemingly annoyed, but I'm not sure why.

'Where do you live?' I ask, struggling to catch up without cracking my shins against the pedals. Her admission when we first met – *I was lucky. Then I wasn't* – has hovered at the edge of my awareness every second I've been with her.

'Somewhere kind of weird,' she says. 'We had to move.'

I give her time to elaborate, but she doesn't. We walk on, faster than before, not looking at one another. I am more or less certain now that she has been bombed out of her home. Her scar dates from that air raid. She has lost at least one parent.

'I'm sorry,' I say.

She nods, not looking at me, and accelerates.

112

'When did this happen?'

'Two years ago. Mum was pregnant. Now she's had the baby.'

'So she can't work?'

'No. Don't ask me anything else. It's a day out. We're supposed to be having fun.'

She suddenly breaks into a run, sprinting away down the street, a burst of exuberance that feels more like an act of will than anything spontaneous or happy.

I know exactly which question she's running away from. Her father. What happened to her father?

I catch up with her at the railway bridge that cuts through a long snake of old terraced houses, leading to the foot of Parliament Hill.

I lock my bike to a half-toppled lamp post which is leaning against the gutter of an otherwise pristine home. When I turn round, Zoe is stroking the head of a scrawny but imperious cat, perched sphinx-like on a garden wall, black from head to toe.

'Is that good luck or bad luck?' I say. 'A black cat.'

I instantly regret using that word 'luck', which must have come out of my mouth because the concept keeps hovering menacingly over us, marking the gulf between my life and hers.

'Neither,' she says, without inflection. 'It's just a cat.'

She turns away slowly, and we cross the railway tracks together, picking our way over the collapsed bridge. A long line of identical laundry-festooned tents, two by two, stretch in both directions along the smooth curve of the tracks, straddling the old railway lines as far as I can see. A few are new, glaringly white, but most have faded to a sickly green, mottled with black streaks of mildew.

A mangy sand-coloured dog lopes out of the nearest tent and looks up at us, assessing the probability that we might be a source of food, then turns away and lies down.

We clamber up the slippery embankment and stand side by side, looking at the ocean of faded tents rising up the wide, high slope of Parliament Hill. Skeins of smoke from innumerable cooking fires are threading into the cloudless, crisp spring sky.

'When did you last come here?' she asks, as we step out on to the bald soil of the hill.

'Not since I was a kid,' I say.

'Was it like this?'

'I can't remember. We have an old map where it's all a huge green heath, but I don't know when that was.'

A mob of children swarms raucously past us, emerging from a semi-functional playground beside the tracks. We set off up the hill, along a line of broad, jaggedly sawn tree stumps. I wonder for a second if it's safe to be walking here, among all these desperate, penniless people, then brush aside the thought. Everyone everywhere is desperate. This place may be a canvas slum, but it's no more dangerous than anywhere else.

As we ascend, without me asking, she tells me about her home, which is a bomb shelter in the book stacks under the British Library. She tells me how the building, when it stood, was like an iceberg. The surface structure was destroyed some time ago, but there's still a vast underground warren, crammed with old books, now also filled with refugees. Hundreds of families live there, crammed together. 'So we always have something to read,' she says, with a resigned, rote tone, as if this is a line she has said many times and no longer finds funny.

'It's one of the only places you don't need to worry about air raids,' she adds. 'We're so far down we barely even hear them.'

She doesn't say what happened to her original family home, but it's clear it must have been destroyed. There's no word of her father in the story, but no mention of his death either.

We're both short of breath by the time we reach the top of the hill, arriving at a small patch of untented land. A low wooden fence, just spikes held together with twisted wire, has been put up to reserve a gravel-covered rectangle of public space, from where you can look down on the whole city, spread out below as far as the horizon.

People must have come here for centuries to admire the scale and extent of London. There's a stainless steel plinth with an etched diagram of the buildings you used to be able to see. A clutch of people is gathered around it, pointing and commenting on the view, hunting for lost landmarks.

Zoe and I wordlessly look down at the huge expanse of concrete, brick and steel. Several drones are buzzing in lazy arcs, one directly above our heads, the bulbous-nosed silhouette unmistakeable. Others further south are just specks in the sky, circling slow and patient, robot-buzzards above a million-mouse feast.

The most striking landmark is the remains of the financial centre – the Square Mile. This cluster of shattered, bombed-out stalagmites was once a millionaire's playground. That's hard to imagine now.

The scar of the eastern buffer zone is the other thing you can't miss, an empty track of bulldozed land stretching all the way to the Square Mile and beyond, punctuated by the concrete cylinders of watchtowers.

It isn't possible to make out what lies on the other side of the fence. I know people live out there, but I don't really know who, or where, or why they won't let us escape this single strip of land.

Behind the miraculously intact dome of St Paul's, a spiral of twisted steel jags high into the sky. People still call it the Shard, though it's no longer a building. The name is maybe more appropriate now.

We stand side by side, silently taking in the view. There's nothing to say. There are no words for what has happened to our city. Out there somewhere lies a heap of brick that was once Zoe's family home.

She turns to me and takes both my hands. A surging pulse

thunders through my body. I can feel it in the soles of my feet. The slice of air between us crackles and fizzes.

The gap shrinks, and shrinks again.

Our lips touch. The most exquisite, delicate pull from her mouth draws me towards her, sealing us together. Her hands rise to caress my neck. The ground, the city, the world vanishes. There is just our kiss.

After this infinitely long, infinitely brief embrace, we are still in the same spot when our bodies separate. I look again into her eyes and see something I never believed I would witness for myself. I never thought this would be directed at me. I see in her gaze, unmistakeably, desire. It is a thrilling, heart-stopping sight.

We look into one another and all awkwardness, all confusion vanishes. It seems as if I know who she is now, and she knows me, and the question is no longer what we might be thinking or feeling, but where this sensation will take us, and how fast. Nothing matters any more, except being with Zoe again, soon, so this can blossom into whatever is next, and whatever comes after that.

I don't know how she's done it, but this girl has plucked me out of my life and deposited me in a new world.

The Base

I'm in a tense and distracted state of mind when my MQ-9 refresher training begins, not because of the work but because it's the same day as my first date with the girl from the mess hall. My instructor starts with hours of talk about weaponry, payload, regulations and procedures, but I find it hard to focus on what he's saying because even though I'm psyched about the idea of finally taking an armed drone out into the field, my mind keeps wandering to thoughts about the coming evening. It's strange how you wait and wait for something exciting to happen, then two huge breakthroughs come along at once, fighting for your attention, stopping you enjoying either of them as you'd like.

My dreaminess only evaporates when they put me on the simulator. There's a zone of absolute focus I used to get into when I was gaming competitively, and it comes straight back to me as soon as I'm at the controls, with targets flashing up on my screen. I haven't had this feeling for a while, and the rush of it floods through me like a blast of caffeine. With remote warfare the simulation is almost indistinguishable from a real battlefield, and the buzz of the hunt and kill obliterates all other thought.

The footage you see on the news is just the clean kills. Only the good ones get out to the press. The training takes in all kinds of complicating factors: visibility, turbulence, collateral damage, blast radius calculations, target identification, and they have ways of injecting stress to put you under combat pressure.

In the simulator you know it's just graphics, but you can't forget you're being tested to make sure you can do it for real. A feed from a drone in the air above a genuine target will look almost the same, so I'm confident I'll be able to step up, though I haven't forgotten that outside the simulator those same pixels will correspond to human beings in terminal danger, facing lethal, inescapable weaponry.

The day I press a button that kills another person, I'm sending myself into a new realm, to a place inhabited by only a select few. Sometimes this idea terrifies me, sometimes it thrills me. I don't know which of those is a more shameful admission. Occasionally I find myself fighting back the stupid idea that crossing this threshold will make me more of a man, though there's no doubt it will make me more of a soldier.

I've had dreams – I suppose you could call them

nightmares – where I'm at the other end of a strike, on the ground among the flames and panic and dust and blood. The dreams, similar to my video feed, are eerily silent, like a movie played on a faulty projector, vivid and present, yet also somehow distant and unreal.

I have no idea if other pilots have these dreams, or similar wayward ideas never mentioned in the training. I don't know if the others have ever imagined themselves living in The Strip, walking the streets that fill our screens, inhabiting the homes that we are ordered to attack. There seems to be no way to discuss how the people in our cross hairs are both impossibly far away and unsettlingly close.

Despite this background unease, despite a creeping fear that an element of the training has somehow not taken root, my work is good, my focus and dexterity tight and sharp. I'm shocked when the instructor tells me it's the end of my shift. I've never known a day at the base to go by so fast.

Adrenalin does a strange thing to time: it lengthens the seconds and shrinks the hours. You see the screen almost in slow motion, calmly hitting the most fleeting sweet spot for each manoeuvre, yet a whole afternoon disappears in a blink.

The instructor doesn't comment on my performance, but I know I've done well. I have a talent and I've been doing this one way or another all my life. It's the job I seem to have been made for. I walk out of the room knowing I'll pass.

I bike home at top speed, shower, shave, put on a good splash of cologne, change, change again a few more times, rinse some of the cologne off my chin so I don't seem like I'm trying too hard, then head out to my rendezvous with the girl.

As soon as I enter the bar that she suggested, the one near the base where everyone goes on a Friday night, I realise how stupid I've been. The place is crammed with uniforms. The girl is in a far corner, so densely surrounded that I can barely get to her. This is absolutely not a date, or a romantic encounter of any kind, or even an invitation with the slightest hint of exclusivity. I'm the only person who has changed into civvies, which makes me feel like I'm the victim of some kind of practical joke.

My first instinct is that I should just leave, right away, before anyone sees me. As soon as I'm spotted, everyone will know what I've been thinking and how I was duped. They'll never let me forget it.

I turn on my heel and retreat. At the exit, before pushing through the heavy swing doors, I take a couple of calming breaths and remind myself how those awful years at school have left me with a hyper-sensitive radar for humiliation. I can sense it coming. I'm primed for an early response, for immediate flight before I can be targeted. I sometimes have to force myself to remember that life has moved on, and nobody is after me any more. I'm an adult.

I turn back, breathe, grab hold of my inner voice and silently intone that I have nothing to fear. Nobody, except maybe the girl, will be able to figure out why I've changed out of uniform. There are any number of plausible reasons. I could be heading to a party later. Yes, that's the explanation I can give if anyone asks. There's no reason to think I'll be the butt of any jokes. I just have to play it cool and behave like a guy enjoying Friday night drinks with his workmates.

There's a bit of ribbing about the cologne – it's lucky I rinsed half of it off – but nothing serious. I make sure I don't rise to it, or blush. I just laugh and say nothing, while discreetly working my way across the room towards the girl.

When I'm within range, I stand at an angle so she can't see my face and is unlikely to spot me, positioned so I can keep an eye on the level of her drink. She's holding a pint glass, and I wait till she's down to the last inch then make my move, cutting through the crowd towards her without, at first, making eye contact.

When I'm right in front of her, I turn my head and act like I've just spotted her for the first time. 'Hey! How are you doing?' I say, hitting the relaxed/casual/friendly tone of voice just right, trying to sound pleasantly surprised to see her.

After a short chat, I offer her another pint. She accepts, and I turn back to the bar holding our two empty glasses, triumphant. I'm in. But when I return, a gang of guys has formed around her, and though she reaches through them to take the drink, looking as if she wants to talk to me, they don't step aside, and I find myself at the perimeter of a crowd of backs, alone.

I stand there for a while, feeling like an idiot, waiting for an opening, pretending to be part of a conversation I can't even hear, then walk away.

I'm too gutted to talk to anyone else after that, so I go outside and join the smokers. I barely smoke – hate the feel of it in my throat and the ghoulish idea of tar lining my lungs – but it's sometimes useful as an option to get you out of a room when you need an exit. Like now.

I take my time out there, then come in for one last drink, which disappears down my gullet much faster than I intend it to. When you're pissed off and not talking to anyone, a pint can more or less drink itself without you even noticing.

I'm about to head home, having notched up another evening of the usual failure and disappointment, when I find myself outside in the car park, with the girl only a few steps away, saying goodbye to a couple of friends.

They leave, I step in, and bingo! It's just me and her.

We talk for a while about what a great evening it's been, and how nice all the guys at the base are, then she launches into an anecdote I can't quite follow about a person whose name I don't catch, but I nod and smile and laugh in what feels like the right places. Then I go for it and offer her a lift home on my bike. I put in the word bike on purpose, and point at my Kawasaki.

She thinks for a second, looking reluctant but tempted, which is just what I'd hoped.

'Are you over the limit?' she says.

'No!' I say, super-confident, though it probably isn't true. 'I'm a pilot. I fly a five million dollar plane all day. You think I can't handle that thing?'

'Er …'

I've gone too far. That was arrogant.

'Have you ever ridden pillion?'

She shakes her head.

'You've got to try it. It's cool. Where d'you live?'

'Right out the other side of town.'

'No problem. You'll enjoy the ride. I promise.'

'If I hadn't been boozing there's no way I'd say yes to this,' she says, as I hand her my spare helmet, which has never yet been used.

I mount the bike, rev up, and she climbs on behind me.

'Ready?' I say.

'I don't know,' she replies.

I rev again. The engine snarls underneath us. 'I still don't know your name.'

'Victoria,' she says, her voice muffled through the foam of the helmet.

Victoria, I mutter to myself, fixing those four syllables into my memory. *Victoria*.

I can't quite hear what she says in reply, but I guess that she's returning the question.

'Alan,' I say, releasing the clutch and easing us into motion.

As we roar out of the car park, my heart is singing. I feel as if everything I have ever done has built towards this moment:

me, on a bike, accelerating away from a gang of mates – colleagues, soldiers, defenders of the nation – outside a bar, beer in the bloodstream, money in my pocket, a girl clinging to my waist.

If anyone who ever called me a loser could see this, they'd choke. Is there any man in the world who wouldn't want to live that moment? Could life get any better than this?

As we fly over the tarmac, trees zipping past, crescent moon smiling down at us from the black sky, with this girl's apartment getting closer every second, I wonder if it is tempting fate to hope that maybe, just maybe, it could.

The City

Just as I'm stepping through the front door my phone beeps. Before I've even looked, I know it's a text from Zoe. I whip the phone from my pocket and read as I enter the house and crash down on to the sofa. *Did you find a place? I've been thinking about it all day. I want to be with you. Z xxxx*

I read it twice, then twice more, smiling to myself, composing a reply in my head, until Dad's harsh, angry voice cuts through my thoughts.

'Where've you been?' he barks.

'Nowhere.'

'Take this,' he says, holding out a folded square of paper. 'Give me your phone.'

I begin to type my reply to Zoe.

'GIVE ME YOUR PHONE.'

'I'm busy.'

He reaches down, snatches away the phone and tosses a piece of paper into my lap. Dad has been edgy lately, veering between gloom and sudden outbursts of anger, his behaviour impossible to predict.

I jump up without touching his message, allowing it to drift from my thigh to the floor. 'I HADN'T FINISHED!'

'What? Texting your girlfriend?' he says with a sarcastic sneer, as if this was the most trivial activity imaginable.

'Yes, actually.'

'Pick up the note. It's urgent.'

'Give me the phone,' I say. 'That's urgent.'

'What?'

'Give me back my phone.'

'Pick up the message! I'm not messing around here! Do you know how important this is?'

'It's always important.'

'Yes! It's always important! Lives are at stake here! Do you think this is some kind of game?'

I don't bend down for the paper, but I stop reaching out to take back the phone. We eyeball one another, motionless.

'What if I don't want to?' I say. 'What if I've had enough?'

It isn't long ago that delivering messages for my dad seemed exciting, seemed like an induction into the adult world, but since finding Zoe that has changed. The pull to spend every moment with her is so intense, anything that comes in the way feels onerous. The school day suddenly seems so long, the evenings and weekends so short. I've bought her a cheap old phone so we can text one another, and being in constant communication now feels as essential as breathing.

Every sliver of time when it's possible to be together, we fly towards one another, as if being apart is a form of suffocation. Some days I've walked an extra two or three miles after dropping off messages, just to give her a brief goodnight kiss.

An hour with Zoe seems to flash by in a minute. We talk about everything and nothing. Only with her do I come fully alive, and every time we see one another, every time we touch, we feed the craving to go further, to have more. It's like living with an insatiable hunger, where the more you eat the hungrier you feel, and the impossibility of ever being alone together, of finding any privacy, drives us crazy with frustration.

It was Zoe's idea that I bike down to the far south of The Strip to look for a hideaway. This is where I've spent the afternoon, cycling around that ghost district, exploring shattered homes and abandoned streets.

It's only way down there, near the devastation surrounding the Brixton Tunnels, that there's any empty space. In every assault, this area is the first place to get bombed. When the tunnels are hit, The Corps waits for the end of hostilities, then digs new ones. Whole blocks have been reduced to rubble, and none of the refugees return, because nobody wants to risk living there.

The text I had begun to type said, *YES! I found the perfect place. We can be alone …*

I wanted to describe the building, tell her how excited I was at the thought of taking her there, but now, before I've been able to send even the briefest reply, Dad has grabbed my phone.

'You're telling me you've had enough?' he says, gripping my arm, staring at me with vitriolic contempt.

I shrug, my anger towards him suddenly tempered by the sense that he's on the brink of tipping into an uncontrollable rage.

'Upstairs,' he snaps, bending to pick up the square of paper from the carpet, then shoving me towards the door, away from my mother and sisters, who are at the dining table playing snakes and ladders.

As I leave the room, I catch Mum's eye. She's always so focused on keeping up a front of normality and cheerfulness in front of the twins that it's usually impossible to detect what she's thinking, but I see on her face a taut expression of strain and alarm. I have a feeling she knows something I haven't yet been told.

I climb the stairs, hearing Dad's heavy, uneven footsteps right behind. He nods towards a bedroom, closes the door behind us and tells me to sit on the bed. I sit; he doesn't.

For a while he looms over me, not speaking, then, in a quiet voice which seems to vibrate with tension, he says, 'I *need* you to send this message, and it has to be done *now*. I'm not asking you, I'm telling you. This isn't the moment to let me down.'

'I will,' I say. 'But I want my phone.'

'You can't have it.'

'Why?'

'You just can't.'

'WHY?'

'I've told you before. They're insecure.'

'I always switch it off when I'm making a delivery. Or leave it at home.'

'That's not enough any more.'

'Why?'

'Something's changed.'

'What?'

Dad prises the back off my phone, removes the battery and places the loose parts in the inner pocket of his jacket.

'I'm sorry. This is how things have to be now.'

'You're taking it off me *for good*?'

'I'm sorry.'

'I was in the middle of writing a text!'

'I'm sorry.'

'I need it!'

'You can't have it.'

'*Why?*'

'I've heard something.'

'What?'

'It might not be true.'

'What is it?'

'It had to happen sometime.'

'What?'

'They're telling me I'm on a list.'

'What list?'

'The drones.'

'What are you saying? What list?'

'I'm a target.'

'What kind of target?'

'They know I'm ... involved. It had to happen sometime. The position I'm in makes me a target.'

'You're saying they're going to kill you?' Saliva rises in my gorge, and I feel for a moment as if I might throw up. A vision of the explosion that shattered my father's leg flashes into my mind. I remember the sensation of throwing myself to the ground, the taste of ash and dust.

'I'm just saying they're watching me more closely than I thought. I can't take any risks.'

'What risks?'

'Missiles can use a phone signal to lock a target.'

'But you don't use one.'

'No. That's one of the reasons why.'

'So why are you taking mine?'

'To keep you safe.'

'You said *you* were on the list. Not *me*.' My vision swims; my head feels suddenly light.

Dad sits on the bed and puts an arm across my shoulders.

131

On the soft mattress, our two bodies tip awkwardly into one another. 'No, not you,' he says.

I stand and look down at him. A disc of scalp is visible at the crown of his head. He takes off his glasses and wipes them on his shirt. I have a sense that he's doing this because he doesn't want to meet my eyes.

He finishes wiping the lenses and looks up at me. The skin under his eyes is pouchy, dark and rough. These last months he seems to be ageing at double speed.

He settles the glasses back on his nose. 'They make mistakes,' he says, his voice little more than a whisper. 'And they use family members to find you. It's not just fighters that die, and it's not just adults. All we're doing is being a little more careful. The most important thing is to keep you safe.'

'But you're still sending me out to deliver messages?'

'I need you to take this one. It's urgent. After that, if you want out, I'll find someone else.'

'I don't know,' I say. 'I want to help.'

'Good. You're a good boy. But I need you to be safe,' he says, his voice wavering. 'You have to stay safe.'

He stands and pulls me into an awkward, sidelong hug. My arms hang loose at my sides as I feel the rise and fall of his chest against mine. Part of me wishes I could comfort him, say something to alleviate the despair that seems to be suffocating him, but the urge to get away, to get out of the house, is stronger.

'OK,' I say, twisting free of his arms. 'Give me the message.'

'I'm sorry, Lex,' he says. 'I'm so sorry. I should never have got you involved. But I could see you drifting, and I know it's hard to find anything to aim for here, so I thought you needed to get out into the real world, participate in something. You're not a kid any more, you need to find your place in something bigger than just the family. I thought I could keep you safe.'

'Thought or think?'

'Both,' he says after a moment's reflection. 'But nobody's safe. Things are heating up. The ceasefire's going to break.'

'They're going to attack?'

'That's the rumour. The Corps has to be ready to retaliate.'

'A rumour?'

'More than a rumour. We have someone. On the outside.'

'Another assault?'

'Seems that way.'

'When?'

'Soon.'

Swallowing this idea feels like drinking a bucket of concrete. It's a couple of years since the last big attack, but the terror of it still haunts me: the sky seeming to tear itself open with the rip of jet fighters; our house almost shaking apart under endless cascades of missiles; the unforgettable soul-shrivelling noise of explosions nearby and far away; every single air raid, night after night, an eternity of lurid, intense hell.

I don't even hear the next thing Dad says. His voice sounds like a dampened hum, a TV heard through the wall.

'What?' I ask, when I sense he is waiting for an answer.

'So when do I get to meet her?' he says, his voice ringing with false jauntiness, a hollow smile pulling at his lips.

'Who?'

'This girl you're always texting.'

It feels crazy to change the subject now, after giving me such dire news, but having mentioned a catastrophe so overwhelming, there's nothing else to say that won't seem ridiculous. Perhaps the only way to deal with this idea is to embrace the fact that it makes every other thing you can possibly utter seem like a joke.

'Oh!' I say, trying to drag my mind towards his question, to follow him away from the abyss. 'Soon, I suppose.'

'Is she nice?'

I nod.

'Is she pretty?'

He raises his eyebrows into a ridiculous parody of excitement, or maybe even of light-hearted comradely lechery, and the beginnings of a smile tug at the corners of my mouth. 'Yes.'

'Are you being careful?'

My cheeks flush red. I think I know what he's saying, and I don't want to have that conversation, not with him, not here, in my parents' bedroom of all places. Not anywhere, in fact.

134

'I'll go now,' I say.

He holds out the message, but when I grip it, he doesn't at first let go. As we both clutch the folded square of paper, he fixes me with an intense stare, and says, 'Thank you. I can trust you, can't I? With this, and with everything else?'

All levity has vanished from his voice. The meaning of this question drips chillingly through me. He's asking me to look after the rest of the family when he is no longer there. I can barely take in this idea, let alone respond.

I pull the message from his grasp and step towards the door.

'There's something else,' he says, just as I'm about to leave.

'What?'

He waits until I've turned to face him before he speaks. 'I'm going to have to disappear for a while. There are a few things to arrange, then I'll be gone. It might be hard to contact me.'

I nod.

'I'll come ba–' he says, but his voice cracks, and he doesn't finish the word.

I spin away, cracking a knuckle against the door frame, run down the stairs, and without a word to my mother head straight outside.

Crisp early evening air fills my lungs. It's that time of day when the sky is still blue, but darkness is beginning to creep upwards from the ground.

The drop is straightforward, not too far away, and I hurry

home with the reply, thinking only about getting to Zoe as soon as possible, to tell her about the Brixton house and to let her know that I no longer have a phone. The idea of her wondering why I've stopped replying to her texts, of her doubting me, twists a knot in my belly.

Dad devours the note I bring him, inhaling the message as if his life depends on it, which maybe it does.

I wish he hadn't told me about the list or about the impending attack. I wish I didn't know. I feel as if there is an irresistible force pulling him deathwards, a rope around his ankle which could at any moment entangle me.

If he really is on this list I don't want to be near him, yet at the same time, just as powerfully, I dread his departure, which I know is imminent and might be final.

I almost reach out and put a hand on his shoulder, but to do that I would need to have something to say, and I can think of nothing. The right words won't come, so I just ask if he still needs me, or if I can go.

He looks up, his eyes unfocused, concentrated on an intense, private thought, and gives a quick nod.

Without looking back, I hurry from the house, unlock my bike and pedal at top speed towards Zoe's corner.

I arrive just in time, as she is finishing work, dusk beginning to pink the sky. I run towards her and we collide into a deep, long kiss.

As I pull out of the embrace I sense someone watching us, turn my head and meet an intense, menacing stare. It's Craig, the man who runs the corner, standing in the central reservation, immobile, the muscles of his jaw twitching under the skin. As traffic passes he flashes in and out of view, unmoving, staring me down.

'So did you find somewhere?' she says. 'Why haven't you texted me?'

'Dad took my phone.'

'When?'

'This afternoon. But listen – I found a place.'

'Down south?'

'Yes. It's a bombed-out house, half-destroyed but still standing, with a complete room hidden away upstairs at the back.'

'A room?'

'Yes. Four walls. A ceiling. There's even a bed.'

She raises an eyebrow. A broad smile spreads across her face, and mine too.

'You want to go?' I ask.

She drops her hands to my waist, kisses my neck, kisses my mouth, and those vivid green eyes blaze at me, so close I can barely focus, as she breathes the word, 'Yes.'

This syllable, on her lips, is the most beautiful sound I have ever heard.

'Tomorrow?' I say.

'Soon,' she replies, pulling me close, her fingers snaking through my hair.

'How soon?'

She draws her cheek away from mine, sweeps aside a wisp of hair that has caught itself in her eyelash, and looks at me, right into me, giving a minuscule nod and a slow, deliriously sexy blink. 'Soon.'

'It's all I can think about,' I say, after a pause that may be five seconds or five minutes. 'I want you.'

'I want you too,' she says, squeezing our tight-pressed bodies even closer together.

'You do?'

'Of course. Can't you tell?'

I can. There's a wild heat in the clutch of our bodies which is somehow heavenly and close to unbearable at the same time – a feeling of hovering, of teetering, of being always somehow on the brink.

'When?' I say.

'I'll have to think about it.'

'What is there to think?'

She smiles, kisses me again, liquefies every bone in my body.

'Walk me home,' she says. 'My mother wants to meet you.'

She draws me away from her corner, guiding me by the hand through the dense crowds on Euston Road.

'Now?'

'You don't want to come?'

'I do, I just …'

'What?'

I'm not sure why I'm hesitating. It could be that I'm taken

aback and unprepared, or perhaps that I sense this is some kind of test. Do I need parental approval? And how am I supposed to behave to get it? I have no idea. But it's clear that the fastest way to fail the test is by refusing to turn up.

'Nothing. That would be great,' I say. 'I'd like to meet her too.'

'Good,' replies Zoe, in a tone of voice that sounds as if she is complimenting me for having chosen the correct tactful lie.

We walk on, soon finding ourselves opposite the vast brick mound that was once the British Library and is now Zoe's home. As we stand at the kerb, preparing to launch ourselves through fume-belching clumps of stuck traffic, she looks at me with intense, melancholy eyes and says, 'Are you sure you want to come in? It's a weird place.'

Something in the seriousness of her tone makes me wonder if the test I am about to face is not what I had imagined. For all the hours we've spent talking together, she has always been evasive about her mother, and has told me nothing about her home. Perhaps this is not about what her family makes of me, but what I make of them.

'I used to live in a house. A nice one. You have to remember that,' she says.

'I know. It doesn't make any difference to me where you live.'

'You say that *now* ...'

'If you don't want me to see ...'

'Just come. Stop talking and come.'

She takes my hand and leads me across the road, then into the library bomb site, past a shrapnel-pocked statue of a seated, armless man, bent double, staring intently at the ground. A flattened pathway snakes over the undulating dunes of brick and down to a low hatch that may once have been a fire escape. Without a word, Zoe stoops and goes in. I follow close behind.

Inside the only light is from a naked bulb, then another dangling a few metres further on, then another beyond that, each casting a patch of brightness along a dark, straight corridor of bare breeze blocks.

Zoe leads the way, her form lighting up then darkening as she passes each bulb, a layer of gritty dust crunching underfoot.

She pauses, turns her head, tucks a strand of hair behind one ear and asks if I'm OK. I stare back, taking in her forehead slightly puckered with concern, her lips ever so slightly apart, and am momentarily silenced by desire.

'OK?' she repeats.

I nod.

We come to a set of metal stairs, flimsy-looking aluminium which jangles and shakes under our feet as we descend past a series of numbered doors: *-1, -2, -3* …

At minus seven she shoulders the heavy door and we emerge into a space both huge and claustrophobic. The ceiling is low, and as we track along the wall we go past row after row of book stacks, each one interspersed with a thin strip of floor space in which a family huddles.

Nobody seems to be speaking. Nobody seems to be moving or even standing. People are crouched, sitting on the floor or lying. Here and there, sheets or towels have been draped as makeshift walls. There are six more floors of this above us. A huge, endless library of displacement and listlessness.

The murky, dank air has soaked up despair like a sponge. The smell of mildew, body odour and over-boiled vegetables seeps heavily into my lungs. I hear the insistent, high wail of a distant baby. From some other direction, impossible to locate, a woman shouts, 'SHUT UP! SHUT UP! SHUT UP!' then falls silent. Something somewhere is tapping, metal on metal, one tinny clank every second. A mixture of floor lamps and ceiling-mounted fluorescent tubes dots the room with uneven patches of glare and gloom. In the dimmest corners, people are wearing head torches.

A middle-aged man with hairy arms and shoulders, wearing a white sleeveless vest, is leaning against the wall ahead of us, half blocking the corridor. He eyes Zoe with a lascivious stare as we approach, sizing up every inch of her. His protruding paunch forces her to turn sideways to pass him, and as she does, he grins, sticks out his tongue and grabs his crotch.

Zoe ignores him and walks on. I freeze, wanting to respond, to defend her, but he stares me down, his dense slab of a body looking ready for a fight. I open my mouth to say something – I don't even know what – then notice a flicker of

141

movement ahead. It's Zoe, rounding a corner, disappearing from view. She hasn't waited for me.

I don't feel I can call after her. In this thick, oppressive atmosphere, I can't open my mouth and shout.

I squeeze past the man, who reeks of old sweat, and hurry towards the last place I saw Zoe, glancing back to check I'm not being followed. As I run, the sound of coins clanking in my pocket seems to reverberate along the library's branching tubes of heavy, suffocating air.

My heart is thrumming with unfocused panic as I round the corner, but Zoe is there, waiting calmly.

'Don't engage,' she says.

'With him?'

'With anyone. No eye contact. Keep walking.'

'OK.'

A sweet, nauseating waft of boiled carrot fills my nose as she tells me to stay close before setting off again at a fast walk.

She begins to weave left and right through the stacks, momentarily dropping out of sight and reappearing at each turn, then I find her with her arms crossed, facing towards me, waiting.

'This is it,' she says.

I nod, but she doesn't move. Her expression seems to be scrutinising my face for a response. I fight to hold my features blank, to conceal that I'm thinking this feels like a place where humans are living like termites.

She takes my hand and leads me into the strangest home I have ever visited. One aisle, narrower than an arm-span, a little shorter than a bus, seems to be her family's allotted space. Four thin bedrolls are stacked at the far end. Her mother is sitting on a low wooden stool, holding the raised arms of a nappy-clad baby swaying on unsteady feet.

A small boy with paper-white skin and wild, straggly hair is sitting close by, seemingly intent on a pair of toy cars, but he leaps up and charges towards Zoe as soon as he sees her.

Zoe lifts him and kisses his neck, then snuffles into him, snorting like a pig. 'I'm going to gobble you up!' she says. 'Gobble you all up!'

He squeals with delight and begs her to stop, but as soon she puts him down, he grabs her by the legs and says, 'Again! Again!'

While Zoe tussles with her brother, swooping him into the air, the mother steps towards me, holding the baby on her hip and patting her hair into place with a free hand.

'So you're Lex,' she says, her mouth spread into an attempt at a smile, though her eyes are vague, exhausted, deadened. 'It's lovely to meet you. I've heard so much.'

'I … er … it's nice to meet you too.'

'This is my beautiful home,' says Zoe.

'It's not home,' snaps her mother. 'This isn't our home.'

Zoe catches my eye, gives me a look that tells me to say nothing.

After an awkward silence, Zoe's mum asks if I'd like a cup

of tea. I wouldn't, but I say yes anyway, because it seems rude to refuse.

She brews from a small kettle squeezed on to a low shelf, filling it from a bucket using a plastic scoop.

As the kettle boils she asks us where we've been, what we've been up to, what the weather's like, if there's any news from outside. Within a couple of minutes I notice that she begins to repeat herself. The same questions return, asked with identical wording and identical intonation.

I glance furtively at Zoe, and she gives me a discreet nod which seems to say, *Yes, this is how it is. This is my family.*

She answers one of the repeated questions with the same patient response as first time round, cueing me in, showing me how conversations with her mother work.

We sip our tea.

We chat through a couple more cycles of the same queries.

Zoe's mother doesn't let silence fall for a moment. Then, abruptly, she does. She falls still, and for a long time stares into her empty cup without moving a muscle, as if she's forgotten I'm there. I've never seen any face look so tired.

When she raises her head she seems different, as if she is looking at me for the first time. With a start, I notice something that chills me. Although rheumy, dim and bloodshot, those eyes are an exact match of Zoe's.

'I have to ask you something,' she says, her voice lower and sharper than before.

'Yes?'

'Zoe has told me about your father.'

'Told you what?'

'She says he's an important man.'

My eyes flick towards Zoe. She looks embarrassed.

'Mum!' she says.

'Can he help us? We're on the rehoming list, but low. Very low.'

'Mum!'

'I'm just asking!'

Zoe directs a minuscule headshake at me, a tiny disavowal of her mother's question. Everyone knows the rehoming list is meaningless. No building materials are coming through the blockade. Nothing is being built, nobody is getting rehomed, and my father has no influence on that list anyway.

I think again about the loop of questions, the eerie blankness in this woman's eyes, the mantle of despair over her cramped living quarters, and the suspicion occurs to me that she barely goes above ground, that her whole world is this cramped, suffocating dungeon.

I could be honest with her, or I could offer a glimmer of false hope. Zoe's face looks tense and alert, but offers no clue as to how I should respond.

I clear my throat, press my hands together and say, 'I'll ask him. He might be able to help.'

Her eyes instantly moisten with tears.

'Thank you,' she replies, barely able to get the words out. 'Thank you so much. So much.'

'He has to go now,' says Zoe. 'He can't stay.'

'OK. Of course. So nice to meet you. So lovely. I hope you come again. Really. If I'd known you were coming …'

'It was lovely. A pleasure,' I say, turning my head, realising that Zoe has already left.

I follow her through the stacks and up the metal stairs, almost running to catch up with her as we climb back to the street. Her pace doesn't slow as we emerge into the cool, noise-filled air of Euston Road, lit now by dim, flickering lamp posts and the slow sweep of car headlights. I have no idea if she is running away from me, or her home, or her mother.

Only when I sprint, overtake her and block her path, does she finally stop.

'Are you angry?' I say, raising my voice over an approaching siren.

She seems breathless, and won't look at me. I can think of nothing else to say, so I wait for her to answer, watching a pair of children cross the rubble of the collapsed library, clattering a dragged sheet of rusty corrugated iron behind them.

Still she doesn't speak.

'What did I do?' I say. 'I tried to … I can't help … nor can my dad, but I just thought she needed to hear something –'

'You said the right thing. Thank you.'

Her eyes are still cast to the ground.

'Really?'

'Yes. I had no idea she'd ask. That isn't why I took you.'

'I know.'

'I just thought you should see. But–'

'But what?'

'It was stupid.'

'Why?'

Finally, she looks at me. 'You think I'm disgusting. I can see it in your eyes. It *is* disgusting. We had a house. We had a proper home –'

'NO! No. I'm glad you brought me.'

'You're lying.'

'Nothing about you could ever disgust me.'

'I don't know why I took you. I didn't want you to think I'm a fraud. That's my home. That's why I have to work on the streets. Dad's dead. It was the missile that destroyed our house. The rest of us got out but not him. Mum can't do anything. Her body escaped but it's like the rest of her was left behind in the rubble. They both died that day, but there's still a shadow of her walking around, talking, eating, sleeping, pretending to be her. She never leaves the shelter. I can't … I hold everything together … without me they'd … I just … have to keep them alive. That's all I'm good for. If you don't know that about me, you don't know anything so I had to show you … before we … if we're going to be together, you have to know who I am. I pretend to be one thing, but I'm another. I pretend all the time. I'm a liar. I've forgotten how to be anything else. I'm sorry. I'm so sorry. You don't have to see me again if …'

I pull her close, haul her into me, cling to her juddering back as she sobs. Pressed together, no air separating our two bodies, I have a feeling of melting into her until we seem fused, and I lose the sense that I could ever release her, or she me.

Yet I still want more. I want all of her. I have never felt any need as powerful as this, even though, having seen her home, having met her family, an alarm is chiming quietly in the back of my head, asking what it really means to fall for someone whose life is so desperate. Is it enough to love her, or am I supposed to save her?

'Come to the house I've found,' I say. 'Tomorrow.'

'I have to work.'

'The day after. Sunday.'

Our eyes meet. She entwines her fingers with mine and grips, hard. 'OK,' she says. 'Sunday.'

The Base

During the ride from the bar, the faster I go, the harder she clings. A couple of times I think I hear her ask me to slow down, but over the engine and the wind it's hard to be sure, and I'm enjoying that cling too much to want to listen.

When we arrive, she leaps down the moment we stop and yanks off her helmet. There's something sexy about a girl removing a bike helmet – the way the hair tumbles out – but when her face comes into view, she isn't pouting or flushed, like I'd hoped. She looks pale and annoyed.

'Enjoy the ride?' I say.

'Why didn't you slow down?'

'I ...'

'I asked you to slow down.'

'I couldn't hear.'

'Bullshit.'

'It was perfectly safe.'

'I asked you to slow down.'

I dismount and remove my own helmet.

'Sorry,' I say. 'I'm really sorry. That's how fast I always go. I suppose if you're not used to it …'

'I was scared.'

'Sorry. I didn't want to scare you.'

I step towards her and put a hand on her shoulder. She doesn't step back. I take another step closer and she still doesn't move.

I bend at the waist and go in for the kiss.

After a moment she pulls away.

'Don't,' she says, turning aside. But that's what she said about the bike ride, telling me it had frightened her, claiming she hated it while obviously standing there, waiting for me to kiss her. Maybe this is how she plays the game – saying one thing, meaning another – testing my confidence and assertiveness to find out how much I want her.

I reach an arm around her back, pull her towards me and kiss her again, strongly, on the lips, pushing my tongue into her mouth. She writhes and squirms in my grip, but I hold her tight, too excited by the thrill of kissing her to think about what her resistance means, not letting go until I feel her nails dig sharply into the flesh of my cheek. As I begin to withdraw, her knuckles shove into my neck and topple me off balance. She immediately sprints away from me, arms flailing as she lurches towards her front door.

I watch, motionless, as she struggles with the lock. She drops her keys, picks them up again with shaking hands, then throws herself inside and slams the door. Through the darkness, I hear a bolt and chain clatter into place.

My mind empties. All thought, all emotion, drains out of me. For a while, I am just a stack of bones wrapped in muscle and fat. I cannot move, I cannot think.

Somewhere down the road, a solitary dog barks. Under my feet, the planet spins at thousands of miles an hour.

Everything is lost.

I have failed with girls many times in many ways, but never like this. I have shamed myself many times in many ways, but never like this.

It does not seem comprehensible how, in a few seconds, something erotic and hopeful and generous can putrefy into violence and disgrace.

I want to go to her door and call through the letter box that she misunderstood, that I would never hurt her, that I didn't know what I was doing, that I'd never use force against her, but I know I will never speak to her again. She will never want to hear a single word from my mouth. She will loathe me, fear me, run from me. There is nothing I can do to explain, justify or retract.

I have to leave. I have to go home. I have to find a way to get through the night without engaging a single brain cell, because there is no thought left for me to think that I can bear. The only way to keep at bay the notion that I will never have a girlfriend, and should not even be allowed to try, is to drink myself into oblivion.

I climb back on the bike and rev the engine, hoping the roar of it will revive me, bring me back to myself, but even that sounds remote and muted, as if it were happening elsewhere.

I kick into gear, slip the clutch and zoom away. Despite a disorienting sensation that I am not fully present at the controls of the bike, I somehow steer from the driveway on to the main road, which is empty of cars and unlit. I wrench the accelerator towards me and click up through the gears until there are no more. A vague awareness trickles into me that the note of the engine is high and strained, the sound of a machine being pushed to its limit, but I keep my wrist cocked, squeezing everything I can from the bike.

Riding this fast feels almost like swimming in an other-worldly essence of pure speed, while at the same time experiencing a curious sensation of being quite still, with the landscape flinging itself furiously towards me.

All I can see is a cone-shaped slice of the world lit by my headlamp, drained of all colour, shooting out of view as soon as it is glimpsed. I could almost be at my desk, flying my drone, watching a screen-shaped patch of some other place, far away.

If I had stayed there, carried on flying, instead of going to a bar to pursue the fantasy of having this girl, I'd be happy. My life would still seem worthwhile.

I ease my bike towards the middle of the road, mesmerised by the on/off flicker of the central line flashing under my wheels, sensing through my whole body the alternating rough and smooth textures of tarmac and paint, tarmac and paint, tarmac and paint.

It occurs to me that I am drunk, and that I might crash at any moment, and that if I do, it won't matter in the slightest.

The City

Dad's going into hiding. He won't tell me where, but he says the assault could be imminent. It might last a few days, or several weeks, and the family will be safer if he is elsewhere. He doesn't say whether he's involved in organising the response, and I don't ask.

He wants us to be fully prepared before he goes, but he can't be seen to stockpile – people watch him and recognise him – so he stays at home with the twins and sends Mum and me to the supermarket. We buy tins of everything plus packet soup, pasta, rice, lentils, beans, chickpeas, flour, piles of all the most boring food imaginable, things that can last without refrigeration. Mum doesn't usually bake bread, but yeast is on the list too, just in case. A delivery of drinking water, by the barrel, has already been arranged.

The whole of Saturday is taken up with this operation,

with Dad stashing food all over the house: in wardrobes, under beds, stacked up in every corner of every room. We seem to have finished at lunchtime, but Dad sends us off again to a different supermarket to get more supplies.

As we pass from aisle to aisle, the feeling of doom hanging between us is so heavy that Mum and I hardly speak. With every tin I take off the shelves, I imagine another day of terror and boredom, trapped in the house, bombs falling. By the end, the trolley is so heavy it takes both of us to push it to the checkout.

The woman at the till gives us strange looks as she scans our shopping, and I can see that she almost asks us what we're doing, what we know, but thinks better of it. It's not that she mistrusts us. It's that our purchases are a warning sign which frightens her.

At the last moment, as she's handing Mum her change, the woman grips my mother's extended hand, leans towards her, and lets out a sharp, intense whisper. 'Is something happening?'

For a second they stare one another down, the shop assistant gazing pleadingly at the cold portcullis of my mother's unreadable face. Mum takes her change, withdraws her hand and gives the woman a single nod.

As colour drains from the shop assistant's cheeks, we turn away and heave our trolley towards the door.

I was fourteen during the last attack, ten during the one before that. The years when it happens are seared into everyone's brain here, with life divided into chunks of time between the assaults. Some people call them wars, others say it's too one-sided for that to be the right word, but what you call it doesn't make much difference when you're cowering in your home with obliteration scorching out of the sky every hour of the day and night, knowing the difference between life and death is just pure luck, knowing that in any given second you might be erased from the planet, swatted like a fly, flicked off like a light. Or wounded, maimed, crippled, burned, disfigured, orphaned …

When I was a child, my parents promised to keep me safe. Even if I didn't really believe them, I wanted to hear it. Now, to utter those words would be absurd.

On Saturday evening we eat in silence. Nothing is said, but with the house fully stocked, prepared for my father's departure, there's a sense he could leave at any moment, and that when he does, he might never come back. Just one knock at the door – a note on a scrap of paper – and he'll be gone.

The twins don't know what's happening, but they absorb the heavy, tense atmosphere. They're hushed at first, then they begin to bicker about which one of them is hungrier, but it feels listless, almost dutiful, as if they are working together to create a soundscape of distraction. Flailing an arm towards her sister, Ella knocks over her water. Mum screams at both of them about their carelessness, their noise, their bad manners, going so far that both pairs of eyes fill with tears.

Dad mutters at her to cool it. She snaps at him for doing nothing to help, stamps out into the kitchen, returns with a tea towel, which she throws on to the table, then vanishes again. For several long, tense minutes, she doesn't reappear. Dad mops up the spillage. We don't speak or even look at each other, until he gets up and clears the table.

I hear a whispered conversation in the kitchen, but can't make out the words.

'It's OK,' I say to Ella. 'It's only water.'

She sticks her tongue out at me.

'ELLA STUCK HER TONGUE OUT AT HIM!' says Ruby.

I put a finger to my lips. 'Not now,' I say.

Ruby and Ella, as they sometimes do, fall without warning into synch, an identical frightened expression crossing their faces.

'What's happening?' says Ella.

'Nothing,' I say.

'Why is there food everywhere?' asks Ruby.

'I ... it was on offer. There was a sale.'

'You're lying,' says Ella.

'Why did we spend all day with Dad?' says Ruby.

'Are the shops going to close?'

'Will there be bombs?'

'I ...'

'Will we have to run away?'

'Will we live in a tent?'

My eyes dart to the kitchen doorway, where Mum and Dad have appeared. Mum steps towards the twins, sits and hauls them both on to her lap.

'I'm sorry I shouted,' she says. 'I'm just having a bad day.'

Watching my sisters snuggle into her chest, I find myself listening intently to their breathing, as if this sound might contain some elusive but important answer to a question I can't identify.

'Maybe you don't remember last time,' says Mum. 'You were only small. There are noisy planes and bombs, and it's very frightening, and it might happen again. That's why we bought the food. Because you have to stay inside. But it might not happen. Either way, we'll look after you. If you're with us, you are completely safe. And I'm going to be right here the whole time. Do you understand?'

Whole houses – whole apartment blocks – can be wiped out in a single strike. Mum knows it, Dad knows it, I know it, and from the look in the eyes of the girls, they also half know it, but they also seem to understand that by pretending to believe Mum, they are doing their bit for the family.

Snuggled in her lap, they both nod and allow her to wipe their wet cheeks with the side of her thumb. They seem comforted, perhaps by her assurances, or perhaps because the situation has now been acknowledged and a role has been assigned to them, which is to pretend to believe Mum's assertion that they are safe. Or maybe what Mum really means is that if they stay close enough, if they huddle together as they are doing now, they can't be parted. The three of them will all live or they will all die, but nobody will be left behind. It's possible this is what has comforted them. I have no idea if they even understand the concept of death. Maybe their only fear is separation.

'It's been a tiring day,' says Mum after a long silence. 'Shall we skip the bath and have extra stories?'

Both girls smile, and she leads them upstairs.

Dad sits.

The room is darkening now, but neither of us gets up to put on the light.

I listen to the muffled rise and fall of Mum's voice drifting down through the ceiling. For the twins, she is a duvet and a shield and a God, a person whose presence can banish any fear, even one that is entirely justified. She must have done that for me once, though I can't remember what it felt like.

As I listen to the familiar, comforting music of Mum's reading, it strikes me how beautiful and also how sad it is that your parents protect you from everything, even the truth, until the day you find yourself standing in blinding light, alone, not quite knowing where you are or how you arrived there.

'I can't take any messages tomorrow,' I say.

Through the gloom, I make out Dad giving a small shrug. 'What are you doing?' he asks.

'Just a little trip.'

His body remains slumped, but I see his eyes flick rapidly towards me.

'Where?'

I wasn't expecting him to quiz me. He can't know about Brixton. 'I don't know yet,' I lie.

'Why? Who with?'

'Zoe.'

He laughs, a low, breathy rumble I haven't heard for ages.

'Oh!' he says. 'The girlfriend!'

I don't want to answer any more questions, but before I can stand and leave, he asks again where I'm taking her.

'Dunno. Out and about. On my bike.'

'Don't go far.'

'Why not?'

'Just … not tomorrow. Stay close.'

I shrug and raise myself from my chair. Brixton is at the southern tip of The Strip, as far as you can go. There's no plan B, nowhere else I can take her, no other place to be alone.

'I'm serious,' he snaps, standing and blocking my path to the door. 'I know you've been all over. That's fine. But tomorrow, don't go far. Promise me.'

I shrug.

He grabs my forearm, digging his fingers into my flesh.

'*Promise me.*'

I twist my arm free and step back.

'I'll be careful,' I say.

The light flicks on. Mum is back in the room.

'What's going on?'

'Nothing,' I say.

'Just chatting,' adds Dad unconvincingly. 'Are the girls asleep?'

'They want a kiss.'

He shuffles out. Mum gives me a searching look, but I turn away and climb the stairs to my bedroom.

If Dad is right about what's ahead, this is not the time to delay anything important. He might think his warning has put me off, but it's had the opposite effect. My main memory of the last war is being trapped inside, stuck, the five of us hiding from raids all the time, then dashing out to stock up on supplies during brief lulls or temporary ceasefires. More than the fear and boredom, I remember the claustrophobia of never leaving the house.

If that really is about to start, tomorrow might be the last chance for me and Zoe to be together. It might be our only chance, because even though these attacks are finite, you don't know what world you will be living in afterwards. You cannot arrange or hope for anything to happen after a war, because you don't know who or where or what you will be. Our trip cannot be postponed or changed.

The Base

I wouldn't say I take it all the way to oblivion, but I'm pretty wrecked when I finally fall asleep, and feel half dead when at nine o'clock on Saturday morning my phone wakes me. The number's withheld, and when I answer I can barely get out a hello. My tongue is parched and thick. The rest of my mouth feels as if it has been vacuumed.

With a jolt that kick-starts my sluggish pulse, I recognise the voice of Flight Lieutenant Wilkinson. 'All weekend leave has been cancelled. You are to report for duty at twelve hundred hours.'

For a terrified instant I wonder if this is something to do with what happened the night before. Has Victoria reported me for … I don't know what the word would be … for some kind of assault?

'Do you hear me?' he snaps.

'Yes, sir. Twelve hundred hours.'

The phone goes dead. I drop it on to my lap and stare at my hands, the hands that grabbed at Victoria the night before, the hands that briefly wrestled with her, refusing to let go. But only for a second or two. Not much longer. Was that really so bad?

'All weekend leave,' Wilkinson said. Not 'your weekend leave'. That was a good sign. And surely this was too fast. If Victoria had made a complaint, they wouldn't come after me so soon, would they? I mean it happened less than twelve hours ago. And what had I done anyway? It was nothing. A stupid misunderstanding. I'm a trained soldier, an accomplished pilot – surely they wouldn't interrupt my career over something so minor.

I drag myself to the bathroom and examine my right cheek, which is giving off a faint throb. There's a small scratch, a speck of blood, but nothing incriminating.

I shave roughly, half hoping to make a comparable scratch on some other part of my face, then pummel my body to life with a scorching shower and head downstairs in my dressing gown. I always get dressed last thing, to make sure I don't spill anything on my uniform.

Mum's there at the table, which is the last thing I need. I grunt a hello and sit opposite her with a bowl of cereal and a black coffee.

'Fun evening?' she asks. 'I heard you getting back late.'

I hate being watched by her. Is this Mum's way of

163

complaining that I woke her up? Is she deliberately using the word *fun* to make me sound like a kid? I shovel in a few spoonfuls and mumble, 'It was OK.'

'Where did you go?'

I look up at her. She looks relaxed and neutral, as if she's making polite small talk with a person who happens to be sharing her breakfast table at a B&B. I can't tell what this means. I have a vague sense that she may be mocking me or putting me down, but I'm not sure why. Or perhaps she's trying to patch things up between us. My brain is too fogged and slow to work this out, so I play it straight.

'Just a bar. With a few of the guys.' Not friendly, not unfriendly.

'Your colleagues?'

'Yeah.'

'Are they nice?'

What a stupid question! 'Er ... yeah. But that's not really the word for it. We're soldiers. We fight together. It's not about being nice. We're a unit. There's a bond that ... I couldn't describe it to you. And I don't know why you're suddenly pretending to be interested.'

Her face keeps the same expression of impersonal courtesy, but tightens a little. 'I wouldn't call it fighting, dear,' she says. 'I mean, it's a desk job, isn't it?'

I stand, pick up my bowl and throw it across the room. It hits the cupboard under the sink and shatters. Shards of flower-patterned pottery skitter across the milk-splattered floor.

I have no idea what makes me do this, and almost immediately feel as if some outside force must have hacked my brain and taken control of my limbs. The overwhelming rage that wrenched away my self-control departs as quickly as it came, leaving behind no explanation, just a slipstream of vacant confusion.

I look back at my mother, whose expression has barely changed, except for a glimmer of victory in her eyes. My arms feel light and faintly tremulous, still not fully under my control.

I hurry out of the room and get into uniform, but just as I'm about to leave I catch a glimpse of myself in the half-open mirrored door of my wardrobe.

I'm not sure why, but this makes me stop, turn and examine myself so intently that after a while I can no longer tell which is me and which is the reflection, who is the watcher and who is being watched. For a moment, I am struck by the thought that neither is truly me – that there is a truer essence of myself elsewhere, either living another life, or perhaps simply unborn. Life has squashed me into an unnatural shape. This is not who I should have become.

Eventually I kick the door shut, walk downstairs and speed away on my bike.

It's not yet eleven, so I drive past the base and kill an hour in a cafe on the edge of town. I dampen down my hangover with a fry-up and a couple of pots of tea, chewing every mouthful to a soft pulp before I swallow, trying to slow down my whirring brain. As I sip at the scalding sweet tea, I banish all thoughts of Victoria and my mum, forcing my mind to settle and empty in preparation for my shift.

I report for duty dead on midday, calm and clear-headed, restored to myself by the hot breakfast. It's immediately clear I'm not being disciplined. There's no sign of Wilkinson or Victoria, just my training officer, who tells me I'm being fast-tracked. I have to run through some final tests, in full combat conditions, and if I pass I'll be going back into service the next day. There's an operation, and they're short of personnel.

'Yes, sir,' I reply, realising that in the few seconds I was listening to him, the last vestiges of my hangover evaporated.

It's out there that things go wrong, that unexpected humiliations leap out of nowhere and ambush me. This base, right here, is my haven. Within these razor wire fences, I am home.

'Wallis will be your sensor operator today,' he continues. 'He's also under assessment.'

I shake Wallis's large, soft hand. If he messes up, I'm screwed. On an armed MQ-9 your sensor operator is like an extra set of limbs. Yesterday the simulator took up the role, but today is the real thing, combat conditions as a joint unit, and for me to pass, he has to be good. There's no buck-passing or special pleading. The two of us, together, have to do the job.

We're barely given time to greet one another before the

first test mission: a follow and strike on a jeep containing six Military Age Males in mountainous terrain. It's a standard daylight double tap, a joint op with a jet making the initial strike, and us on a Reaper detailed to mop up the squirters.

There are only two, and I ice them with a single Hellfire. Easy. The only difference between training and real combat is that on a simulator the screen goes briefly blank when you're done, then instead of the endless hours of waiting and watching, you're straight on to the next operation. They pile them up to measure your stress response.

We do a night run, using the heat sensors, then move on to urban, with a safety officer added to the team for collateral damage assessment. We're given day and night, pedestrian and vehicular, open and concealed, the usual mix. Urban ops are more delicate, with a less clear success/failure profile, but Wallis is solid, and between us we put in a strong performance.

We go straight into a debrief and I'm surprised to notice darkness outside the window. I've been so focused I had no sense at all of the day passing. My eyes are bleary, straining to adjust back to three dimensions.

With a curt nod we're told that we've both passed, and should report for duty the next day at twelve hundred hours. 'Good job,' the instructor says as we're walking out. 'Same drill tomorrow, and not on a simulator.'

Wallis and I walk a short way down the corridor in silence, then without any particular cue, we turn towards each other and grin. I don't know who starts it, but next thing I know we're hugging. It's only quick – more a mutual slap on the back than anything else – but even though we've barely spoken I know he's thinking what I'm thinking, which is that in a single day we've forged an intense connection.

People outside the military can't understand the way soldiers risk their lives for one another on the battlefield, but when you go through what we go through, it makes perfect sense. The bonds you make with your fellow men are instant and unbreakable. Obviously your life isn't really on the line in remote combat, but if it was, I'd do anything for these guys. I really would.

In the car park Wallis admires my bike, and I almost suggest a Saturday night adrenalin-comedown pint, but it sounds like the mission tomorrow is a serious one, and with a midday start that could mean we'll be working till the small hours, so I hold back. I want to be on top form.

We part with a knuckle-crushing handshake, telling each other we did great, and head home.

The memory of flinging a cereal bowl drifts into my consciousness as I ride, but I push it away. Not far behind comes a queasy re-enactment of my disastrous lunge at Victoria, but I banish that thought too.

Today was a watershed, a significant promotion at the base. I forgot to ask about the figures, but there's bound to be a pay rise. Maybe enough, at last, to move into a place of my own.

As I toe-click the bike into a higher gear, sending a surge of acceleration from the motor to the wheels to my body, I tell myself that last night and breakfast this morning were the final humiliations in a period of my life which is now over. I have been too weak, too insecure, too hesitant. The time has come to leave that person behind. This promotion is the cue to inhabit a bigger self, to step up as a man.

The City

It feels like the first hot day of the year. As I ride southwards towards St Pancras the whole city seems to have an atmosphere of relief. Some people are still in ragged overcoats – the hungry ones, permanently chilled to the bone – but most have set out for the day in T-shirts and shades. The crowds are thicker than usual, bodies filling every inch of pavement, hurrying or strolling or just basking like sunflowers, their faces turned towards the delicious heat.

Near Camden Lock I see the grey-haired man who once grabbed me accost another teenage boy, yelling at him, '*I knew you'd come back, I knew you'd come back!*'

The boy tolerates this briefly, says something I don't hear, then shoves him away, perhaps pushing harder than he intends, or failing to account for the weakness of the man, who stumbles backwards and falls to the ground.

The boy hesitates, contemplates helping him up, then turns and walks away. The old man remains on his back, motionless, so I pull over at the kerb to see if he needs help. As I'm dismounting, he sees me, becomes suddenly alert, rolls on to his front, hauls himself to his knees and drags his body upright, all the while yelling the same desperate chant, this time in my direction. One eye is swollen shut under an eyelid the colour and size of a ripe plum.

I climb back on to my bike and set off.

Zoe is waiting for me in the usual place, standing in her particular way, right leg bent, heel balanced on the inside of her left ankle bone. Yes, that's how she stands. That's how I expect to find her.

Every time I see Zoe I get a delicious feeling of her gradually unfolding herself to me, the web of quirks, traits and habits that makes her who she is becoming each day more familiar and somehow more thrilling. The more she reveals, the more hungrily I want to know what is still concealed.

She's wearing her usual scuffed sneakers, with a white vest top and faded jeans. Her hair is tied back, in a style I haven't seen before, though her forehead is hidden, as always, behind that slanting fringe. My pulse accelerates as I picture how later today we will arrive at the house I have found, and there we will lie down together, and we will kiss, and undress, and if she hasn't changed her mind ... if she hasn't changed her mind ...

The moment is breathtakingly close, but still I cannot imagine it. Even though the trip was Zoe's idea, part of me can't believe she will really go through with it. And if she does, if we do, what lies on the other side? What will change? Who will we be? I have no idea.

As I approach her, Zoe seems lost in thought, perhaps asking herself these same questions. When she spots me her face comes alive, snapping into the moment. I weave through the clogged traffic and squeeze her against me, drinking in the sweet taste of her, filling myself with her scent, oblivious to where I am or who might be watching.

She opens her eyes slowly as our lips part, like someone resurfacing from a dream. We stare at one another, the universe pausing for us as we do.

'Are you ready?' she says eventually. 'Shall we go?'

I turn for my bike and steady it in front of her. As she's about to climb on, a flicker of doubt crosses her eyes. 'This place you've found, is it safe?' she asks.

I have never wanted anything as much as I want this trip to happen, but since waking up a queasy hum has unsettled my mind, rising and falling but never fading away. I am afraid. Of the journey? The bombed-out Brixton streets? The semi-derelict house? Of what we are intending to do when we get there? I don't even know. Or perhaps it's just my father's warning which, though I shrugged it off at the time, now keeps ricocheting through my thoughts.

But can I confess any of this to Zoe? Can I admit my fears? Can I really come this far, get this close, only to say, 'No, it isn't safe'?

She watches me, immobile, waiting for a response, then says, 'Is it near the tunnels?'

This is a question I can answer. 'Not too near. It's that area.'

Zoe's body is turned aside, paused in the act of climbing on the bike.

'We don't have to go,' I add. 'I mean ... if it's not the right day. Or if you want me to look for somewhere else.'

She draws in her bottom lip, rubbing it against her top incisors as she thinks.

'What do you think?' she says.

'I don't know. It's a risk, but ...'

'But what?'

'If we don't, I think I might ... explode,' I say.

She smiles and presses her lips to mine, her soft tongue flicking briefly into my mouth. 'Me too,' she says, pulling away from me and climbing on to the bike. 'Let's go.'

I stare at her, my brain fogged with lust. The urge to kiss every part of her, to explore every millimetre of her body, is so powerful that I feel almost drunk with it, delirious, crazed.

'Come on!' she says, slapping the saddle. 'Let's go!'

I climb on and steer us out into the queue of traffic inching towards the West End. We manage the bike well now, balancing easily, leaning together into each swerve and turn. As we travel southwards through London, I glance back every few blocks to check on Zoe, whose eyes are always scouring the streets around us, drinking in the city.

There doesn't seem to be any pattern to the bomb damage. Some areas are worse hit than others but even though older bomb sites are more overgrown than newer ones, it's hard to tell what has been destroyed, or when, or why.

The physical effort of cycling helps me empty my mind of anxious thoughts, but as we pass a weed-knotted ruin in which a twisted row of cinema seats is visible, pointing towards the sky like a giant gnarled finger, Dad's warning pops up again in my mind. *Tomorrow, don't go far. Promise me.*

I can see again the pleading look in his eye as he repeated those last two words. This wasn't an empty threat or a general warning. He was talking about this specific day. Today.

I didn't promise. I shrugged and evaded.

With each passing minute we stray into more unfamiliar territory, and in increasingly unknown streets I feel my confidence teeter. My back is slick with sweat, yet something in my core feels as if it is getting colder.

We continue on down Shaftesbury Avenue, turning left at a huge, ornate theatre which is pitted with shrapnel and boarded up, but still standing. There are only a few missing buildings around here but further south, beyond Trafalgar Square, whole blocks are gone. Whitehall is a wide avenue through nothingness, the stone of old government buildings stretching in all directions, like a jagged, pale sea. Further on, one end wall of the Houses of Parliament is still upright, the rest is flattened. Towering over the whole area, seemingly untouched, is Westminster Abbey.

By the time we cross the river my throat is dry and a chill certainty is pulsing through my veins, warning me this is too risky. Going any closer to the tunnels is a mistake. But I can't turn back. If an attack really is imminent, that should be a reason to carry on, to hurry, to live as much as I can before the sirens sound and life is indefinitely postponed, or cancelled.

I can't even bring myself to share this dilemma with Zoe. Nothing can be allowed to go wrong. This might be our last chance. When we arrive, I tell myself, when Zoe and I are alone together, my fears will evaporate. She has the power to sweep away all worry. In our long-awaited solitude every anxiety, every thought of the outside world, will dissolve. The last leg of this journey is no time for self-doubt, no time to infect Zoe with my own apprehension.

South of the river the city is less badly damaged, but with fewer bomb sites to draw the eye, it's here that you notice the decay and decline. Here, where not so much has been blown up, the slow, crumbling slide into dilapidation is what hits you. Nothing is new or clean or freshly painted; little looks solid or durable.

For the whole ride, Zoe and I don't speak. Silence seems like the only response to the overwhelming, unanswerable questions of how these streets would once have looked, and how they'd be now if war had stayed away.

Usually you can hide from the pointless, outlandish fantasy

of imagining normality, of picturing life in a safe, unbombed, peaceful city; sometimes this thought charges at you like an angry bull.

It's a long slog down Kennington Road with the heavily laden bike, but my weakening legs get a jolt of extra energy when we cross the invisible line from relative normality to absolute destruction. Suddenly, perhaps half a mile from the tunnels, there's barely a house standing.

I stop the bike, and we stare in silence at the devastation, which is so complete that side streets have entirely disappeared under a thick, undulating layer of rubble. It's an urban desert.

Unlike everywhere else in The Strip there are no scavengers, no pedestrians, and an ominous silence hangs in the air, underpinned by the usual ever present buzz of drones. I look up at the cloudless blue sky and see three of them, possibly in formation, aligned along the southern fence. I've never seen them cluster together like this.

Tomorrow, don't go far. Promise me.

'What's wrong?' says Zoe.

I turn to her and arrange my features into a smile. 'Nothing. Do you want to go on?'

'Where?' she says.

We should turn back. We should go home. Something lethal is in the air.

We *should*, but I cannot give up now.

'I'll show you,' I say.

We dismount and walk side by side through the ruins, which are dotted with fragments of furniture, the odd mattress, shreds of curtains, a few rotten shoes and clumps of unidentifiable mildewed fabric. Bricks have tumbled inwards, covering the pavements, reducing the road to a narrow snake of bare, dusty tarmac.

A plump rat skitters in front of us, shortly followed by several more heading in the opposite direction. Zoe places a hand on my forearm as we pause, watching the ground, but no more appear, so we carry on, heading away from the main road, along what would once have been a residential street. Long brick terraces must have stood here, but there isn't enough left to picture how it would have looked, or to imagine people really living here.

The area must have been destroyed a while ago, since most of the bomb sites are dense with weeds, but a cloying poison seems to waft out of the rubble, as if the slaughter that took place here is so recent it is still somehow happening, just out of view, half glimpsed in flashes at the corner of an eye. Amid the emptiness, I can feel an unsettling tingle of human presence, of ghost residents fleeing for their lives or lying, crushed, close by, invisible under layers of masonry.

This place seemed eerie enough on my last visit, but now, with the threat of another attack looming over us, a stark deathly chill pulses through the streets.

We walk on, past a complete chimney breast with its TV aerial still attached, standing in the middle of the street as if on top of a buried house. There are cats everywhere, eyeing us as they prowl the ruins, looking at the same time regally calm and murderously alert.

As we stop in front of a short stretch of terraced housing that has remained more or less upright, from somewhere to the north I hear the guttural roar of a passing fighter jet. This isn't particularly unusual, but is hardly commonplace either. The sound of it sends a trickle of dread down my spine.

I tell Zoe that the last of these bombed-out houses is our hideaway. Most of the front wall has been blasted away, revealing a naked, shattered living room, arrayed with the scorched remains of a sofa and two hollowed-out armchairs. A warped and blackened flat-screen TV is still attached to the wall, hanging at a skewed angle.

My heart is thumping so forcefully that I worry Zoe might hear. Despite the planning and preparation that has filled my mind for weeks, all desire and anticipation now seems to have clotted inside me, but I can't see a way to turn around and back out.

'Here we are,' I say. I'm on the brink of telling her we should run away now, fast.

She steps ahead of me, approaching the house. I lock my bike to a half-buried iron railing and follow her. Our steps seem unnaturally loud on the loose bricks, which clank together underfoot.

A distant thud, audible more in the chest than the ears, brings us up short.

'What was that?' she asks.

'I don't know.'

We wait, unmoving, but there are no further explosions, or clues.

She moves on towards the house, picking her way steadily over the uneven surface. The door is a couple of inches ajar, exactly as I left it when I scouted the place out. It doesn't yield to her first push, then scrapes against a warped floorboard as she shoves harder.

I follow Zoe into the dim, sour air of the abandoned house. The hallway is thick with dust and debris, but there are still pictures hanging on the dark green walls: a faded child's painting of a donkey and an angel, a tiny ink line drawing of a rural cottage with smoke snaking from the chimney, and a framed photograph of three grinning children in swimming costumes showing off a sand-sculpted mermaid with seaweed hair and shell scales. In the background, between sand and sky, is a stripe of open water.

Zoe lifts the photo from the wall, exposing a rectangle of unfaded wallpaper, and for a while we both gaze at it, transfixed. Neither of us has ever been to a beach, or set foot in the sea. We have no idea how it would feel to run on sand or plunge into a wave or sculpt a mermaid with seaweed hair. Until you see a photo like this, you forget that such places even exist.

'Can you imagine?' she says.

I can't, and don't really want to try, so I gently lift the picture from her grip and rehang it, then take her hand and lead her upstairs, to the room I have found for us. It's empty except for a pine wardrobe, a dressing table with a cracked mirror, and a double bed coated with crumbled fragments of ceiling plaster.

The windows of a small bay are shattered but one curtain still hangs from a partly detached metal rail. A chair is at the window, tipped on to its back.

Zoe stands in the doorway, examining the room with an inscrutable expression that could denote anything from contentment to dismay.

'I brought a sheet,' I say, pulling the pilfered item from my backpack.

She doesn't move.

I lift a corner of the bedspread and drag it slowly to the floor, folding it in on itself to contain the filth. A pale blue sheet is still on the bed. I can make out two dents in the mattress, one slightly deeper than the other, husband and wife, who may or may not still be alive.

'Let's put the sheet on,' Zoe says.

We take more care over this job than is really necessary, pulling it taut, smoothing out every wrinkle. I can't tell who is creating this delay: me, her or both of us.

She sits on the end of the bed. I sit next to her. We aren't touching, and I have no idea what to do.

Around our feet, I notice a scatter of mouse droppings.

I cannot quite believe the thought that is still lurking in my mind: an insistent, cowardly incantation telling me I do not want to be here, telling me this feels too clinical, too fake, too planned, and somehow callous in the half-destroyed home of a family who may be dead.

Through the silence that hangs between us, I can feel Zoe thinking the same thing.

It's me who eventually speaks. 'My dad says there's going to be an attack.'

Zoe turns her head. 'When?'

'Soon.'

She looks at me gravely. After a while she says, 'You're shaking.'

'Am I?'

Only now do I realise that a faint, barely perceptible tremor has colonised my body. This has never happened before. 'Sorry,' I say.

She places a hand on my cheek. 'Don't be sorry,' she says.

'I'm sorry about this,' I add, meaning the dismal atmosphere of the room, but making no gesture to explain myself. 'I'm sorry about everything. I just …'

My voice tails away as she pulls me towards her, wrapping both arms around my head, clutching me into the side of her neck.

Slowly, as she holds me, the tremor recedes.

I breathe her in. I breathe her out. My arms reach around her waist and I pull her closer towards me, kissing the soft, private skin of her neck, swamped by a wave of relief and gratitude, by a warm, exquisite, enveloping sensation of being understood, cared for, maybe even loved.

I am beginning to feel weightless as I kiss her again on the lips, then without knowing why I am doing it, I raise her lopsided fringe and pass my lips, kiss after kiss after kiss, slowly along the length of her scar.

Our bodies topple backwards on to the bed, and every thought, every fear, every anxiety dissolves.

When my hand slides between her legs, she reaches down, not, like before, to push me away, but instead placing her cupped fingers on top of mine, guiding me, slowing me down, softening the pressure of my touch, until her body loosens, yields, transforms into something liquid and pliable, yet with a focus and a drive to do more, to go further.

I scrabble frantically for the condom I have brought with me in the back pocket of my jeans, then I am above her, wondering, for a moment, if this is really happening. Her eyes stare into mine, seemingly focused on a spot deep inside my skull, looking at me, into me and through me. She guides me inside her.

The sensation is of every nerve firing at once – it's like being turned inside out – like plummeting and flying – it's a wild, infinite song of life itself.

The universe beyond our bed ceases to exist. Locked together, we rise; explode; descend.

Our naked bodies knitted together, sleep drapes over us.

Dusk is leaking in through the windows when the world finds its way back to us. It is the cruellest, most brutal transition. The silence of our secret room in this abandoned house in an empty street is broken by the shattering roar of a low-flying jet, immediately followed by an explosion so loud and so close it lifts us off the mattress.

We throw ourselves under the bed as another jet thunders past. Between the explosions my ears scream a high-pitched yowl of protest.

My mind races over futile calculations for self-protection. Downstairs there'd be more cover from a direct hit; upstairs less chance of being buried if the house collapses. Zoe pulls me towards her. I stretch an arm across her back and squeeze her hand. A choking, juddering sob pulses from her throat with every breath. I wish we weren't naked. I wish we weren't here. I wish I'd listened to my father.

The raid goes on and on, every explosion a deafening, diabolical hammer blow that punches up at us through the floorboards.

When quiet descends we remain under the bed, shivering with terror and cold. I'm the first to crawl out.

I dress hurriedly and shuttle myself, hunched, to the window. It's dark now, though a few falling flares are lighting the sky. The street outside looks the same, but since the whole view is of old bomb sites, it's hard to tell if anything has exploded nearby.

Thicker darkness descends as the final flare extinguishes. A low arc of sky glimmers with a sickly orange glow, illuminated by fires that must be just out of view. The only other light is high above, malevolent circling dots, The Strip's evil stars.

Zoe crawls out from under the bed and with shaking hands begins to pull on her clothes.

'They've gone for the tunnels,' I say. My voice sounds tinny and strange over the persistent, high ringing in my ears. I become aware of a chorus of sirens, but my senses are too battered to distinguish how many, or where they might be.

Zoe's face is white, blank, as if she has been erased. Her eyes are glazed, her lips colourless. I can't tell if she has heard me, or even if she can see me.

'Are you OK?' I ask.

I realise that she is holding on to the end of the bed, seemingly incapable of standing unsupported.

'Are you hurt?'

She shakes her head once, very slowly, staring beyond me, through the windows, out at the glowing sky.

'We should go,' I say.

She doesn't respond. I step across the room, place a hand on each of her shoulders, and stand so close she can't avoid eye contact, but she looks through me.

'Zoe?' I say.

'My father's dead,' she replies, in a flat, low voice that I barely recognise. 'Did I tell you? It was the raid that destroyed our house. The rest of us got out. Did I tell you?'

'Yes, you said …'

'They used to discuss over and over different plans for

184

how to sleep during an attack. They argued about whether to leave and stay with relatives, about whether this area or that area was safer. Every night they'd have the same conversations round and round. When they finished with which house to sleep in, there'd be arguments about which room. Which direction were the bombs coming from? Should we all stay together or should we divide up? Dad wanted me with him on one side of the house, and Mum with my brother on the other, to spread the risk, give more chance that some of us would survive a hit. Mum wanted us all together. I was supposed to be with him, but I got scared that night and went into Mum's bed. I should have been with him. I should be dead. Maybe I could have helped him. I don't know. We just ran for it and he never came out. Mum was screaming and digging with her bare hands. He never came out.'

I hold her as she talks, but her body is rigid and unyielding, as if she's bracing herself against a gale. Even after she goes quiet her body doesn't loosen or react to my touch. I sense that, for her, I'm barely there.

'We have to go,' I say eventually. 'We have to get out of here.'

I hand her the jeans that she still hasn't put on, and help her into them. I sit her down, put on her socks and shoes, tie the laces, stand her up and lead her by the hand out of the room.

She freezes at the top of the stairs, as if terrified by the drop in height.

'Come on,' I say. 'You can do it.'

She shakes her head, and I notice that she's trembling, losing control of her limbs. I turn, enfold her in my arms, and lift.

She's a dead weight, and I can't see past her to find the stair treads, so I shuffle my way down, feeling for the ground with an extended leg like a blind man using a stick. Near the bottom, a rotten floorboard gives way under us and we almost fall, but I grab at a banister before we topple. Zoe remains limp, seemingly unaware of our near accident, her face hot against my neck.

We squeeze through the stuck front door and I carry her out, staggering in the darkness over the uneven, wobbling surface.

When I put her down it seems at first that she will crumple to the ground, but she manages to stand as I unlock the bike, then to walk with me, stumbling like a sleepwalker as I lead her through the undulating shadows of the ruined street, back towards the main road. Above us, the lights of circling drones seem low and fast. A polyphonic wail of sirens fills the air, rising from every direction, but I hear no more bombs. The jets, for now, seem to have gone.

As we emerge on to Brixton Road, I lower the bike to the ground and place my hands gently on Zoe's cheeks, trying to make her see me.

'We have to get on the bike,' I say. 'Can you do it?'

She nods, but I'm still not quite sure she has heard.

We mount tentatively, Zoe placing herself in the right

position, but her grip on my back is weak, her balance wayward and strange, and I can't get more than a few metres without the bike toppling. I step off, bracing the frame under Zoe's flopping weight, and speak to her again, more loudly, an edge of sharpness in my voice. 'Zoe! The planes could come back. We have to get out of here! I can't ride if you don't hold on. I can't do it.'

She gives a vague nod, still far away.

'Do you understand? Please hold on. Tight.'

I place a kiss on her cold, pale lips.

At last, eye contact. She nods again, this time showing a glimmer of understanding.

I climb back into the saddle and we set off again, more successfully. As we cycle homewards, streets that were busy during the journey south are now empty except for a few zooming ambulances. My legs soon burn with the strain, and we're still miles from home.

There is no time to rest, no opportunity to take cover from the drones, which must have spotted us. I can picture us on the screen of some pilot somewhere, the only fools out on the street during an air raid, an impossibly tempting target, like a single piece of popcorn on a coffee table, begging to be taken. My effort and desperation must look so futile, laughable even, to someone who can wipe me out at the push of a button.

Up ahead, somewhere near the river, a streak of white light shoots through the sky, starting in The Strip then arcing eastwards, out over the fence. A missile. Not a missile like the vast payloads of a jet fighter, but a weapon, no less lethal for being home-made. This is the response – the retaliation from The Corps – the next stage of the tit for tat. Out there too, beyond the fence, people will be running for cover.

'This isn't safe,' I say, flicking my eyes towards Zoe, causing the bike to wobble as I turn. She's staring blankly at my back. 'We need to get under cover. Let's head for Waterloo and look for a spot under the station. OK?'

She doesn't respond.

It's the longest mile I have ever cycled. Every second I keep expecting to see the inescapable, fiery dart of a Hellfire missile corkscrewing towards me. But we get there.

I let the bike crash to the pavement and haul her pliant body into a railway arch of graffiti-covered Victorian brick, cut deep into a high structure of overlapping bridges. At last, we are hidden from the drones, protected from missiles.

I ask Zoe for her phone, desperate to tell my parents where I am, and that I'm safe, but when she hands it over there's no signal. I remember from last time how the network was often blocked during raids, either jammed from outside or overloaded, nobody seemed to know which.

I give the phone back, but she doesn't put it away or use it. She just stands there holding the phone in an outstretched hand, staring out at the dark, empty street. Her family, deep underground, must also be uncontactable.

'Are you OK?' I ask.

She doesn't respond.

'We got out,' I say. 'We're safe. We can spend the night here.'

She doesn't look at me, her face doesn't move, her breathing remains slow and steady, but tears begin to run down her cheeks. She does nothing to wipe them away.

I've never seen anyone cry like this, as if it isn't actually happening to them, as if their tears are somehow detached from all emotion. I stare, frozen, sensing that she doesn't want to be touched, or even spoken to.

'Come,' I say, leading her by the hand to the back of the railway arch. The furthest corner is spread with flattened out cardboard boxes, where someone has slept, but this makeshift bed is stained with patches of dark fluid and gives off an acrid sinus-pinching stench. The ground is covered with beer cans, food wrappers, pigeon feathers and bird crap, so I use my foot to sweep clean a patch beside the wall, away from the worst of the smell.

I sit and draw her down to me, laying her head on my lap. I feel exhausted but utterly awake, stretched taut like a piano string. With my hands around Zoe, I sense her settling into a state that isn't sleep, but isn't wakefulness either. I remain upright, alert to the slightest sound, waiting for the beginning of the onslaught that will bite new chunks out of my city. That first raid was only the beginning – the sound of war clearing its throat before breaking into full demonic song.

I have never before spent the night out of the house without my parents knowing where I am. Dad will know I ignored his warning, know I lied to him, and with every hour I don't return, he'll become more convinced that I must have been killed. The cruelty of inflicting this torture on him makes me want to break cover and battle my way home, just to let him know I'm still alive, but I have to stay put. To die for that would be madness.

The hours crawl past, our two bodies shivering together as cold seems to seep out of the old, dank brick and into our bones. After that single attack on the tunnels, a menacing quiet fills the city. I hear only sirens, distant burglar alarms, buzzing drones, and the occasional squeal of an outgoing missile. The usual background rumble of traffic has gone. Everyone must be sitting out the night, under cover, waiting for the next onslaught.

I constantly expect to hear the screech of incoming jets, to feel the ground shake as bombs strike, but the night inches by, and the sword does not yet fall.

Long before dawn, a fox, casual and untroubled, trots diagonally across the street. He pauses, perhaps smelling me, and we stare at one another. Two fox eyes glint through the shadows. I stupidly wish, for a moment, that he would come and join us under the arch.

His heavy-looking tail lifts for a second, then the fox turns away and on silent paws scurries out of view.

I try to think of this as a sign, a blessing, a communion

with a higher power. His calm and elegance seem like a visitation from another world, from a parallel universe in which war is a passing inconvenience, like a thunderstorm or a flood, but I know in my heart there are no signs, and the higher power who decides if a bomb will find you is just dumb luck.

Luck is almost a deity here: a callous god who doesn't care in the slightest whether you have sinned or prayed or obeyed your parents or helped your fellow man. If he wants you, he'll come for you, and that's that.

I look down at Zoe. Her eyes are closed but her body feels rigid and tense. If she's asleep, it is only lightly. I kiss her on the forehead. She doesn't stir. I press my lips into her hair and inhale.

A flash memory of our afternoon on that white sheet flares up in my mind's eye, of her head tilted back, the underside of her chin beaded with sweat, her mouth slightly open, gasping for breath.

I inhale again and transport myself deeper into that vanished moment, so recent, but now on the other side of an appalling chasm.

If I keep breathing her in I can try to override the present, this brick arch so far from home, the stink of urine, the pain in my back and legs, the fear that is chilling my blood. I must reverse time, reel it in and pause my life elsewhere. Then, perhaps, we will make it through until morning.

The Base

Sunday is another late start – four hours after my usual shift time – but I don't manage a lie-in. My eyes pop open at seven, and I sense immediately that I'm too excited, too psyched to stand a chance of getting back to sleep. This is the day. The culmination of everything I've worked for. No more simulators. No more surveillance and reconnaissance. No more watching and waiting. A Reaper MQ-9 will already be out there over the skies of London, armed and prepped, ready for a combat mission with me at the controls.

If the anxious and bullied teenage Alan had known this was coming, everything would have felt different. If someone had told me this day would arrive within a few years of leaving school, I could have sailed through everything, impervious, knowing I'd soon prevail.

I lie still for a while, basking in thoughts of the day ahead, but I feel too restless to stay long in bed, and can't face the possibility of seeing my mother, so I shower, pull on my uniform and head off to a cafe.

There's nothing better than being at your leisure over a slow breakfast, paging through a newspaper, feeling idle but not idle, taking your sweet time over everything while knowing you have a solid day's work ahead of you. If you're in uniform, you always get great service and the biggest portions you'll ever be given.

At the base, where everyone is doing the same thing, it's easy to forget what a sacrifice it is to serve your country. You have to mix with civilians to be reminded how grateful people are. Extra sausages and constant coffee refills are the least I deserve quite frankly. It's only bleeding heart snowflakes like my mother who think otherwise.

I go in early and give myself an hour or so in the mess room to hang out with some of the guys and get myself ready. It isn't good to be too amped. Adrenalin is no help when you're piloting an armed drone. You're dealing with extreme velocities and precise targeting, with controls that are perfectly designed but sensitive to every twitch. It's meticulous, delicate work. You have to be like a Formula One driver and a silversmith at the same time. You need focus, dexterity and a cool head.

The atmosphere among the men waiting to go on shift is buzzing. A few of the older guys are sitting quietly, lost in private thought, others are in noisy groups cracking jokes, but everyone seems somehow alert and poised for action.

I help myself to a coffee and circle the room, avoiding the loudest gangs, scanning to check for the presence of Victoria. I need to talk to her, frame some kind of apology, but I don't yet know what to say, and it feels too soon. I'm prepared to leave immediately if I catch a glimpse of her, but she doesn't seem to be around. A couple of pilots from my usual lunch crowd wave at me, summoning me to their table, but I just wave back, realising that I'm slightly shaky, on the brink of nausea. I should have gone easy on the coffee.

I walk to a window and look out, suddenly craving solitude, clutching my mug in both hands but resolving not to let myself drink any more caffeine. A breeze is releasing petals from a single blossom-laden tree, sending white drifts across a rectangle of manicured lawn. A small bird is pecking the ground for worms. The reflection in the glass makes it look as if rows of fluorescent tubes are lined up in the grey-blue sky.

Wallis arrives ten minutes before we're due in the flight room and makes straight for me. There's an odd moment when I think we might greet each other with another hug, but at the last moment he reaches out for a handshake.

'You good to go?' I say.

He nods.

'Any news?' he asks after a silence.

I shrug. Stick monkeys are never given any strategic information. Our job is just to press the buttons.

For all the closeness we forged the day before, there doesn't seem to be much to say, so I suggest heading over to the flight room.

I let him walk a couple of paces ahead so it doesn't seem weird that we aren't talking. His boots give off a small, mouse-like squeak with every step. All the way there my mind flickers between wondering if Wallis likes me and berating myself for caring.

We switch over with the outgoing crew on the dot of twelve.

'Anything?' I say to the departing pilot, a guy with blond hair and an oval birthmark under his left eye. I've spoken to him a few times before, but can't remember his name.

He shakes his head as he coils the headphone cable and claps me on a shoulder. He's clearly frustrated to be leaving before the action kicks off, and I can't say I blame him.

As soon as I've taken my place in the still-warm chair I get a short briefing through my headphones. I'm on an armed MQ-9, with identical controls to yesterday's simulator. We're observing a stationary target in the south of The Strip. Strike zones have been identified and final checks are being carried out. The goal is to knock out all of The Corps' supply tunnels in one raid. The entrances are concealed in various devious ways, but weeks of surveillance have flushed out the key locations. The question now is one of timing. When the go-ahead comes, a jet assault is going to do the bulk of the work. My assignment is to mop up. Anyone in the target zone is assumed to be a terrorist, and is pre-authorised for a strike.

Of all the training scenarios we worked through this is the easiest, but knowing it's for real sends a prickle of anticipation to my fingertips. I'll be doing nothing I haven't done before, over and over again, yet on every previous occasion I merely sent electric pulses through banks of microchips. This time, when I press the launch button, fuel will ignite and a fifty kilogram missile in a blast fragmentation sleeve will shoot through the air towards human flesh.

I conduct the usual system checks, a nervous smile pulling at the corners of my mouth, but it's a long time before anything happens. I'm watching what looks like a dilapidated garage. Nobody goes in or out. If I didn't know what was coming, this would be the most boring day ever.

Then word comes through my cans that we have ten minutes. I turn to Wallis and ask if he's ready.

He glances back at me, gives a minuscule nod, his expression unreadable.

I take a sip of water, and as I unscrew the cap, it occurs to me that the next act of these same hands will be to unleash an awesome, lethal force.

Minutes pass and nothing moves on my screen, then, in an instant, the garage simply ceases to exist. It's obliterated so completely that when the dust clears there's little sign it was ever there. Nobody emerges. I zoom out, widening my target zone, and circle over the area, which at first reveals not much

196

more than drifting dust clouds from other blasts, until a figure appears on screen, staggering, attempting to run down a cratered, debris-strewn street. I can't tell where he's coming from or heading to, but he looks like a Military Age Male, so authorisation is in place.

Wallis locks on to him and I fire, guiding the missile bang on. It's a perfect bug splat. There's no question as the dust clears that the guy's toast.

As I stare at the screen, transfixed by the devastating effect of my actions on that faraway street, a wave of relief crashes through me. Throughout my life, at key moments, I have crumpled under pressure. The more intensely I prepared, the more likely it was that my goal would elude me, because again and again, in the seconds that matter, I've made flustered, stupid choices. I've always feared that something in the core of me was too unsteady to really succeed in this job, to succeed perhaps at anything. But this task, this solemn, godlike undertaking of wiping out another man, an enemy of my country, has now been achieved. I am not, after all, too weak.

I knew I could get through the training, but only now, with my first kill, can I finally be assured of my abilities. It took me years to get here, and now I have arrived. I'm blooded.

I survey the area for the rest of my shift, looking to clean up more bad guys, but there's nothing.

The moment when the new crew arrives to relieve us feels like being jolted awake. I've been living through that screen, weightless and omnipotent, so intensely at one with my task it's almost like dissolving out of myself into the realm of flight, as if my body in this quiet air-conditioned room has evaporated and somehow metamorphosed into a bird of prey.

As I unplug and stand, the process of how to move in human form rises sluggishly from my brain: these are your legs, this is how you straighten them, gravity will pull you downwards ...

The new pilot asks me a question I don't even hear. For a second, I'm unsteady on my feet, not prepared for human interaction.

I grunt a vague non-answer and walk out alongside Wallis. After the dimmed, intense atmosphere of the flight room, the white corridor is so bright it makes us blink.

We look at one another for a second before wordlessly shaking hands. He looks like I feel: wide-eyed, dazed, elated.

'See you tomorrow,' I say, releasing myself from his grip.

'Yup.'

He walks away, lumbering down the corridor with the heavy, uneven gait of an ex-sportsman, his boots still squeaking. He's exactly the kind of guy who would have given me a hard time at school, but now we are partners, soldiers, fellow fighters.

I step outside into the illuminated, fenced-off smoking area, not really wanting a cigarette, just a reason to stand still, be alone, and breathe.

The flash of my lighter's flint summons a neat, perfect

flame, blue at the heart, encased in orange, which I hold for a while in front of my face, admiring its simple beauty. Tobacco crackles momentarily as I light up.

I blow my first exhalation skywards. It's a cloudy night, only a few stars glinting feebly through the darkness. Above my head, a flurry of moths are beating themselves relentlessly into the floodlight. It's so quiet, I can hear the patter of their wings against the hot plastic.

As I suck another throat-clenching puff into my lungs, I find myself pondering whether I am a changed person, now that I've killed a man.

This ought to feel entirely new, but do I, at this moment, actually feel anything at all? When they look almost identical, how am I supposed to find a response to the shift from zapping pixels to ripping apart skin and bone?

I know I ought to have an emotional response to what I have done, but what that should be, I don't know. Guilt? Triumph? Grief?

Was that scatter of limbs on my screen *really* a man, who woke up this morning to his last day on earth? Who did he have breakfast with? Are those people still hoping he will come home? When will his body be found, his family told? Is somebody far away weeping for him right now, while I stand here smoking?

Who's the hero, me or him or both or neither?

The questions keep on coming, but I have no answers, no idea what to think or feel.

I killed a man. This fact hangs emptily in front of me like a lurid balloon that means nothing, tells me nothing, answers nothing.

I can detect only one change in me, which is that I can't quite get the sensation of weight back into my body. As I crush my half-finished cigarette and walk away from the compound, I still feel lighter than I should, less than entirely present, fractionally detached from the ground, though my footsteps on loose gravel, crunching through the hushed darkness of the base, seem strangely loud, ominously clear.

As I stand in the silent, empty car park, sliding a cool motorcycle helmet over my head, a half-memory from distant childhood drifts back to me, of looking up and realising that everyone has left, and I don't know where they've gone.

The City

I must have fallen asleep eventually, because an arrow of low dawn light wakes me. A solitary burglar alarm is wailing persistently somewhere down the street, but there are no bombs and no sirens.

Zoe is awake, standing at the mouth of the railway arch, staring motionlessly along the empty road. One hand is planted on a hip and her face is turned to the sun, which is casting a white glow into wisps of her hair.

She turns slowly towards me. A long, skewed shadow moves with her, slanting out from her feet, along the filthy ground and up a wall of the arch. Her lips curl into a small, tentative smile, not an expression of happiness, just a word-less greeting. The chilling absence that hollowed her eyes the night before has gone.

For a few hours, the essence of her disappeared. Only now

can I acknowledge to myself the sheer terror of looking into Zoe's vacant unseeing eyes. Only now can I admit to myself that I truly feared she had reached her breaking point, snapped, joined the ranks of the broken people.

I scrutinise her face more closely, and allow myself to bask briefly in a relief so intense it feels like stunned, addled joy, as if I have watched the girl I love return from the dead.

No cars pass. The city's usual background hum of traffic is absent. Dust motes and tiny feathers drift lazily through the air between us, twinkling into invisibility as soon as they leave the narrow beam of sunshine.

'Are you OK?' I ask.

She nods, reaches up with both arms, tilts her head skywards and stretches luxuriantly, emitting a low moan.

'I'm starving,' she says.

'Me too. Let's get home,' I say, standing and brushing the worst of the filth from my trousers. 'I thought they'd bomb last night,' I add.

'It'll happen.'

Blinking in the harsh sunlight, I lift and steady my bike, but before we get on, Zoe drops a quick, tender kiss on my lips, and I feel a thread of joy plait itself into the terror and dread that is knotted within me. Despite the bombs, despite the imminent attack, I feel sure, for the first time, that she is mine and I am hers.

I kiss her again and we fall into an embrace. Locked together, afloat on the miracle of this girl's affection, it occurs to me that it's inaccurate to say you feel love in your heart. You feel it in every part of you, to the tips of your fingers. It trembles and sings through every artery, vein and capillary. It dances across every pore and follicle.

I almost say this. If I had paused to contemplate the onslaught that was about to fall on the city; if I had remembered who my father was and let myself consider that a missile circling somewhere above was destined for him; if I had calculated the transformed odds of that day being my last, I would have said what I was thinking. But the words that come out of my mouth are just 'Let's get home.'

The Base

It's brutal going from a late shift to an early. Even after a long, blisteringly hot shower, I'm still half asleep as I drag myself downstairs.

Mum is at the breakfast table with a newspaper in front of her bearing some lurid headline about The Strip and an image of exploding ordnance. Her face is pale and severe. She looks up at me with grief-stricken, accusatory eyes, but doesn't speak.

I'm already in uniform and only want a bowl of cereal. There's barely time for breakfast, let alone the conversation I can feel she's about to inflict on me. I almost turn on my heel and go, but, to my surprise, she looks at me and doesn't open her mouth.

I wordlessly fetch a bowl. The sound of the cornflakes tumbling in seems to fill the room.

I don't want to get any closer to her. I eat standing up with my back against the fridge, avoiding eye contact.

But of course she can't contain herself. I've wolfed down a few mouthfuls when her prim little voice pipes up and says, 'Don't go.'

I turn to face her, seeing her pinched mouth etched with sorrow, and shrug. I have no idea what she even means, and no particular desire to find out.

'Don't go in today,' she says.

'What are you talking about?'

'Don't take part in this.'

'What, you think I can just not turn up? Tell them I don't fancy it?'

If I didn't feel sorry for her, I'd be laughing.

'Please,' she says. 'Think about what you're doing.'

'I'm doing my job. I'm serving my country.'

'Nobody can make you do anything. You have the choice. You can walk away.'

'Of course I can't. I'm a soldier.'

'You can though,' she says, rising to her feet and rushing towards me, then stopping herself awkwardly mid-step. 'You still have a choice. Every moment of every day, you have a choice about what you do!'

I turn and rinse out my empty bowl so she can't see the smirk that is tickling at the corner of my lips. 'I don't know what planet you live on,' I say. 'You've lost the plot. I'll see you later.'

As I manoeuvre my bike out of the drive, I notice through a window that she is still in the kitchen, standing motionless in the place where I left her, with the same crushed, weary expression on her face. It must be hard being that old. After a certain point, I suppose you can't keep up with how the world changes, can't make sense of what seems obvious to everyone else.

Riding fast towards the bright, low sun, with my visor up so I can enjoy the brisk air whipping past my face, it occurs to me that while I zoom towards the base, my brain is revolving at a lower, calmer, more contented speed than ever before. The semi-permanent background noise of anxiety and doubt is turned down low, drowned out by a simple, clear thought which rings slowly through me, replete with meaning, even though at the same time I sense it may be utterly banal. All I can think, over and over, is *I am who I am*.

Wrapped around this idea is a sudden liberating incomprehension of how much I allowed my mother to upset me in the past, how much time I spent pointlessly craving her approval. Now, at last, I genuinely don't know why I even cared.

Weaving through the car park and slotting my bike into its usual spot, it becomes clear to me why this day feels so good. All my life I've been looking for a place where I belong, where nobody expects me to be anything other than who I am, and now I've found it, right here.

There's little time to spare, so I hurry across the gravel and head straight for the flight room. All tiredness has been blown away by the ride, replaced by a skittering, almost jaunty excitement.

When you join the military, you know almost every working day will be spent waiting, training and preparing. What you're waiting for comes along very rarely. And it's this. Days like this.

The skinny guy who relieved me the night before is still at the controls. I've only been away one shift.

'Anything?' I say at the changeover.

He shakes his head. 'I guess you're in for the big one,' he replies.

There's no sign of Wallis, but the outgoing sensor operator stands to leave straight after his pilot.

'Wait,' I say. 'My guy's late.'

'Your guy's not a guy,' he says, pointing to the uniformed figure who is poised to take his place. 'She's here.'

My whole body feels as if it has been dunked in ice at the moment I look across and see Victoria take a seat next to me.

'Where's Wallis?' I say, not to her, not to anyone in particular, but she's the only person who listens.

She doesn't look at me. Plugs in her cans. Shrugs.

'I thought you were a …' My voice tails away. I can barely speak.

She shakes her head. 'Training status is classified. You should know that. But some people like to brag.'

I haven't yet put on my headphones, and I hear a tinny voice rise up from my lap. I clamp them on.

'Yes, sir. I read you,' I say.

The briefing is swift. I've never heard any emotion in Wilkinson's voice, but today he speaks fast, crisp and loud, faintly short of breath. I'm back to #K622, but on an armed MQ-9, not a Watchkeeper. He gives me formal confirmation that #K622 is on the kill list, fully authorised, scheduled for a coordinated strike. I must wait for the order.

The same house I've watched for thousands of hours is on screen. Wilkinson confirms that he is in the building, and that I must stay on him wherever he goes.

I ask for the collateral damage parameters, and I'm told that's not an issue. He's a High Value Target. There's no mention of who else is in the house with him.

'Sir?' I ask. 'With respect. Where's Wallis?'

'He's needed elsewhere. You got Hicks, another newbie off the programme, but she's fully trained.'

There's an audible click as Wilkinson signs off.

I glance across at Victoria. Her eyes are fixed on our screens.

Ever since that moment outside her house I've tried to avoid thinking about this girl and what happened between us. Whenever she pops into my mind, a cascade of words comes with her: apologies, explanations, strategies for how to avoid her or how to approach her, a mad din of useless speeches I know I'll never give. Now she's within touching distance, by my side for the next eight hours, with everything we say audible to our superior officers.

I feel as if every tendon in my body has been tightened. Just knowing she's there, next to me, has seized me up. It's like sitting next to a grenade.

Her face is unreadable, blank, professional, but I can feel pure loathing pulse out of her, irradiating me with embarrassment and shame.

This is the biggest day of my career, the culmination of everything I have worked for, but my mental focus is shot. I can't think straight, can't concentrate. The screen in front of me is a blur.

I blink, force myself to snap to attention. My eyes flick towards Victoria. She's watching our primary screen. Calm, inscrutable.

I tell her to go wider on a secondary display.

She pulls back the view.

'Full scope test,' I say.

She draws the view wider. The target house shrinks away, becoming a grey square within a line of tiled roofs, which in turn slides back to become part of a tangle of streets, old bomb sites standing out like missing teeth. The broccoli speckles of The Strip's remaining trees shrivel to nothing as street after street crowds into view, endless hordes of buildings rushing in to fill the screen from every corner, a deluge of lives. Only the parks stand out among the grey: patches of brown criss-crossed with neat grids of tents which, from this height, look like the layout for some kind of board game.

I don't know if it's the presence of Victoria or a sudden upsurge of battlefield nerves, but my mood has flipped, excitement and anticipation curdling into a sour, unsettling brew. It occurs to me that my screen is filled with hundreds of thousands of people, some of whom will soon be killed, their deaths orchestrated from this room.

The morning's surge in confidence, which seemed like a transformative revelation, has left no trace. Despite my successful kill the day before, the haunting old questions are suddenly back, fizzing through my skull. *Can you kill this man? Can you kill his wife? His son? His twins? Do you have the steel? When the moment comes, will you find the nerve to pull the trigger?*

NO, I tell myself, the words almost slipping aloud from my lips. *NO!* Not these thoughts. Not now. Not on this day, of all days. These questions should have been trained out of me. My focus must be entirely on the target. I have a simple job to perform, which requires no analysis. The family are not my consideration. Any seepage of empathy must be banished.

There isn't much more time. I have to concentrate and master my thoughts. Yet a nauseating simmer of self-doubt is bubbling within me.

Can I do this?

If I cannot do this, who am I?

Whatever made me think I could hold my own in this place, among these people?

210

Why have I put myself under exactly the kind of pressure that makes me crack?

What will happen to me if I fail?

I reach for the bottle on my desk, fumbling the lid, spilling a gobbet of water down my chin as I sip. The roof of my mouth feels dry and sticky, my throat tight. Although open containers aren't allowed on the consoles I don't replace the lid, fearing that Victoria, or someone else, will notice my trembling hands.

'Restore,' I say.

She zooms the image back in towards the target house. London flings itself out of view as we zero down towards #K622's home.

I try to throw myself into the shrinking image, to mirror its movement, to zoom my concentration into the task at hand. My job is not to think or feel. Just to act. My task is to see the world through a drinking straw, and obey orders. Nothing beyond the screen is my responsibility. Doubt is immaterial. No element of reflection or choice belongs here.

I run these thoughts round and round my head as if I'm exercising the wildness out of a cooped-up dog.

My mind begins to settle. My pulse slows.

I breathe.

I watch the house.

If a thought buds, I snip it off.

I allow myself one simple, comforting idea, which is that every soldier in history has probably experienced similar fears on the way into battle, and when the order comes to fight, reflection is obliterated.

I am calm. I will perform. I won't fail.

'Heat,' I say.

She gives me the heat view, popping the screen into monochrome.

'Back,' I say.

She goes back.

'It won't be long now,' I say.

She nods.

'Frustrating, isn't it?' I say. 'Waiting for no reason.'

I'm hoping that by saying this I might mean it, but I feel myself blush, and turn aside to conceal my face. Better not to talk. Better just to pretend she is Wallis. I have to shut her out of my head and focus on the assignment. After this shift, I can request a different operator.

A flicker of movement on screen draws my eye. It's the son, arriving home, getting off his bike. The sight of him immediately pulls me out of myself and nails my attention to The Strip, to this house, towards which I will soon be ordered to launch a missile. Another figure is with him, a female, who also dismounts.

He doesn't carry the bike through to the back, where it's usually kept, or even lock it. He leaves it under the front window, and hurries to the door.

They pause, kiss, then stand facing one another for a few seconds, perhaps speaking, perhaps not. He takes a key from his pocket and opens the door with his right hand, his left remaining entwined in the fingers of his girlfriend.

He lets go of her, and they enter.

My screen again shows nothing more than the usual image of this infinitely familiar brick terrace house, which must have stood there for at least a century. In a short while, at the push of a button over which my finger is already hovering, it will be destroyed.

My pulse is hammering now. I had been trying not to think about whether the boy was in there with his father. Now there's no denying it.

I wish I could tell him to leave. I would do almost anything to find a way to scream at him to get out. But all I can do is watch, and wait.

Please let the boy leave. Please let #K622 go for a walk, or to a meeting with his accomplices.

Why is he still there with his *family*? Is he using them as a shield? Because it won't work. He's the target, and wherever he is when the order comes, that's where the missile will strike. He must know that.

After all the anticipation and eagerness, all the months of training and preparation for this moment, the order that is about to come through fills me with pure dread.

Please. Not just yet.

Not yet.

Please.

The City

The roads are empty as we cycle northwards. No cars, no lorries, no buses and certainly no other teenagers sharing a bike. The occasional figure comes into view on foot and scurries from doorway to doorway, staying close to the walls. It feels as if the entire city, a metropolis of millions, is dangling by a thread, and every one of us is waiting to see how far we will fall when the thread is cut.

The only sound is the grind of my bicycle chain and the buzz of the drones as they slice their patient laser-eyed arcs through the sky, watching and waiting.

My body, swirling with dread and bliss, has never seemed more alive, or closer to death. Every cell is alert, brimming with intensity. It's almost as if I'm not cycling through the city, but high above it, along a knife-edge, with the whole world apart from Zoe and me far below.

The tide is high as we cross Westminster Bridge, water lapping against the partially crumbled retaining walls, almost covering the collapsed Ferris wheel whose rusted hulk nearly blocks the bend in the river. We're the only people on the bridge, and after a right turn next to the ruins of parliament, we also have the whole of Whitehall to ourselves. The emptiness is strange and unsettling, but to be north of the river feels like a leap homewards.

Everything looks sharper, brighter, more real than it did yesterday. But back then, I was a different person. A virgin. Today, I feel as if I'm knitted into the world as I've never been before. Zoe has suffused me with more life than I ever thought I could contain.

This is life.

This is life.

I am.

She is.

We are.

The only places we see other people are around the tube stations, some of which seem to be full, with crowds at the entrances fighting to get inside, to find a way underground before the bombs fall.

We come to a stop outside Zoe's home. She gets off, but doesn't make any move to go. A small mob is clustered around the entrance to the underground shelter, engaged in an angry dispute with a pair of armed security guards.

The buzz from the sky seems louder now, the drones lower, closer, bigger.

'Are you going to be able to get in?' I ask.

Zoe eyes the crowd, deep in thought.

'We should get your family,' she says.

'What do you mean?'

'Bring them here.'

'There's no space.'

'There's always space. Just till this is over. Even if they have to stand, there's space. They should be underground.'

'We won't get in.'

'Our area is assigned. I have ID. I can get you in.'

This idea freezes me. I can't think what I should do. My ability to calculate options, assess risks, has vanished. I feel as if I can't grasp any plan more complex than just getting home and telling my parents I'm still alive. I know my father will have access to some kind of shelter, but anywhere associated with The Corps is a likely target. This would be far safer.

I look up at the nearest drone, sensing that it's watching me, then remember that it contains no human being. No eyes, no hands, no skin or sweat, no heartbeat, no conscience. But somebody somewhere is looking down on us.

Zoe places her fingers on my cheek, gently drawing my attention back to her. 'We don't have much time,' she says.

'My father won't come,' I reply, without having any idea what I might be agreeing to.

216

'Your mother. Your sisters. They should be here,' insists Zoe.

'We have to ask your family,' I say.

'No. There's no time.'

'But …'

'And no point.'

She fixes me with those vibrant green eyes. An image of her distraught mother flashes across my mind. In that family, there is no higher authority than Zoe.

'Are you sure?'

'Yes. Hurry.'

'They don't know you. They don't know this place. They won't come.'

'Take me with you. I'll explain.'

'But …'

Zoe grips my arms and shakes, as if she's trying to wake me up. 'I can't go down there without you, and you can't go without them, can you?'

'No.'

She gets back on the bike.

'So come on,' she says. 'Stop wasting time.'

We set off. The strange elation that half numbed me at the start of our journey has evaporated. I can feel desperation in the air now. As we approach home, passing through residential streets, more people are outside. Everyone we see is hurrying, close to the walls, pushing trolleys, hauling carts, carrying bursting bags or crammed suitcases, many with children or old people on their backs. With each revolution of my pedals, each advancing minute, cold, sharp terror sinks its hooks deeper and deeper into me. I feel as if annihilation is riding with us on the bike, a hostile stowaway squeezed between us, exhaling its icy breath on my neck.

When my pace slows, Zoe gets off the bike and tells me to keep riding. She runs alongside, fighting to keep up, and by the time we get to my home we're both sweating and breathless.

I lean my bike against the house and am about to open the front door when Zoe touches my shoulder and turns me to face her. She places a kiss on my lips, which brings the prickle of almost shed tears to my eyes as a lurch of something that feels like grief wrenches at my belly.

There's no time to contemplate what I might be grieving for, or even to think of a response. I turn my key and push open the door.

My parents are instantly upon me, rushing out into the dim hallway. Mum grabs me into a rib-crushing hug while at the same time screaming at me, a long howl of outrage, relief and anger. 'Where the hell have you been? We thought you were … we thought you … we've been up all night … we've sent people out to search … nobody wants to be on the streets but we've been out there looking and looking and asking everybody and there was nothing … nothing … Where were you? What were you doing? How could you disappear like that? Didn't you hear the bombs? There's going to be more. We thought you were … We thought …'

Her mouth is so close to my ear that I can see my father's lips moving, but can't make out his words until Mum finally lets go of me. As soon as her grip loosens, he steps between us. His face is twisted into an expression I have never seen before – as if he detests me.

'WELL? WELL?' he spits, demanding a response to some question I haven't even heard.

'Well what?'

'WELL WHAT? Are you making fun of me? How could you? Do you know what you've done? I shouldn't be here. I'm putting every one of you in danger … your mother, your sisters, our neighbours … I'm not supposed to be here. Not now. But your mother's been crazed with fear all night … I've been the same … We thought something had … We knew it had to be something bad … something terrible … and now you just walk in here with some girl as if nothing's wrong!' Spittle is collecting in the corners of his mouth. His eyes are pinched and bloodshot. 'You should be ashamed! How could you be so selfish?' He grabs my chest and pins me against the wall. 'Things are happening right now. Last night. Today. I can't be here. I cannot be here now, but because of you I couldn't leave. Because of you.'

His hands are gripping my T-shirt, twisting it in his fists.

'I told you. I TOLD YOU!' he yells.

I'm speechless for an instant more, then something in me seems to burst. I shove back against my father. He staggers, almost falling to the ground. 'DON'T TOUCH ME! GET

YOUR HANDS OFF ME! YOU HAVE NO IDEA WHERE I'VE BEEN OR WHY. YOU THINK I'D DO THAT ON PURPOSE? YOU THINK I HAD A CHOICE?'

I step forward, nose to nose with my father. My chin is tilted ever so slightly downwards as I eyeball him. I'm taller. 'Don't push me again. Ever. You don't know where I was. You don't know what happened to me. I was trapped. I'll explain later. The important thing is, I've found a place. Zoe is from a shelter. She says we can go there. Now.'

My father's eyes flick towards Zoe and I turn to face my Mum. 'Now. Now! Me, you, and the twins.'

Mum is frozen, her face blank with confusion at the sudden onslaught of conflicting emotion.

'There's space for you. For a while,' says Zoe. 'A bag can go on the bike. We'll walk.'

'NOW!' I say.

Mum spins on the ball of a foot and runs from the room.

I turn back to Dad, who is staring at me as if I'm a violent stranger who has broken into his home.

'I warned you,' he says. 'I warned you and you ignored me.'

I shrug.

'You didn't listen. You never listen. You could have killed your sisters, me, your mother. I had to be here all night. At the worst possible time. How could you do that?'

'*I* could have killed them?' I say, my words slicing through the air.

220

He turns his face aside as if I have slapped him on the cheek.

'Are you really trying to tell me it would be *my* fault?' I say.

He doesn't move. Every tendon in his body seems to slacken, somehow shrinking him in front of my eyes. His head remains motionless, turned to the wall.

Mum punctures the silence, bustling into the room with a single suitcase and my two sisters, who look sleepy-eyed and confused.

'OK, let's go, let's go,' she says.

She steps towards Dad and kisses him once on the cheek. 'Good luck,' she says, her voice clipped and fast, carrying undertones not just of hurry, but of hostility and blame. She may have tolerated or even supported his work for The Corps, but I can feel now that she will never forgive him for where it has led them.

Dad hugs and kisses the girls, saying over and over, 'See you soon. See you very soon.' It is obvious, even to them, that his words are a wish, a prayer, not a promise.

Then we are out of the door, hurrying awkwardly with the children, the suitcase, the bike, getting away from that house as fast as we can.

The Base

He's out! He's out!

I want to jump from my seat and dance. I could almost shout for joy. He's out and away from his father, with the sisters and the mother and the girl.

I watch them stagger away from the house, almost counting their steps, willing them away from the blast zone, and within a few seconds they're safe. The boy, it seems, figured out what was coming and has rescued them.

I almost comment to Victoria that the family are out – which is a positive step in terms of collateral damage – but I fear my voice would give too much away. If anyone around me knew what I was thinking I'd be a laughing stock.

I'm not sure what the nature of my connection to that boy is, but I know it's unprofessional, verging on a dereliction of duty. I will never admit to anyone the degree to which my sympathies have strayed from their allotted path.

Perhaps others feel the same way. We pass more time watching these people than we spend with our own families. Or maybe I'm the only one. I'll never know, because I couldn't ask another pilot, and if anyone asked me, I'd deny it.

I say nothing. I keep my face as neutral as I'm able, even though my first thought, when the order comes through to lock the target, is simple delight that the boy and his family have escaped.

I execute and a red icon appears at the top left of my screen.

A bristle of excitement sweeps across the row of consoles, a palpable intensification of the room's poised hush, which makes me glance over my shoulder. Screen after screen is now bearing the same red icon.

It's a coordinated action. All the High Value Targets are being taken out at once.

There will be no more than two minutes until the strike order, then, after I launch the missile, a few seconds more until impact.

The heady to and fro of anxiety and self-doubt has gone now. I feel absolutely prepared, poised in that sweet spot between anticipation and calm alertness. Until a flash of movement at the lower edge of the screen jolts me upright.

The boy.

It's the boy! Running back. *Towards* the house.

Why?

Why would he do that?

He was out – away – safe – and now he's running back!

Why now?

Not now!

Not now!

Out of the corner of my eye, I register that Victoria is watching me. I've given something away.

I must stay calm. Whatever thoughts are boiling through my head, I can reveal nothing.

My role is very simple, very clear.

I cannot stray from my procedure.

I must not display the slightest hesitation or qualm.

The boy opens the door and steps in.

The City

We are at a safe distance, halfway to the corner, when Zoe stops me.

'You didn't say goodbye,' she says.

'There wasn't time.'

'You … if you …'

She seems to be struggling to get the words out. Her throat is tight, her eyes wide, her fingers digging into my forearm.

'What is it? Are you OK?' I ask.

'If you don't say goodbye … if that's your last …'

I suddenly remember her father. Zoe knows that any conversation in wartime could be the final one. I sense that her last words to her own dad are spooling through her mind, maybe a dispute or a sarcastic comment or a meaningless trivial exchange, but she wishes they had been something else, and this haunts her.

The last thing I said to my dad was the harshest, most painful accusation I could have made, one that nobody in the family had ever dared voice. The last time I touched him was a shove in the chest. Our last look was one of hatred and anger.

'Wait here,' I say, stopping my mother and the twins, passing the heavily laden bike to Zoe.

I turn and sprint back to the house.

'WHERE ARE YOU GOING? WHAT ARE YOU DOING?' Mum screams.

I turn my head but don't stop running. 'Just stay there. One minute.'

I burst through the front door and sprint up the stairs, finding Dad hurrying out of the bedroom, carrying a small bag, already on his way out.

We stare at one another, but I haven't prepared what it is I came to say. There's no way to express any of the emotions that are pounding through me.

Then he's on me, arms wrapped around my back, hauling me into his embrace. We stand there at the top of the stairs, clinging to one another like drowning men clutching at driftwood. There's no sound but his breath in my ear, the ticking of our hall clock and the distant buzz of a drone.

Then a new sound intrudes. Not exactly close, but not far away either. A missile strike.

'It's started,' he says. 'Go. Go now. I'll give you a minute to get away from me, then I'll leave. Go.'

The Base

A momentary click and hiss through my headphones, then, 'Prepare for launch.'

I enter the launch code. 'Roger.'

The boy is still in the house.

'Confirm target lock.'

'Confirmed.'

The boy is still in the house.

Click and hiss. 'Five seconds … Four.'

The boy is still in the house.

'Three … Two.'

He's still in the house.

'One.'

He's still in the house.

'Launch.'

My finger hovers over the launch key, but my body and

my brain seem paralysed. Nothing is moving.

'Launch!'

Behind me, clusters of noise bubble up – a few cheers, some clapping, the odd whoop. I glance behind and see screens filled with dust, smoke and fire.

'LAUNCH! LAUNCH!'

I look back at my screen. I turn my head to Victoria. She's staring at me but I cannot read her expression. Puzzlement? Revulsion? Scorn? Concern? I have no idea.

There are always alternates on site for medical or psychological emergencies, but for the mission today there must be one in the room, at the ready, because after a strange, vacant gap of time in which I have no idea what happens, or what I am thinking, two pairs of arms haul me from my seat and another pilot takes my place.

I'm face down on the floor with a knee in my back when the handcuffs come out. I feel suddenly sleepy, detached, as if the wrists sensing the bite of hard plastic are not quite my own.

For a while I see only shoes. Clean, black military shoes, standing on grey carpet tiles whose roughness I can feel against my cheek. I have walked over this carpet countless times but have never felt its surface, or noticed that it smells like a new home.

I watch a spider walk unhurriedly away through a crack under the skirting board.

I am falling. Although I am on the floor, there is much

further to go before I land. My instant of hesitation has opened a trapdoor underneath my life, and a plummet has started into another world. Every hope or ambition I ever held is gone. Everything above me now is out of reach forever. I have no idea what is below.

I'm hauled to my feet and marched from the room by two men who grip me at the elbow and armpit, half lifting me from the ground. I am neither walking nor being carried, the balls of my feet stepping across the floor but bearing no weight. I twist my neck, craning to see one last glimpse of my screen.

It is grey. Nothing visible but smoke and dust.

The City

I turn from my father and run down the stairs, taking the whole flight in three bounds.

I hear more explosions all around, each blast coming before the sound of the previous one has faded. They're not just taking out the tunnels now. This is everywhere. The assault has started.

My hand fumbles with the door latch. The next missile will land any second. It could be on this house.

The door yields under my trembling hands. I push it open and turn back for one last look at my father.

'Don't wait!' I say. 'Come. Come now.'

'GO! GO! GO!' he replies, shooing me away with a thrust of both arms.

I step out into the blinding sunshine. Zoe, Mum and the twins haven't moved. They are wide-eyed, the girls clinging to their mother's legs, flinching from the blasts.

I take my first step towards them, trying to break into a run, but there is no run. There is no second step. I hear nothing; I see nothing; I become, in an instant, nothing.

The Base

I don't lose consciousness – there's no blow to the head that knocks me out – but I do lose awareness. There is a gap I cannot remember. I don't recall any prison admission, being stripped of my uniform, having my pockets emptied; nor is there a moment of waking up, in which I look around me and realise I am in a cell.

The guards do not speak to me. Sometimes they spit in my food.

A lawyer appears and explains that I am awaiting court martial for misconduct on operations and disobeying a lawful command. I hear him, half understand him, and even reply to his questions, but mostly I just watch his lips move.

The days do not pass slowly or fast, because for a while time seems to have become static. Every moment is both endless and infinitesimal. It seems, in my cell, as if nothing happens or ever will happen.

It may be days or weeks before I'm told I have a visitor. I have no idea.

I don't really want to leave my cell, but my wishes no longer have any bearing on what happens to me.

It's my mother. She looks somehow younger, taller, more alive than I remember. Around the home she always wore shapeless old trousers and frayed knitwear, but now she's dressed in a blouse and skirt. Her grey hair is styled, falling elegantly over her shoulders, no longer tied back in a ponytail.

Tears well up in her eyes when she sees me, but something in her bearing and expression speaks of happiness, or perhaps relief. She tells me she knows what I did, and she's proud of me. She tells me I am brave. She tells me people are calling me a hero. There is a campaign to raise funds for my defence. A group of activists wants to turn my protest into an example, a test case, the beginnings of a challenge to the drone programme under war crimes legislation.

My protest?

This word, at first, means nothing to me.

As I slowly come to understand what she thinks I did, it occurs to me that she feels herself to have been a participant. She thinks she persuaded me not to fire. And the more she talks, with an enthusiasm and intensity to her voice that I can barely recognise, mentioning events and speeches and press conferences, the more it becomes apparent that she has claimed for herself a public position as spokesperson and mentor of the conscientious objector.

I have, at long last, given her something she wants. This is why she suddenly looks smart, driven and alive. She finally has a role, at the heart of a cause she believes in.

In truth, I can't understand what I did, or why, nor do I have any hopes for my defence. I know she has misunderstood, and has hijacked my dereliction of duty for her own purposes, but since I can't summon any coherent explanation for what froze my hand at the controls of that missile, I have no objection to somebody else finding a meaning for me.

I am equally indifferent to both punishment and help, unable even to care which is which.

I watch her talk, nodding, unsure whether to feel betrayed or helped, speaking only when she threatens to send in my 'supporters' to visit me. All I can say to her is that I don't want other visitors. She can come, nobody else.

She hugs me tight before she leaves. The guard tells her not to touch me, but she silences him with a glare and he seems to give up. In her arms, inhaling her heart-wrenchingly familiar scent, a strange teenage emotion wells up in me – a mingling of childish pleasure in receiving comfort, and revulsion at her stifling miscomprehension and stupidity.

There's a new lawyer after that, with no tie, unkempt hair and a gleam in his eye like a dog who's sighted a squirrel. He talks and talks, tries to coach me as to the line we are taking in my case, a challenge to the notion of what constitutes a 'lawful command' in the case of an assassination from an Unmanned Aerial Vehicle, but I don't really listen. He gives the impression there is huge interest in the case, as if it's not really me who is on trial, but the military itself.

On the day of the hearing I imagine banks of cameras, being mobbed as I step from a van, reporters screaming at me for a quote, but it turns out courts martial are held in private.

There are a few observers who may or may not be reporters; it's hard to tell. My mother is right at the front, upright and expectant in her seat, with an excited look on her face as if this were my wedding day.

The proceedings are all done within a few hours. I don't really listen, and I'm not called on to say much. The 'lawful command' challenge is thrown out, and I'm given a dishonourable discharge, but no further imprisonment.

Mum cheers and leaps towards me. She hugs me, grabs one arm and lifts it in the air like I'm a victorious boxer after a fight.

As soon as we're outside, in daylight, I hear shutters click. Mum doesn't let go of me, so we walk out of the base hand in hand. I don't really want to hold her hand – it seems embarrassing – crowds of people are watching – but she grips so hard I don't have a choice.

After the quiet solitude of my cell, the jostling throng of TV cameras, flashbulb-popping photographers, shouting

235

journalists and chanting well-wishers is terrifying. When we come to a stop, I stand behind Mum and the squirrel-chasing lawyer, fighting the instinct to flinch and the urge to run away.

The lawyer removes a piece of paper from his pocket and clears his throat. A hush descends on the crowd, punctuated by clicking cameras each time he looks up between phrases. He says the decision is a travesty, an attempt to bury the problem, and vows that it will be taken to a higher court. He says vital questions have been asked about what should be legal in modern warfare, and that these questions will not go away. He talks and talks and talks. Eventually, he says the most important thing is I am free again, but this is clearly an afterthought.

The moment he finishes, a cacophony of questions is fired at us. He answers a few, but the tirade is endless and deafening. He says something about post-traumatic stress disorder, tells the crowd that I will be giving an interview in due course, then with the help of a couple of policemen, I'm bundled into a car and driven home.

A short while later, it's me and Mum across the kitchen table with cups of coffee. She's elated, so electrified by her triumph she seems to twitch with the effort of sitting still.

I can think of little to say.

The silence is unbearable, so I tell her I'd like to go to bed.

She says of course.

The crowd of journalists on our front lawn gets smaller

each day. By the end of the month there are none. I never give that interview.

I feel tired and confused for a long time.

Mum's friends visit a lot at first. It seems as if they are excited to meet me, but when they do, I sense their disappointment. I try vaguely to say what they want to hear, but it never comes out right. I have learned to call what I did 'my protest', but it never sounds convincing coming from my lips.

After a while they stop coming. It turns out there's not enough money for a legal challenge, which is fine by me.

I start going to the shops, running basic errands, but Mum cooks for me, looks after me, changes my sheets.

The old dynamic returns. I am not her hero for long. I spend most of my time gaming.

'How can you still do that?' she says one day from the doorway, gesturing at the on-screen gore.

'I'm good at it,' I mumble.

Not long after that she starts nagging me to get a job. She stops cooking for me, stops changing the sheets.

Eventually I cave in. There's a hardware store run by the husband of one of Mum's friends which is in need of a shop assistant. The job offer appears to be a favour, a sympathy call, but as long as I turn up and do as I'm told, they pay me real money.

It's not enough to get my own place, but I can at least get my bike back on the road. The wage allows me to eat in cafes and fast food joints, instead of at home. It's a lot easier when

I only have to use the bedroom and bathroom there. If I have money, I barely need to set foot downstairs.

Slowly, I realise I like the job. Our customers are all making, repairing or building something. I find them what they're looking for: a tool, some screws or nails, paint, timber, sealant – we have an enormous range in a small space. I come to understand the details of ordering and stock control, of customer satisfaction and product rotation.

With a daily routine, time seems to accelerate, my period in the military falling away into an almost forgotten past. I become assistant manager. I interview and train a young guy to take my previous job. The boss turns up less and less, trusting me to take charge. The shop doesn't expand, nor does it shrink. I maintain a steady profit.

We have a noticeboard where tradesmen can put up cards touting for work. One of the regulars is in a band. He asks to put up a flyer for a gig, which isn't what the board is for, but he offers to put me on the guest list so I say yes.

On the night of the performance, I pull the flyer down, shove it in my pocket and head to that part of town. I ride past the venue, which looks more like an abandoned warehouse than a night spot, and take shelter in a nearby bar to build my confidence. After a couple of beers I almost turn for home, but at the last moment force myself to go in.

The noise and density of the crowd is alarming at first, until I realise this is a place in which you can disappear. Nothing is expected of you; nobody will even notice you are there. The music is raucous and clumsy, but by the end of the gig I find myself swept up by the volume and atmosphere, bouncing up and down in the middle of the room among a crowd of sweating strangers.

It's the best night I've had in years. I wouldn't normally be so forward, but after the show I go over to the guy who invited me and tell him how much I enjoyed it. He's surprisingly delighted by my compliment, even puts an arm around me, and I soon find myself drinking among a gang of his mates. That's where I meet Crystal.

It's amazing how your whole life can turn on tiny choices that seem insignificant at the moment you're making them. The decision to congratulate someone for their moderately competent guitar playing can divert your future on to a new path. Crystal is a shy girl with pale skin and thin blonde hair which half hides her face, but I like her straight away, and we end up talking until almost midnight, by which time I somehow have the courage to ask for her phone number.

We take it super-slow. Neither of us are talkers, so at first our dates are a little awkward, but after a while we realise that we're both comfortable with friendly silence.

We're at her place, a few months after getting together, when I finally tell her I used to be a pilot, and what happened to me. She already knows I served, but I have never confessed about breaking down on duty, or being imprisoned and court-martialled.

I plough on through the whole story without looking at

her, thinking all the while how strange it is that I have never before related these events all the way through, fearing that as soon as I get to the end she will walk out on me. But when I finally fall silent and sheepishly meet her gaze, she kisses me on the cheek, pats my thigh and tells me I worry too much. It all happened a long time ago, and far away. Life moves on.

She's right of course, but not entirely. I've never been able to resolve whether to be ashamed of failing as a soldier, or of almost succeeding. I can never forget the screen image of that man staggering alone down a dimly lit street during the seconds after I'd launched the missile that would rip apart his body. Nor can I forget that I froze during my second kill order. Killing or freezing, I still don't know which was the crime.

If I had launched that missile and remained as a pilot, who would I have become? I could so easily have slipped into that other skin, lived another life entirely, as a man who would have been both the best and the worst of me, a man I both admire and abhor: a confident, successful, untroubled assassin.

Crystal and I have been together more than three years, and she is newly pregnant, on the day Victoria walks into the shop. She's looking for a hook to hang a child's mobile. She's pushing a buggy containing a dozing toddler, a boy in a sky blue coat decorated with propeller planes flying loop-the-loops across his chest.

She flushes red when she sees me. I'm not sure what my face does, but I avoid eye contact and sell her the hook and a matching Rawlplug.

She pays cash and as I return her change, she says my name, with an intonation that seems to be halfway between a statement and a question.

I stare across the counter at those brown eyes which haven't looked into mine since that awful moment outside her flat, years earlier.

'How are you?' she says.

'Fine,' I say. 'I'm assistant manager.' It's a stupid answer. Absolutely the wrong thing to say. I swallow, try to smile. 'And you? How's things?'

'Good.'

'It's been a long time.'

'Yeah.'

'You've got a kid?' I say, nodding towards the buggy.

'He's two.'

She places her hand on her belly, which I notice is bulging, and seems about to say something, then stops herself. I want to say that it's OK, that I can see the pregnancy, that I have a girl-friend, and she too is pregnant, but I don't know how to get the words out. I can't think how to say this without embarrass-ing myself, without looking as if I am trying to prove something.

There's an awkward silence.

'I'd better be off,' she says, reversing down an aisle to turn the buggy. 'It was nice to see you.' She's facing the door now, smiling tentatively at me. I don't want her to leave.

'So … you left the military,' I say.

She nods. 'A while back.'

'To have kids?'

'Before that.'

She looks down. Lets go of the buggy. For a moment, she's lost in thought.

'It wasn't long after you were ... after you ...'

She tails away. Thinks. Looks up at me.

'After you did that, it changed things,' she says. 'I carried on for a while, but ...'

'But what?'

'I should have stopped sooner. I should have left straight away. I should have visited you when they locked you up. I wish I'd supported you.'

I shrug. I can think of no response. The person who was ripped from the controls of his drone because he couldn't fire a missile is no longer me. That man, not much more than a boy, is a stranger I can barely remember.

'I'm sorry,' she says.

'I'm sorry too,' I reply. 'I've wanted to apologise to you for a long time.'

I see a flash of recognition in her eyes. She remembers.

The bell above the door punctures the silence. A man wearing paint-splattered overalls walks in, barking instructions into his mobile.

'Bye,' she says.

I nod and scurry around the counter to hold the door.

She leaves, pushing her sleeping child, carrying another inside her.

The City

The front door opens. Lex steps out. His chin lifts and he squints in the daylight. Relief surges through Zoe, and at the same instant a fleeting screech is audible above her, from the drone overhead.

The next thing she knows, she's on her back. Her ears are howling and she doesn't know where she is or how long has elapsed since she was on her feet.

A dull sensation of what might be pain throbs in her left arm, which is streaked with red. Her entire body is covered with fine grit. She stands, brushes at her face, blinks the dust out of her eyes.

She can still hear nothing, but as her vision returns she remembers where she's found herself, and understands what has happened.

In front of her, a woman is inaudibly screaming at the top

of her voice, her face crazed and savage. It is Lex's mother. She is pulling her girls to their feet, checking their bodies. Then she's yelling at Zoe, pushing the twins towards her. They're crying, refusing to let go of their mother. Zoe watches as she prises the children off her and gives them to Zoe, gesturing at her to hold on, to hold tight.

The girls launch themselves again at their mother, but Zoe holds them firmly by the wrist. Though she can see screams in their round, howling mouths, she hears nothing except a high shriek between her ears.

The mother turns and runs, arms flailing, each step a lurching topple. She runs towards the bomb site – where her house used to be – where her husband and son still are.

There is no Lex.

Bricks, wood, roof tiles, glass, a broken and twisted door, but no Lex.

There is no Lex.

Lex's mother is the only person moving towards the strike. A few others are on the street, all of them hurrying away. Everyone fears the double tap. Nobody will approach a recent drone hit unless they have nothing to lose or are mindless with grief.

The drilling wail in Zoe's ears begins to fade. She hears the rumble of distant bombs and the screams of Lex's mother as she reaches her destroyed home and climbs the rubble, tearing at it with her hands.

The twins pull away from Zoe, twisting free of her grip. They sprint for their mother.

Zoe watches, numb, as these two children scramble up the smoking mound that has buried their brother and father.

She falls to her knees. Her face drops into her hands. She can't watch; she can't speak; she can't move; and she can't cry.

Zoe has little idea what happens next. She knows there was no follow-up strike. The mother and twins survive, because she sees them a week later at the hasty funeral. Thousands are there, for the father not for Lex, and the atmosphere is wild with rage, but the proceedings are fast because everyone knows the next raid could come any minute.

Zoe does not approach the mother, but one of the girls glares at her during the burial with angry, accusing eyes as if she is somehow to blame for what happened.

And perhaps she is. If Lex had been home that night, instead of with Zoe, perhaps they all would have been else-where by morning.

Zoe has no memory of how she got back to her family that day, though she does remember standing in the shower that evening, watching grey water streaked with red swirl around her feet.

She's not sure how she got through the fifty-one days of the assault. She remembers seeing terror in the eyes of every-one around her during the raids, but not really caring, feeling nothing. Her mother must have stepped up, found some of her lost resources, because they didn't starve.

When the onslaught ends another new normal begins, with less of the city still standing; more grieving ghosts staggering through the streets; the power grid half-destroyed; and a blockade just as severe, preventing the city rebuilding or recovering.

The time comes when Zoe has to work again. She doesn't know if Craig, the man in charge of the corner where she used to sell, will give her back her slot, but she knows he always liked her, always gave her preferential treatment, so she thinks there's some hope.

When she sees Craig, a strange look flashes across his face, as if he is shocked by her appearance, as if just the sight of her has startled him. He keeps asking if she is OK, if she is ready to work again. She tells him she has no choice.

He gives her back a prime slot, but she cannot sell.

She stands there in the traffic, carrying the same wares, pulling her face into what she thinks is the same smile, but drivers don't open their windows for her, and if they do, she can think of nothing to say. She has no banter, no act. Sometimes a whole cycle goes by from green to red to green, and as the cars inch back into motion, she realises that she didn't move, never approached a single customer.

The other vendors ignore her. She can see them thinking she should be sent away; that if it was anyone else, she would be.

Craig takes her for a coffee. He's never done this before. He asks her several times how she is, how she's getting on, how she's managing. She gives short answers. This is the first time for weeks that she has talked to anyone outside her family, and she can hardly remember how.

He slides round to her side of the table.

He kisses her.

It isn't revolting. She doesn't really feel anything.

He talks and talks after that, a long and excited speech, about how he can look after her; about how he thinks of her every night; about how long he's had feelings for her; how he can find somewhere for her family to live. She vaguely hears him making promise after promise, nods, tries to smile.

She doesn't recall ever saying yes to Craig, nor does she ever say no. She never chooses him, but the rising tide of his intent picks her up and carries her into a new life. After years of fighting for survival, fighting to protect her mother and siblings, her strength is gone, her willpower is shot. She makes no effort to keep Craig at bay for the same reason a passenger on a sinking ship accepts a life jacket.

His flat is small and comfortable. It is above ground, which is a way of living Zoe barely remembers. There are windows, through which daylight comes, beyond which night falls.

Witnessing the slide of day into night and night into day at first mesmerises Zoe. It's the first thing since the missile attack that she truly sees, an initial nudge out of herself, back towards the world.

Zoe no longer works the corner. A tutor comes to the flat every morning to give her the schooling she missed and prepare her for exams she never sat. The tutor is a woman with short grey hair who never smiles and always wears the same necklace of dark blue beads. Zoe likes her, finds the work easy, is pleased that she is never required to chat. She enjoys filling a page, silently, with numbers or words. The puzzle of a foreign language unlocking itself fills her with fascination, makes her begin to dream of places she knows she will never visit.

After a long chain of excuses about the new place for her family, eventually a single room in Paddington is made available. At first, Zoe visits every other day, helps her mother unfurl, come alive again. Back above ground, her younger brothers snap to life instantly, noisily filling the space as if they never lived any other way.

Zoe doesn't find Craig repulsive, despite his size, his aura of canny menace, his heavy slabs of muscle. He looks after her, attempts to please her with occasional gifts and surprises, appears genuinely pleased when she remembers to show him affection in return. What he asks from Zoe she can give without excessive discomfort, because she has no hope of reawakening that part of her which died with Lex.

Craig wants her to look good and he wants her to seem classy. He loves to show her off, never telling anyone she was once one of his street sellers. If anyone does remember her from that life, they all apparently choose to forget.

Though the tutor was originally hired only for Zoe to catch up on her lost years of school, she refuses to stop studying after sitting her exams. Without this work, she feels as if she might sink into the ground and disappear.

Craig reluctantly allows her to take up a place at college. Although a degree serves little functional purpose in The Strip, where there are few meaningful jobs, fragments of two universities still run, always oversubscribed. In a place where material ambition has become pointless, since there is so little to buy, education is more passionately sought than ever. What else, after all, is there to seek?

Craig prefers Zoe to come home immediately after lectures, because he doesn't want her mixing with other students. He tracks her timetable carefully, checking that she is always where she ought to be, which Zoe finds irritating in principle, if not so much in practice. She dislikes the grinning boys who come bounding up to her, making small talk about this lecture or that essay, trying endlessly to get a response out of her, to garner a flicker of interest.

Girls seem to have little time for her, quickly sensing and resenting her aloofness. Zoe has no desire to join the excited gaggles that populate local coffee shops and campus libraries. She knows she'd have nothing to say, and would be unable to laugh at their jokes and anecdotes.

She isn't lonely. She doesn't really know what it would mean to be lonely.

The day after she completes her finals, Craig asks her to

come off the pill. Without even giving much thought to the incalculable magnitude of the decision, she tosses her strip of pills into the bin.

It is during her pregnancy that Zoe develops a first understanding of the concept of loneliness, because as this human being forms and grows inside her, she senses that something hard and cold in her heart seems to be softening, melting away. The life swelling inside her slowly, gently, eases aside a kernel of death that has lodged in her core. A new human takes shape within her. An everyday, universal miracle.

During these months of being two people – two hearts, four kidneys, eight limbs – Zoe begins to nap in the afternoons, a pillow supporting her swollen belly. A strange recurring dream often descends on her during these naps, in which this foetus is enveloping her, feeding her, pumping bursts of red, vivid life into veins that have calcified and blackened.

When this baby, crumpled and puce, fights its way out of her, howling himself into the world, she knows that she too is newborn. She loves this boy instantly, at sight. She has been, she knows, part dead since the day Lex died. Now she feels the deadness may have loosened its grip, might begin to fall away.

She still has little interest in friends, or perhaps just no time for them, with every hour of the day now ruled by this tiny creature. Her dual body may have divided, but her son at first seems no less dependent than when he was inside her. They are two separate bodies now, but for the first months still seem like one person. She eats to feed him. He gorges himself on her body, greedily, passionately, pumping the air with minuscule angry fists when hunger descends.

Even when she can barely stand from exhaustion, the caramel scent of his neck is bliss. His first smile is the greatest work of art she has ever seen.

Zoe never tells Craig, or anyone else, about Lex. She knows Craig suspects she has been grieving for more than just her father, but she never mentions the boy she loved, who died in front of her eyes.

Even though the name would mean nothing to Craig, she never considers calling the baby Lex. The idea doesn't occur to her. But when she falls pregnant again, she knows immediately this is the name she will use. The first child brought her back to the world; in some way she hopes this second child can give Lex another life.

In the end, the baby is named Alexa. She is born by emergency caesarean, a sudden panic in the middle of the night, umbilical cord around the neck, but survives. She seems the most fragile of babies, with blonde, downy hair so light it flutters under the faintest breath. Her eyelashes are translucent. She has a birthmark the shape of a strawberry on the back of her left hand, which she stares at in amazement every day for the first weeks of her life.

She feeds; she crawls; she walks; she grows; her hair darkens; the birthmark fades; she goes to school; and a few days after her sixteenth birthday, she walks into the kitchen and Zoe, for an instant, wonders if two decades have evaporated, if that girl is not her daughter, but herself.

Zoe is in her late thirties now, and she rarely thinks of Lex, but in this instant when she mistakes her daughter for herself, a nanosecond's electrical charge lights up her heart, as she half thinks for less time than it is even possible to hold a thought that she might be on her way to see a boy she loves, who is also still sixteen.

'Why are you looking at me like that?' says Alexa. 'What's wrong?'

'Nothing,' replies Zoe, returning to the stove.

This year, when Alexa turns sixteen, is momentous for another reason. It's the year in all the history books. You will probably know the date.

Zoe never listens to the news. In a city where every radio seems to be constantly on, where everyone has an opinion about negotiations, non-negotiations, military manoeuvres, resistance, the date of the next assault, Zoe's is a home where the news is banned. She doesn't want to hear a single thing about the men whose posturings dictate the fate of The Strip, or about the peace process that never produces any peace. But that year, even she knows something is up. After a stalemate so long that nobody thought it would ever end, negotiations have finally taken place. Concessions are being agreed. Yet Zoe still refuses to allow a radio in the house, and the TV is switched off as soon as the bombastic chords of current affairs title music begin.

The fourteenth of June is the day everyone remembers. Zoe is at home when, at ten o'clock, she hears the bells. Every church bell in the city is ringing.

She has never heard this before, has no idea what it might mean.

She goes to the window. The street, rarely busy with pedestrians, contains a stream of people all walking in the same direction, heading south.

Zoe steps out. She asks a passer-by, a young man with a neat beard, what is happening. He looks at her like she is mad. 'Haven't you heard? They've opened the gates in Brixton. People are just walking out. The checkpoint's open!'

The man's face is alight with excitement. He dances away, spotting a friend who he greets with a bear hug. Zoe notices that all around her, people are hugging. Walking or hugging.

She follows the flow of people. The crowd swells as they approach the centre of town. She tries to call her children and Craig, but there's no signal on her phone. The network is overloaded. Everyone is trying to phone. She'd like to be with them, doesn't want to experience this without her family, but to head back against the flow of the crowd would now be impossible.

Every road is jammed with stationary cars which are hooting in celebration. Some people have abandoned grid-locked vehicles and continued southwards on foot. Zoe crosses Waterloo Bridge, which is so crammed she can't get to the edge or see the water. Beyond that, all roads are a flood of humanity, everyone heading in the same direction. Strangers hug her. Clusters of people burst into song. Above, revellers hang out of windows, cheering, clapping, waving flags. Upbeat music wafts into the street from all directions. Bubbles of dance grow and burst around her as the procession travels slowly south.

A young man with high, handsome cheekbones, his face alight with joy, takes her by one hand and tries to dance with her. She does a small jig, smiles apologetically and breaks loose.

She must have been walking for hours by the time she reaches Brixton, but she feels only a faint ache in her feet, no tiredness. She could walk all day to get to those gates.

At one particular corner, not far from the tunnels, she stops. The crowd flows around her, heading onwards, but Zoe stands motionless.

This is the street where she came with Lex.

She takes a few strides off the main road, stepping out of the tide of bodies, down this street she hasn't visited for twenty years.

It still looks the same.

Nothing has been repaired or rebuilt.

The same narrow path snakes through the rubble, perhaps wider now, after two decades of use.

She has never before considered coming here. Even knowing she was walking towards Brixton the thought had not occurred to her, but now, pulled by a force she cannot resist, her feet are leading her to a place she has never been able to forget, dropping her down a chasm of memory.

The house is still there, still recognisable, still standing, with the same half-destroyed living room exposed to the street. Zoe turns from the path and clambers over the mound of loose brick.

The door, barnacled with blistered grey paint, is ajar. She pushes it but the hinges have rusted solid. Flecks of paint come away on her hand. A shoulder barge creaks the door a little wider, enough to squeeze herself in.

An acrid, musty smell rises into her nostrils. The floorboards have gone, exposing partially removed pipes and wires. A few pictures still hang on the walls, one a photo of three children in swimming costumes, on the beach, displaying a sand-sculpted mermaid.

Zoe balances on a joist and looks up at the staircase, which has come loose at one side. The treads are still connected together but loll away from the wall, looking too fragile to bear her weight.

She places her foot on the first step, as tight to the skirting as possible, and stands. There is a creak, but no collapse. She moves up one more step, holding tight to a rusty banister that is screwed into the brickwork.

The seventh tread gives way under her but she keeps her balance, steps over it, uses the eighth, and inches her way on to the landing.

There are no panes on any of the bedroom windows. A buddleia has snaked in through the bay, its sickly grey-green leaves pressing against the ceiling. Every surface is dark with grime, yet for Zoe it is as if nothing has changed. The white sheet, no longer white, which Lex carried here in his backpack, is still on that same bed, in the same place, as if it has been waiting, all these years, for Zoe's return. Near the centre, visible through a thick coating of dust, is a single spot of blood.

Her pulse thunders. Her brain whirls. That day with Lex, on this bed, explodes like a firework in her mind, returning with absolute clarity: the feel of his hands on her bare skin; the scent of his neck; the weight of him above her; the sensation of her body opening like a flower; the certainty that the future was a landscape into which they would walk together, hand in hand. She realises she can barely stand.

That day, after making love, they heard the first bombs of a new assault. Today, through windows that may have been shattered by those very bombs, Zoe hears the sound of a distant crowd, singing.

By the following night, he was dead. Zoe sent him back to his home, to die. She remembers her words exactly. They had been halfway down the street, safe, when she said, *You didn't say goodbye.*

This is what turned Lex back. It was her fault. If she hadn't spoken, he would have lived.

If she'd said nothing …

If they had kept walking …

If …

If …

For twenty years, Zoe has had two pulses. Her heartbeat and this, constant, half heard, pumping every second somewhere in her skull.

If …

If …

If …

Zoe opens her mouth. She cries; she wails; she howls.

This is the first and only time she ever cries for Lex.

When she has finished, she wipes her face, stands, and walks from the house, down the destroyed street, into the flow of bodies heading south, towards the open gates.

Acknowledgements

Heartfelt thanks to Atef Abu Saif, whose searing and unforgettable book about the 2014 Gaza War, *The Drone Eats with Me: Diaries from a City Under Fire*, was in part the inspiration for this novel.

My thanks to the authors of the following books: Andrew Cockburn, *Kill Chain: Drones and the Rise of High-Tech Assassins*; Medea Benjamin, *Drone Warfare: Killing by Remote Control* and Eyal Weizman for the chapter 'Targeted Assassinations: The Airborne Occupation' in *Hollow Land*, which gives a revelatory account of the capabilities of a modern air force.

Thanks also to: Felicity Rubinstein, Rebecca McNally, Hannah Sandford, Lizz Skelly, Richard Sved and Adam, John and Susan Sutcliffe. And above all, as always, thank you, Maggie O'Farrell.

About the Author

William Sutcliffe was born in London in 1971. He is the author of the international bestseller *Are You Experienced?*, *The Love Hexagon*, *New Boy*, *Bad Influence* and *Whatever Makes You Happy*.

His first YA novel, *The Wall*, was shortlisted for the CILIP Carnegie Medal in 2014, and his next YA novel, *Concentr8*, was shortlisted for the YA Book Prize in 2016.

His work has been translated into more than twenty languages. He lives in Edinburgh.

@Will_Sutcliffe8

Everyone on Joshua's side of the Wall
knows one thing: the Wall keeps you safe.
You must not cross to the other side.
Joshua kicks his football into a building site and
discovers a secret tunnel. It leads through pitch
darkness under the Wall and into forbidden territory,
where a boy like him shouldn't stray. When Joshua
emerges into the light of the other side, his world
is turned upside down – with kindness, terror and
violence, and a debt he can never repay.
One thirteen-year-old cannot tear
down a wall. But why should
he have to choose a side?

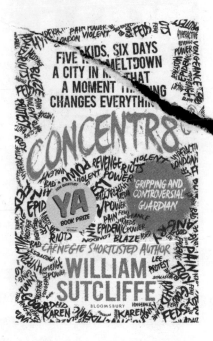

FIVE KIDS, SIX DAYS
A CITY IN MELTDOWN
A MOMENT THAT
CHANGES EVERYTHING

CONCENTR8

'GRIPPING AND
CONTROVERSIAL'
GUARDIAN

YA
BOOK PRIZE

CARNEGIE SHORTLISTED AUTHOR

WILLIAM
SUTCLIFFE

Bloomsbury

Troy, Femi, Karen, Lee and Blaze were looking
for trouble, but not this kind of trouble.
They didn't expect to get famous.
Now the world is watching to see what they will do next.
This is the story of what happens when angry,
overlooked teenagers find themselves face to face
with the powers that be. This is what happens when
you take a city off its meds.

'A clever, compulsive read that shifted my world'
Patrice Lawrence

'A brilliantly written novel – thrilling, frightening and all
too real and relevant. I urge you to read it'
Sarah Crossan

'A powerful, fast-moving dystopian novel'
Metro

'Shockingly suspenseful'
New Statesman

'Fast moving and brave, with lots and lots of heart'
Ahdaf Soueif

'A chillingly authentic account of a near-future London'
Irish Times

'A terrifying glimpse of a potential future'
Scotsman

'Sutcliffe maps beautifully and movingly Lex's
experience of falling in love'
Guardian

'A hard-hitting dystopian thriller'
Daily Mail

CHAPTER TWENTY-FOUR

NEVER EVER . . .

Within days I began to feel better about the reviews. I was experiencing what the phrase 'tomorrow's chip paper' refers to. No sooner had the reviews been printed, the journalists were digging their pens, opinions and knives into the next poor sod. As cruel as it may sound, I was relieved it wasn't me!

Life slowly went back to normal. I began to eat properly again, I didn't have so many sleepless nights and I began to look forward to doing some more styling work.

Just after the series had finished airing, Carol received a call from EMI music. The head of A & R told Carol that the girl group All Saints had reformed and they were interested in hiring me as their stylist. The girls had seen *Naked* and they wanted to meet me. WOW! I couldn't believe the programme had worked as a PR drive and that even celebrities had tuned in to watch the show. What a head-fuck! Did this mean that perhaps even the Queen might have settled down with a microwave dinner on Tuesday nights and watched my show? Wicked!

Channel 4 hadn't decided whether they were going to re-commission the show so the All Saints job came at just the right time. The band had signed a one single and one album deal and had a ruthless press schedule ahead of them. They needed a stylist who could re-brand them and give

241

them a new look for the video, press shots, interviews and CD covers. What a touch!

* * *

I was nervous as I entered the recording studio in Primrose Hill for my meeting with the girls. All Saints had been a huge band in the nineties and had made famous their casual look of combats and vest tops—I had certainly emulated their look on more than one occasion.

I had spent a few days researching and preparing what I envisioned for their new style. I knew I had to keep them looking 'poppy', but they had also grown up and had children. There was no way they could be slung back into combats and ponytails. They needed a new, sexier look that was casual enough for a back reference but was more of the moment.

I decided I would give the girls a 'sexy skater' image; that way, I could keep the casual image they were famous for. I would replace the combats and sneakers with skinny jeans and high heels but keep the sweatshirts, hoodies and urban sport-lux jackets. It would be a perfect mix of Gwen Stefani meets Avril Lavigne.

As I stood in the studio reception, a flash of confidence soared through me. Why was I so worried? They'd called me! If they didn't like what I had in mind for their new style, then I would simply turn round and go after the next job.

I realised then that *How To Look Good Naked* had given me a back-up plan; I had a second string to my bow, now, and I was no longer entirely reliant on my styling career for money or success because there was the possibility of a new career as a TV presenter. But just in case that didn't happen, I did still have my stylist work.

Feeling strong, powerful and confident, I was shown into the studio where the girls were laying down a track. As the door opened to a darkened studio, I got my first glimpse of the girls in the flesh. Instantly, my new-found confidence drained out of my body. Fucking hell, I thought. It's All Saints!

Nicole and Nat were sitting behind the mixing desk, Mel was perched at their side and Shaznay was standing behind them. The girls all looked towards me and in perfect harmony they said, 'Hi, Gok!' It was like I had gate crashed the set of *Charlie's Angels*.

'Hi,' I replied shyly as I walked through the doorway. I was so transfixed by the girls, I hadn't noticed there was a small step leading into the studio. I tripped down the step, lost my balance, fell through the door, stumbled forward two or three paces, throwing both arms into the air, and finally landed face down on the mixing desk.

It was truly the most humiliating moment of my life.

The girls screamed with a mixture of excitement and embarrassment and then fell about the studio in fits of laughter, clapping their hands together gleefully. I couldn't believe it. Sore faced and panicked, I tried quickly to regain my composure, pulling myself up from the desk but knocked backwards into a swivel chair, which threw off my balance once again. I must have looked like a six-foot, red-faced Chinese Frank Spencer!

After finding my feet, I apologised for my

clumsiness. The girls were still laughing as they told me it was fine and asked if I was okay.

I told them I was, but I was lying. My pride had been seriously wounded in the fall and I wanted to run from the studio, find a quiet corner, curl up and die. Never, ever have I felt so ridiculous. (Recently Mel told me that they knew they were going to hire me the moment I fell over. 'It proved you were one of us,' she said.)

Once I'd re-gained my equilibrium, I raced through my ideas for their new style. The girls seemed to like the looks I'd come up with but I hardly noticed. I couldn't wait to get out of the studio.

A few hours after I'd managed to escape, Carol received a call from the girls' management telling her All Saints were very happy with me and I was booked. It looked as though the girls had fallen for me as hard as I had in front of them.

*   *   *

One of the first jobs we did together was the girl's come-back video, 'Rock Steady'. I had several meetings with the director, label, management and, of course, the girls. The story of the video was a 1920s, Bonnie-and-Clyde-style bank robbery with the girls pulling off a heist. Thankfully, I came up with an idea they all loved. I designed some vintage-looking costumes inspired from the thirties, forties and fifties and had them made in black-and-white PVC. It was rather like a bondage tribute to *Breakfast at Tiffany's*! The concept worked and the video looked amazing, very glam and stylish. The girls loved their sexy new image.

After the single was released, we went on a press tour around Europe. The girls had been booked on to all the breakfast, chat and music shows. They needed a different outfit for every appearance and I was the person responsible for making sure they always looked perfect, never duplicated a look and, more importantly, felt great in their clothes.

I decided it was better to take the girls shopping with me to fit them for their press tour outfits, as that way the girls could give me input into what they wanted to wear. I figured it would be easier to take the girls two at a time, so Mel and Nic went first. Naturally, all of the shops wanted the girls to be dressed in their clothes, so we were treated to five-star service with a team of personal shoppers on hand, and a couple of bottles of champagne on ice. Now that's what I call shopping!

In one shop, we were going through the rails of clothes and out of nowhere a gaggle of screaming and giggling teenagers came running up to us. Assuming the teenagers wanted autographs and pictures with the girls, I stood to one side but to my amazement, and Mel and Nic's shock, the group of teenagers rushed towards me and asked me for MY autograph! The look on Mel and Nic's faces was priceless. I blushed, gave the kids my signature and saw them on their way, then turned to Mel and Nic, grinned and said, 'Come on, girls, we've got eight outfits to find today, keep looking!'

With that, we all burst out laughing.

*   *   *

I loved working with the girls. We had our differences and sometimes it would result in fashion blows, but on the whole, it was great fun. I loved the dynamics of the band: Shaznay was the quietest of the girls but always in control; Mel and Nicole had re-kindled their childlike friendship and were always up to mischief; while Nat remained focused and determined.

All Saints were in demand and everyone wanted to interview them. The press were on the hunt for a scoop and sniffed about for gossip on why the band had originally split in the nineties, but the girls had been brilliantly trained to bat away any intrusive questions. I watched and learned a lot about how to handle the press when they were in full bloodhound mode.

The first single 'Rock Steady' did very well and peaked at a very healthy number 3 in the UK charts. The girls were overjoyed but they knew they had a long way to go before they had the same level of success as they'd had before. I was proud to be a part of their comeback.

*   *   *

Meanwhile, Channel 4 and Maverick were also working hard re-developing *How To Look Good Naked*. Although I didn't yet know it, Sue Murphy had re-commissioned the series and had decided to make it an hour-long show.

When Carol called to tell me they wanted me to film the second series, I couldn't believe it. I had slipped easily back into the familiar world of styling where I'd felt safe and secure, and I'd assumed *How To Look Good Naked* had been canned after one series. I wasn't aware the show had done surprisingly well, clocking up viewing figures of over three million households per episode. *Naked* was a huge success and was set to return in the spring of 2007!

It was brilliant news and I was hugely excited. I'd felt sure we'd done some amazing, groundbreaking telly that was able to touch hearts and change minds, and Channel 4 obviously thought so, too.

Fuck, though . . . What about All Saints?

I spent days panicking about how I was going to tell the girls I was leaving. I was worried they would think me a traitor and a user. Would they think I had just taken the contract with them while I was waiting for something better to come along?

Although the band had employed me as a freelancer and I had the option to leave whenever I wanted to, I didn't want to let the girls down. For a brief moment I contemplated filming the new series as well as styling the band, but I knew it would be too much. I even contemplated not filming the show and staying with the girls, but there was no way I could turn down this opportunity. I had had a fabulous time working with All Saints but deep down, I knew that I was no longer happy simply being a stylist. I'd had a taste of the limelight I'd always yearned for and in the five months I'd spent with the band, I'd missed performing for the camera. Although there were aspects of presenting I didn't like—the media attention, the really long hours—I was hooked.

*   *   *

My greatest fear was that TV work would cause an onset of my anorexia; it had certainly affected me badly during the first series. But I'd had a few months out now to think it over and to understand why the disease had come back. It was because I'd felt out of control. Added to this, the show had made me re-visit my body hatred vicariously through the contributors; I was made to question what *I* thought when *I* looked in the mirror. I knew if I was ever going to make peace with my anorexia then I needed to *not* run away from what scared me.

*   *   *

All Saints took my departure really well—so well, I could have been slightly insulted if they weren't so lovely. In the lead-up to Christmas 2006, I told them I was leaving and with lots of kisses and promises to keep in touch, we said our goodbyes.

We began filming *How To Look Good Naked*, series two, in January 2007. I had decided I was going to make this series bigger and better. There was no way I was going to let the press beat me down: I was stronger. I knew I'd finally found the career I wanted to pursue and I was prepared to give it everything I had.

I wanted to learn everything there was to know about making a TV show. I wanted a say in the editorial decisions and I wanted the country to know that this show was about to change the shape of British fashion. The show's message was to become my personal vendetta against all those bastards who'd told me I was not good enough. I was going to prove to them I had been a good person when I was fat and I was the same good person now that I was thin. If anyone ever told me again I was not good enough, then I was prepared to fight them, bare knuckled, alongside my new naked army.

*   *   *

I was duly empowered and firing on all cylinders, but I began to notice that filming series two was different from series one, mainly because the women that had been cast on the show had watched the first series and knew what to expect.

The format of the show is built on surprises and without shock tactics we would never be able to get big genuine reactions from the ladies. To combat this, the producers decided they wanted to introduce a new finale: a catwalk for the ladies in nothing but their underwear.

I was worried this was too much for the girls. What if they said no? What if we got complaints from the viewers saying we'd pushed it too far? What if the press thought it was gratuitous and blamed me for it? Fuck!

I raised my concerns with the producers but they reassured me the ladies would be protected and we would never allow them to come to any harm, and I trusted what they told me because I'd seen how they'd looked after the ladies in the first series. Their naked photo shoots were carefully managed so that the women felt comfortable throughout and nothing was shown that would have embarrassed or offended anyone. I knew that the naked catwalks would be handled in the same way. The show's fashion producer, Jane Galpin, was hugely responsible for making sure the girls were cared for without compromise. Jane quickly became the show's conscience.

Once filming was underway, I fell in love with the show again. I slept well at night knowing *Naked* was an important TV show with a vital message of the zeitgeist, and I disagreed with the journalists who thought it was rude and inappropriate. I knew we were making a difference and challenging the fact that the fashion industry had, for a long time, been both elitist and promoted an unhealthy ideal of the female shape. For far too long women had been told they had to undergo masses of cosmetic surgery or they wouldn't be beautiful. What a load of old shit! Series one had already proved that with reassurance, guidance, some decent underwear and some well-chosen clothes, a woman could feel a hundred times better about herself. You didn't have to be a supermodel (i.e. impossibly thin and weird-looking in real life), or a beautiful actress (carefully shot in a professionally lit studio with the help of a make-up artist, hairdresser, stylist and our friend-the-airbrush), or a teenage beachbabe, to be a gorgeous woman proud of her natural assets.

Series one had been our pilot series and it had proved a hit; the second series was now going to be an hour-long show and Channel 4 was going to invest a lot more money in what would be a big, prime-time programme.

When we were making the first series, I'd sometimes been alarmed at the amount of emotion the ladies were revealing. Once or twice, I'd panicked and felt we were going beyond what a television show about getting some nice new clothes and a burst of confidence should attempt. But once the shows had been edited together and we'd seen them, it was clear that *Naked* was about much more than some new dresses. At its heart was the emotional journey the women were going on and the results of this journey for the ladies proved it was all worthwhile.

In series two, therefore, we decided to go deeper, really getting to know our ladies, their lives and their body hang-ups. Not all of our girls were curvy, either. There were plenty of smaller-figured women out there covering up because they were convinced they were hideous. The show was creating a community, helping people to understand that they were not alone when they hated their bodies and felt dowdy and worthless.

There were some other format changes, too. Now the women came with me when I displayed their underwear shot at the start of the programme—resulting in some quick sprints for me as they ran away from it! We tackled issues like how to deal with body hair, tans and other treatments, and what lingerie suited which body shape. We had huge consumer tests, with a hundred ladies trying out the promises of different lotions and potions. We looked inside the girls' underwear drawers and I threw ancient, greying pairs of pants out of windows or on to burning braziers, urging them to find knickers that fit and flattered.

And, of course, we had our catwalk. It came as a shock to the ladies when I broke the news to them that I wanted them to model in front of thousands, ending up in only their underwear. Everyone could read the fear and apprehension on their faces, but they all gathered together their courage and did it, and I was amazingly proud of my brave girls. That moment—as my lady strode down the catwalk to cheers and applause (and maybe some tears) from her proud family and friends.

When the series aired, the viewers found it as moving and happy as I did. In fact, series two was to be a huge success and my life would turn yet another corner.

CHAPTER TWENTY-FIVE

THE BIG TIME

The next six months were insane! The second series of *How To Look Good Naked* became one of the most talked-about TV shows in the country: we must have garnered more column inches than a Katie Price wedding! The newspapers and magazines loved it, the online bloggers loved it; even some of the critics who had doubted the first series were now backpedalling and praising the programme.

Carol's telephone was ringing off the hook. Offers seemed to come flooding in from every direction. Clients wanted me to open shopping centres, speak at charity shows, attend premieres and endorse washing machines, hair products, glasses, clothes and underwear. Carol and I would joke together that there wasn't a part of my body that couldn't sell a product. I trusted her judgement in the things that we chose to do: she advised me on what I should accept and what wasn't right for me. We remained selective about the clients we chose to work with, as we didn't want to sell out to the industry and I wanted to retain my integrity. I became a spokesman for SpecSavers, who sponsored the show, and wrote a book to tie in with the programme, also called *How To Look Good Naked*.

It wasn't just the commercial market that wanted to speak to us. Paul O'Grady wanted me on his sofa, Gordon Ramsay wanted me in his kitchen and even the prime minister wanted me in his home. I couldn't believe it. The fat, bullied kid from Leicester was now one of the most wanted boys in the country—how fabulous!

Along with all the excitement of success and the buzz of feeling wanted, I realised that my fame had hit a level no one could have expected. I would get stopped anywhere and everywhere I went and be asked for my autograph, a photo and, in many cases, advice. 'What dress shape am I?' women would ask. 'I'm going to a party on Saturday, what do you think I should wear?'

It felt like the country had taken ownership of the show. *How To Look Good Naked* was about real people *for* real people, so everyone felt they had a piece of it. In many ways I agreed with them—it *was* their show! We couldn't do it without our wonderful ladies, their friends and families and the members of the public whose opinions we canvassed or who attended the catwalk shows.

I think that my accessibility came from the fact that I didn't put on a performance that turned me into a different person—I was simply myself. In theory this was a good idea, but in reality it had its drawbacks. For one thing, everyone who had seen the show felt as if they knew me. I loved meeting fans and talking to them. I didn't say no to autographs and pictures as a rule, because I understood that I had a responsibility to the people who were my viewers—without them, I wouldn't have my career—so I always tried to be friendly and approachable, and I often indulged in a bit of chitchat. People were generally lovely to me—friendly and complimentary about the show and how much they loved it.

The viewers had quickly picked up on my language. I'd always talked on the show as I would in real life. I called breasts 'bangers' and told my ladies we were going to use 'knicker know-how'. This became the public's way of communicating with me. I was standing on Oxford Street one day when a taxi drove past me with two women hanging out of the window, both with their tops pulled up showing their bras, screaming, 'Grab my BANGERS, Auntie Gok!' I laughed for about a week!

*   *   *

But fame had started to change the dynamics of my friendships. It was now impossible to go on a night out with mates and not be approached all evening for autographs and pictures. Rightly, my friends were frustrated with the constant attention I was getting. They weren't jealous of the fame, they simply didn't want to share the time we had together with the rest of the country.

While I tried to be polite and do what I could for people who wanted autographs and photos, sometimes it just wasn't possible because I had a life to live as well. One night, E'lain and I had gone out for a drink and ended up having an argument as we stood on Shaftesbury Avenue. It was pretty intense and we were trying to work things out, both of us in tears, when a couple stopped and asked if they could have their picture taken with me. They could see we were both upset, but it didn't stop them. For the first time I said no, saying I was sorry but it was a really bad time. The man called me a wanker and as they walked off, the woman said, 'I knew he wasn't like he is on TV, what a fucking fake!'

I couldn't believe it and was left even more upset than I had been in the first place. I realised that fame had now eaten its way into my personal life. After this episode, I promised myself I would do as much as humanly possible to protect my family and friends from this new world of mine.

*   *   *

There were other changes, too. For the first time in my life, I began to have some proper money. When I'd first started on *How To Look Good Naked* I was earning less than I had been as a stylist, but this was now improving. My sponsorships, my books (I'd signed up to do two more style books) and the success of the show were starting to bring in some good money, and I was looking at other business possibilities, such as my own underwear line. It was a strange feeling after being skint for most of my life, but my approach to it all was not to go out and splurge.

My working-class caution was too ingrained for that and I continued living frugally. I bought a few nice things, and allowed myself a good car and some designer clothes—but my rule was that everything had to be paid for upfront. No credit. I knew that TV presenters could have a short shelf life, and I was too frightened that it all might come to an end and leave me with nothing to start wasting my hard-earned money. I carried on renting flats and saved up my cash because I wasn't going to buy a property until I could afford it outright.

With series two, viewing figures had grown and Channel 4 knew they had a winner on their hands. We were soon back in production for series three, now with even more episodes per series. Maverick had also worked hard on developing my relationship with them. Alex Fraser, Maverick's creative director, became my confidante when I was unsure about an editorial decision. She always convinced me the producers were right, but just the fact she listened to me made me feel she had my interests at heart.

The press continued to support us, and *Naked* was still being picked up by other countries. Australia, New Zealand, Canada and Poland—to name but a few—had bought the show, and our message of 'Size hero, not size zero' was being preached round the globe and in many different languages. It was a strange feeling to think that people in countries I had never visited knew who I was!

I developed various strategies so that I could lead as normal a life as possible. I began to customise my routines. Shopping trips into central London were strictly limited to the 9 till 10 a.m. slot when the stores would be virtually deserted. When I needed clothes, I would run into Topshop and grab a whole load of stuff and buy it quickly so that no one had time to recognise me. I also styled up a disguise of tracksuit, cap and sunglasses to assist in making my visits to Sainsbury's less interrupted. No one needs an audience when deciding which toilet roll to buy.

But as *How To Look Good Naked* became a prime-time phenomenon, I had to come to terms with the fact that I'd entered the next phase of celebrity. It wasn't simply a matter of being hassled—it was now more serious than that.

One example of this was when a friend of mine had managed to get a couple of tickets for the *Spice Girls'* comeback tour at the O2. He asked me if I wanted to go with him and, of course, I agreed. I didn't consider where we might be sitting; I was too excited to be seeing the girls' costumes.

When we arrived at the O2, I realised I might have made a mistake. Getting into the building was like trying to get through a football match riot. Mothers and daughters rushed me for autographs and pictures, and the more people that crowded us, the more attention I received.

Once we were finally in the building, drinks bought and popcorn stashed, we went to find our seats. The tickets were amazing! We had a fabulous view of the stage, right in the centre of the main circle. As we walked towards our seats, the most enormous cheering erupted round us. I thought the girls had arrived on stage early, although that was strange since the house lights had not gone down. I very quickly realised that it wasn't the Spice Girls the entire arena was cheering for, it was ME!

Within moments, a swarm of people had rushed towards us again; it was incredible! Camera flashes popped in every direction, a chanting of 'Gok, Gok, Gok . . .' filled my ears and hundreds of Spice Girl programmes were being thrust towards me for my signature. Luckily, the security guards had clocked this situation and pulled me and my friend from the crowds. We were placed in a private box to stop any danger to Health and

Safety in the arena. We were gutted, however, as the private box had the worst view of the stage! If I didn't know it before, I certainly knew it now—*Naked* mania had arrived.

Zigazig ah!

*   *   *

A few more episodes like this made me realise that my safety—and my friends'—could be at risk if I didn't take more precautions. I was mobbed at airports, and going into clubs and restaurants became a nightmare. One night in Liverpool, I went out to a club with some of the team and we ended up having to leap over the bar and run out the back to prevent ourselves from being squashed. After that, I knew I would have to be more sensible.

Nights out with mates were now organised like military events, with VIP areas booked and doormen warned of our arrival. Hotels were given a pseudonym to stop the staff from telling their friends about my stay (this was after a receptionist told her best mate, who then told the whole town that I was staying in the hotel. After checking in, I went to my room and was greeted by four girls, who had camped outside my door waiting for a photographs and signatures!).

Filming the show also had to be carefully organised. No longer could we slip discreetly into a store and not be noticed beyond the odd curious glance. Security guards were now booked to help usher the hundreds of fans who wanted to watch us film—and it's hard to concentrate with camera flashes and kids screaming your name.

There were other aspects of fame I hadn't

expected—the downsides that went beyond simply losing my privacy. Meeting guys was no longer a simple 'Fancy a drink?' or 'Do you come here often?' Potential dates needed to be vetted with expert precision to ensure honesty and the right intentions. I had spent my life not really attracting too much male attention, and all of a sudden I was inundated with offers from men who wanted to 'get to know me better'—only to discover their tender would be laced with lies about their profession, martial status and age. On the other hand, I was also committed to making sure that past, current or potential boyfriends would not be subjected to public scrutiny, even if it had become a part of my daily schedule.

Friends would email me and ask if I knew that there were t-shirts for sale with my picture on them, or that I was featured on birthday cards and unofficial calendars. I would hear myself talked about on the radio or my name would crop up in conversation between characters in *Coronation Street*, *Hollyoaks* and *EastEnders*, or in comedy shows. I had entered the national consciousness to the point where my name became synonymous with a kind of caring campness. I discovered that someone was working as me at a lookalike agency, going along to birthday parties and hen nights and whatever, being paid to pretend to be me. I have to say, that freaked me out.

*　　　*　　　*

My family was inevitably caught up in the ripple effects of my fame. While I'd been following my path through make-up to styling and then on to television, my family had been pursuing their own lives.

After university, Oilen had fulfilled her academic promise and had become a solicitor specialising in childcare cases, a world far removed from mine. Of course, Oilen has to keep the details of her work confidential, but I know how much good she is doing saving families and young children from danger, and I feel humbled and honoured to call her my sister.

It took Kwok-Lyn a little while longer to discover what he wanted, but when he did, it was amazing. He had managed to keep his head above water, getting through college and then working in the restaurant, and not falling into crime or loafing round town like so many other kids with similar backgrounds to us. Instead, in a weird mirroring of my father's life, he left Leicester for a year, going to Portsmouth to work, and returning with his gorgeous wife, Lisa. When he got back, he was reinvented and ready to take on the role of eldest son.

It wasn't easy for Lisa to find her place in our fold. It took her years of patience and determination to break the watertight seal surrounding our family, but I'm happy that she did. Lisa has shown us that we can, as a family, exist around other people. She has undoubtedly added a new layer to our lives.

As Kwok-Lyn and Lisa began to raise their two gorgeous daughters, Maya-Lily and Lola-Rose, Kwok-Lyn found the path he'd been searching for and became a martial arts instructor and specialist. He created his own business and discovered he had a masterful business brain. He wrote for combat

261

magazines, taught in America and started up one of the country's biggest martial arts expos at the NEC, which he runs every year. He is incredibly well respected in his field, but by none more than me.

Mum and Dad had finally closed The Gong and had moved out of Chinese food altogether. Instead they took on a fish and chip shop called the Whetstone Fish Bar and they carried on working as hard as they ever did, running their business six days a week.

When I started to appear on the television, they were very excited for me and watched every minute of it . . . twice! Mum and Dad decorated the chip shop with pictures of me, and cuttings from magazines and papers about the show. I was now able to afford to treat them to some holidays, which I loved doing.

But my fame had its downside for the family, too. Oilen found that she was suddenly known as 'the sister of' instead of as a person in her own right, which was rightly frustrating for her. My parents were constantly asked about me by customers, and their friends and friends of friends were forever requesting books, autographs and merchandise. They hated letting anyone down, so when I went home, I would find a great pile of books and pictures by my bed ready for signing.

Nor could I enjoy time alone with my family any more. On the rare occasion when I made it home to Leicester, most of our socialising and catching up was done in my uncle's restaurant eating dim sum, just as we always had done. But long-gone were the days when we could overorder, scoff our faces and be left alone together. We were now mobbed by 'old friends' of the family or distant relatives, who wanted autographs or a quick picture.

My family was very gracious and would always stand aside for me to have my picture taken but secretly I resented it. I didn't mind having photos taken, doing autographs or chatting at any time other than when I was with my family. My life had become so busy that the small amount of time I had with them had become as precious as diamonds to me. I felt obliged to sign the bits of serviettes or pose for the photos and very seldom would I say no, but I felt guilty when I did.

I wanted to go home precisely so that I could get away from the madness of fame and my TV life. I didn't want to be working there, too, so I made a rule that I wouldn't do any signing at home. But my mum would always come sneaking in last thing with a book and a pen, begging for just one signature so she didn't have to disappoint someone, which I understood but couldn't help finding frustrating. Like I said, fame is a head-fuck.

It was my business-brained brother who coped best. He realised that he couldn't stop all this from happening, so reckoned he might as well turn it to his advantage. He's worked me hard, pimping me out to help his business and using my fame as much as he can. Brilliant! Go, Kwok-Lyn. I don't mind—in a small way, it feels like repayment for the meals he and Lisa fed me when I was ill. Fame is an ongoing situation that we've learned to cope with as best we can. I'm still a son and brother before I'm anything else, and if it all goes away tomorrow, my precious family will still be there, loving me just the same, no matter what. I know

what they put up with for my sake, and I love them
all the more for coping with it.

Comfort Risotto

INGREDIENTS

1 pack of bacon
1 onion
1 oz butter
10 oz risotto rice
1 pack of cherry tomatoes
1¼ pint chicken or vegetable stock
2 oz Parmesan

METHOD

Heat oven to 200°C/gas mark 6. Chop bacon into small pieces and fry in a casserole dish until crispy, then add the onion and butter. Cook for 3 minutes, then add the risotto rice and stir. Add the cherry tomatoes and the hot stock, cover with the lid and bake for around 20 minutes. Stir it through again and grate the Parmesan on top.

Total comfort on a plate!

Recipe by: Make-up artist extraordinaire, Charlie 'Pleasure' Duffy

CHAPTER TWENTY-SIX

A NEW DAWN

I had almost given up my styling work to devote my time to making the show, but when Carol told me that French and Saunders wanted me to style them for their 25th birthday anniversary at the BBC, I jumped at the chance.

I'd always been a huge F&S fan. Simply having the opportunity to meet the girls would have been enough, but to get to style them was like a dream come true. I had followed their career since it began back in the eighties with their sitcom *Girls On Top* and my time at Central had been made more bearable by the thought that they had attended the school and even been on my course— fuck, I was a super fan! Who would have thought that one day these great comedy icons would ask me to style them?

The girls booked me for all the shoots they had in the lead-up to the anniversary. Every magazine and weekend supplement wanted to interview them and, of course, they needed pictures.

Dawn's manager told Carol it would probably be a good idea if I went to Dawn's house and had a rummage through her wardrobe, as she had her own clothing line and had a fabulous collection of outfits.

Oh my God! Someone pinch me! How exciting!

*   *   *

I geared myself up and set off to Reading, where Dawn lived with Lenny Henry. Their house was hidden in beautiful, picture-postcard-perfect countryside. As I drove up the gravelled driveway towards their house—described to me as a 'cottage'—nerves began to make me giddy. The house was far grander than a regular cottage but it still retained a natural, rural feel—not unlike a house from *The Vicar of Dibley*. Wisteria climbed up its walls, perfectly complementing the manicured garden.

As I made my way to the front door, I stopped for a moment to gather my confidence and have a quick rehearsal of my greeting: 'Hi Dawn, I'm Gok', or 'Hello, Ms French, I'm Gok . . .'

Before I had time to knock, the door opened just far enough for Dawn to pop her head out: 'Hello, Gok Wan!' she said, with the biggest, warmest smile I have ever seen. She swung the door open and before I had a chance to say 'Hi' back to her, Dawn leaped from her doorstep, wrapped her arms round me and gave me the biggest hug and kiss in the world.

OMG . . . the Vicar of Dibley just kissed me. *Praise the Lord!*

I tried to keep my cool but it was hard not to be star-struck. With a beaming smile and slightly flushed cheeks, I walked into her home. It was as if Dawn had known me for years as she led the way to her kitchen, offered me a cup of tea and asked if I was hungry. Her easy-going charm and warm hospitality totally put me at my ease and I only just managed to stop myself from blurting out how much I admired her. After a mug of very sugary tea and a couple of chocolate bourbons, we decided it was time to take a look at her wardrobe.

Before I'd put down my mug, Dawn rushed out of the kitchen screaming, 'Come on, Gok Wan!' (I loved the way Dawn used my full name; it made me giggle.) I followed her into the hallway and suddenly there she was at the top of the staircase, her top off and the cheekiest of smiles on her face!

I burst into fits of laughter. Was this really happening? It was as if this scene was a sketch from one of her shows and I was Dawn's stooge! Then, with such perfect timing it was almost as though it'd been choreographed, the front door opened and in walked Lenny bloody Henry! Rooted to the spot, I grinned inanely at him, gestured to his wife by way of explaining my presence in his hallway, and said, 'Hi, Lenny, I'm Gok.'

I was blushing like a child who'd been caught by his parents kissing the babysitter. With an equally cheeky smile, Lenny replied, 'Hi, Gok, what are you doing with my wife?' Then he walked into the kitchen, laughing to himself.

I LOVED THIS HOUSE!

Our afternoon was like a dream slumber party. Dawn tried on a million outfits while I lounged on her bed critiquing her clothes. We got on famously. Dawn made me feel totally comfortable in her home and spoke to me as if I was a member of her family. I was so in awe of her that when she told me she loved *Naked* and admired what the show had done for women all round the country, I burned with pride!

After we'd gone through Dawn's huge walk-in wardrobe, she said she had something special to show me. She led me to the spare room, where she had a closet filled with old costumes from her amazing comedic career. It was like flicking through fashion porn! I almost cried when she pulled out her vicar's robe and crucifix.

My time with Dawn and Jennifer was amazing. I didn't get to meet Jennifer until the first shoot we did but, just as Dawn had been, Jennifer was simply gorgeous and welcoming in her own way. Where Dawn was ballsy and upfront, Jennifer was softer and more reserved. When I suggested what Jennifer should wear from the rails of clothes I had prepped, she thought about the clothes more methodically than Dawn did and seemed to have a more cautious approach to her wardrobe. Perhaps her research for *Absolutely Fabulous* had given her a greater understanding of how clothes can instantly work for or against you. This was made apparent by how she decided if she liked or disliked one of my suggestions. She knew what clothes suited her body shape and she also knew what she wanted to wear.

Jen was definitely the calmer of the two and allowed Dawn to deliver most of the punch lines, both on and off set. I loved how they had allowed their relationship to evolve over the last twenty-five years and how it still worked like a faithful tandem bicycle.

When we'd finished our press run, the girls invited me to their last live show at the Drury Lane Theatre. They performed amazingly and were fabulously hospitable to me at the after-show party, introducing me to their families and close friends. Meeting and working with the girls was definitely a huge career highlight for me. For a brief moment, I imagined myself to be a girl who had hit the top.

Dawn gave me one piece of advice I will always remember: 'You always have control. It may not feel like it, but you do.'

*　　　*　　　*

As we filmed series three of *Naked*, I had never felt more confident of my work. We were still re-working the format every series, as it was important to keep refreshing it so that it didn't become tired and formulaic. Besides, our ladies always thought they knew what to expect because they'd seen previous series, and we wanted to make sure they were taken by surprise. In series three, we went a step further and asked our ladies to go on the catwalk not just in their underwear with their naked picture displayed above, but actually naked. It was a lot to ask, and I was worried we might have gone too far, but as usual my girls did me proud.

How To Look Good Naked is actually built in a huge way on humour. I would gently tease my girls because even though I was building up confidence, I couldn't be too smarmy or so compassionate it spilled over into cloying sentiment. Humour helped me to lead the ladies to question themselves, and to see the funny side of the situation. It also helped to lighten the really quite terrifying prospect of getting naked on national television.

I had always been in awe of television comedians who could deliver great gags with perfect timing and when I was younger, I would try to learn from them. At school, ever on the quest to make people laugh, I would listen carefully to conversations and look for places I could jump in and shock, or finish the story with an unexpected, amusing ending. It all proved to be perfect training for my job.

I loved using my sense of humour while I was presenting—the gags and stunts that were very funny. It felt like I was contributing more to the show than just my knowledge of fashion. The more I made my ladies laugh, the better our performance was on screen.

I also developed my live comedic skills when we filmed the catwalk shows. In one day, we would film four catwalks and we could have in excess of 8,000 audience members who would tirelessly stand all day and watch the shows. We needed the audience to be upbeat and join in, clapping and cheering, so we warmed them up before we started to film. I would go out on to the stage for about fifteen minutes and talk to the audience. I loved it! I'd crack gags, flirt, do some gentle teasing and get them all laughing and cheering. It was the best buzz in the world. I absolutely loved being in front a live audience and I loved experimenting with my improvisation skills. It was the actor inside me who was finally getting a chance to come out and play.

*   *   *

These skills also came in handy for the live work I was doing outside *Naked*. Whether Jonathan Ross was interviewing me in front of a live studio audience, or I was hosting an awards ceremony, as people had started to ask me to do, live audience work was where I was happiest.

Towards the end of 2007, Maverick called Carol and me into their offices to pitch an idea to us. They wanted me to consider doing a live stage show of *How To Look Good Naked*.

Live shows had proven to be a great way of supporting a TV brand. *Top Gear*'s live show had been a great success and *Strictly Come Dancing* and *The X Factor* were exploring the concept as well. I was nervous because it was something I had never done before but I knew that I couldn't pass up this opportunity to test these skills and see whether I was up to the challenge. So I said yes, what the hell, I'd do it.

We decided we would take some of the elements of *Naked* and develop them into a live performance: cutting up clothes to demonstrate how to show off your silhouette; hair and make-up transformations; a five-part catwalk show and, of course, a naked finale. We'd also have a live question-and-answers session with the audience and as much humour as I could muster as I shook in my size-nine boots! I was absolutely petrified. What if the tickets didn't sell? What if people walked out because they were bored? What if I wasn't funny enough to host a two-hour live show?

The production company decided we should hold the show in Glasgow as the company was based there, and they knew the audience would be lively. Happily, the tickets sold out, and before I knew it there was no turning back.

The lead-up to the show was intense. My nerves kept me from sleeping and when I did sleep, I had nightmares that I was booed off the stage. I couldn't help feeling I had bitten off more than I could chew, but my fear of failure meant I wasn't prepared to back out.

On the day of the live show, the technical crew had a complete run-through of the lighting and sound cues, and their rehearsal overran by more than two hours due to a lighting disaster. As time ticked on, I grew more and more frantic. I didn't care if I couldn't be lit on stage, I just wanted—no, *needed*—a couple of rehearsals. But there was no time. By 4 p.m., I still hadn't had a full run-through of the show and I my nerves were frayed beyond repair. Carol and my parents were there, but there was no way anyone could calm me down I was feeling so frantic.

At 5 p.m. I was able to block the show through—basically run through all my exits and entrances and where I needed to be and when—but there was not enough time for a full rehearsal.

I sat in my dressing room, shallow breathing and feeling desperate. Then I reminded myself that this was the kind of thing professional actors had to deal with. And what did they do? No matter how nervous and terrified they were, they went out there and did it. They winged it, relying on their innate talent and the knowledge that things could go quite wrong and often the audience would be none the wiser. I would have to call on all my experience and all my resources. Fuck! Could I do it?

By 7 p.m., the stage manger was giving me my half-hour call. I decided that this was the worst day of my life. I couldn't remember the sequence of the show, I couldn't remember my lines and the earpiece they had given me so that I could hear the director was falling out of my sweaty nervous ear.

I was about to go on stage in front of thousands

of PAYING people and die!

Standing backstage and looking out of the wings was the most horrendous experience of my life. The theatre was packed to capacity with people, including groups of tipsy women who were all chanting my name. I wanted to vomit.

Suddenly, the introduction music began to play and smoke filled the stage. The 'voice of God' began to introduce me and I took my position at the centre of the stage, hidden by two huge, floor-to-ceiling, red velvet curtains.

'Ladies and Ladies . . . Please be upstanding for your host for the evening . . . He's the Sultan of Style, the Master of all Makeovers and your best mate . . . Get your bangers ready . . . It's GOK WAN . . . !'

The audience went absolutely berserk. They screamed, shouted, clapped and chanted my name so loudly, it reverberated through my chest. The curtains lifted, more smoke poured from behind me and a giant spotlight hit me. My silhouette filled the entire stage as well as the two enormous screens to the sides of the stage. I stood in the centre of the stage with my back to the audience while they shouted and chanted my name ever louder. My heart was beating like a drum, and my arms and legs shook with excitement. This was what I had dreamed of all my life—to be on stage in front of a live audience.

As I slowly turned round and faced the audience, I remember thinking, *If you die right now, then it serves you fucking right, you silly twat!*

*   *   *

The show was . . . INCREDIBLE! The first half ran twenty minutes too short as my nerves made me race through the schedule, but I made the time up in the question-and-answer session. The audience remained engaged throughout the entire show, laughing and crying in all the right places. The makeovers were a triumph and the catwalk finale got the entire audience out of their seats, dancing and singing. When I did a saucy semi-strip, taking my pants off from under a black leather kilt, they went absolutely mad. The audience was amazing, every single one of them!

WHAT A FUCKING BUZZ!

*   *   *

Another highlight was when I was asked to present live from the *Sex And The City* premiere at Leicester Square. I couldn't believe it!

I'm a self-confessed *SATC* addict. I have watched every single episode at least a hundred times and, like so many women in the world, I live my life by the girls' mantra: Fuck it and let's go shopping.

I adore everything about the show: the costumes, the situations and, of course, the 'girlfriend' camaraderie. I was so excited to be chosen to present one of the most anticipated premieres ever! *Thank you, Father, Son and Holy Chanel!*

*   *   *

On the day of the premiere, I'd been filming all day on *Naked*. When I arrived at Leicester Square at

5 p.m., dressed head to toe in Vivienne Westwood, I was exhausted.

No sooner had I put my manbag down, I was being given cue cards, scripts, directions and a double cappuccino. By 6 p.m., the square was filled to capacity with hysterical *SATC* fans (myself included).

I discovered that I was the only presenter allowed on the red carpet so it was my responsibility to interview *all* the main cast (OMG—SJP!), the director, producers and all the A-listers. It was like I had won the lottery.

As I rehearsed my opening link, it suddenly dawned on me that I had never presented a red-carpet event before, and what the hell was I supposed to do? What if I ran out of questions to ask the girls? What if they hated me? What if I went to double kiss one of the girls and they only wanted one? What if I forgot Sarah's real name and called her Carrie? My mind was filled to bursting point with 'What if's', but there was simply no time to get too nervous.

At any red-carpet event, the cast is expected to spend as much time with the fans as possible and as little time as they can with the journalists, without appearing rude. My director told me I needed to keep the girls talking for as long as humanly possible since they were our 'money shots'. If the PRs tried to pull the girls away early, I had to continue interviewing them until the very last second. There was only one chance to make a connection in the interview and since we were making the only official premiere show for the UK market, it was imperative the interviews were interesting and informative. No pressure then!

276

Flustered and panicked, I was shooting the first few links but I was finding it hard to concentrate, which made my presenting look like the video recording for my GCSE Media Studies. Just then, through the masses of PRs, security guards, hysterical fans and nervous film execs, I saw it. Like a gorgeous green bird of paradise, Sarah Jessica's Philip Treacy hat rose from a blacked-out Mercedes.

I thought I was going to be sick with nerves and excitement. Sarah Jessica 'the Goddess' Parker was now standing on the same red carpet as me, waving to thousands of screaming fans. She looked amazing in a knee-length silk tulle, flared chiffon dress by Alexander McQueen, and her hat was a magnificent confection of a green silk rose, meadow flowers and butterflies.

The square had erupted. I have never heard cheering like it. It was like being at the fashion World Cup! I found myself grinning madly and clapping like a idiotic seal when I saw her, until my director quizzically shook his head at me, urging me to try and control myself—*shame!*

* * *

As she worked the crowds of photographers and fans, I waited obediently at my camera for my chance to interview her. The longer I waited, the more nervous I became, my hands shaking with total euphoria.

After half an hour, Sarah Jessica finally arrived next to me. She was tiny but perfect in every single way. I couldn't believe I was standing next to Carrie Bradshaw! I wanted to scream, 'I LOVE

277

YOU!' down her neat little ear and then hold her until the last day of eternity, but I guessed the security guards would probably pull me to the ground and Taser me to death before that happened.

The questions on my cue cards that I'd been rehearsing for hours seemed to melt away and all I could do was look at her. I wanted to prod her on the arm and make sure she was real, but I didn't dare to touch her. This was it! My one and only chance not to balls up the best moment of my career to date. Sarah Jessica smiled at me, the camera swung round and my director screamed, 'Action!'

I was smiling so hard I must have looked deranged, but I managed to hold it together just long enough to get my first question out: 'Sarah Jessica, you look amazing, darling! Who are you wearing?'

The interview lasted about three minutes. What I asked after my first question is beyond me; I was trapped in a star-struck womb where I could only hear the sound of my own beating heart. Before she was whisked away to the photographers, she turned to me, placed her hand on my arm and said, 'Thanks, Gok, that was a nice interview. I hope you like the film.'

Fuck me backwards with a plastic fish slice! I LOVE YOU, SJP!

*   *   *

Over the next hour I interviewed Kristin, Cynthia, Kim, Michael and a handful of very groomed celebrities. Patricia Field, the *SATC* stylist,

278

recognised me as her British equivalent; Vivienne noticed I was dressed head to toe in her gear; and Davina McCall hugged me so hard, I think I may have farted. It was truly a fabulous evening.

After that night, I realised I'd found a confidence with my work I never thought I would achieve. Perhaps I was never going to be the best presenter in the world, but now I'd been in some demanding situations and I'd managed to rise to the occasion. At last I began to trust that I could do this job. Maybe now I could relax a little bit and let myself be happy.

'Last night I got to thinking, when does meeting SJP ever stop being an OMG . . .?'

CHAPTER TWENTY-SEVEN

WOOOOAAAH—FASHION!

When Carol called and told me Channel 4 wanted a meeting with me, I assumed it was to speak about *Naked*. I thought they might want to thrash around the format and see if there were any ideas I could contribute to re-developing it.

So I was completely blown away when they told me they wanted me to host a different show called *Gok's Fashion Fix*. My initial reaction was WOW! I was excited and pleased in equal measure that the channel thought me experienced enough to carry two of their shows. This could be just what my career needed as I'd become very comfortable with *Naked*. I was far from bored but I was aware that a new challenge would be good for me. The channel offered a few days for me to think about it before they would give the production company sign-off confirmation.

After my excitement wore off, I began to consider the downsides. What if *Fashion Fix* wasn't as good as *Naked*? What if the viewers hated me for trying my hand at another show? What if *Fashion Fix* flopped like an eighties fringe?

I wondered if this show was too much, too soon. After all, I'd only just found my feet with my presenting career and *Naked* was still getting top ratings for the channel. Did I need a new show?

Carol and I had lunch and we discussed the pros and cons. The upside was that *Fashion Fix* would be a programme where I could show off my skills as a stylist on some real fashion situations. And I would be able to avoid being pigeonholed as only the *Naked* Gok; a new side to my personal brand might lead to a whole host of new opportunities. But there was a massive downside. They wanted me to have a co-presenter—pop princess, Alexa Chung.

What?!

I didn't think there was any way I could present with Alexa. She was a million years younger than me, a billion times prettier than me and she had a trillion times more experience shooting in a studio—I was used to out-of-studio presenting. Arghhh!!!

But I kept my fears to myself and agreed to speak to the producers and find out more about the show.

Colette Foster had moved from Maverick TV by this time, and set up her fashion TV camp at Endemol, who had come up with the idea of *Fashion Fix*. I was pleased the show had been commissioned from Colette, and as we met over a cocktail she told me what she had in mind for the series.

Fashion Fix would be a fast-paced magazine programme that celebrated all genres of fashion. The main segment would be The Fashion Face-off—four big-wigs from the world of fashion would compete against me to assemble four looks to put down the catwalk. The twist was that I would be limited to high-street fashion with a budget of £200 for each outfit, while the fashion girls would be able to spend as much as they liked on designer labels. At the end of the show, the studio audience would decide which collection they liked the best, and vote, not knowing which collection was designer and which was high street. We would also have a celebrity wardrobe inspection, a travelling catwalk where I would go to a different town in the UK searching for the country's best-dressed person, and a road test, where Alexa would put a selection of products through their paces. On top of this, there would be the designer interview, where Alexa would go to a different part of the world to interview a high-end designer—Cavalli at his villa in Florence, Lagerfeld in his iconic Rue Cambon office in Paris and so on. *How come she got to do the best job?!*

I listened carefully and then thought: ARE YOU FUCKING MAD, COLETTE?

I couldn't believe she wanted me to go head-to head-in a fashion face-off with some of the biggest names and most influential buyers in the fashion industry. They'd have a limitless budget and access to the most incredible designer labels, while I'd have my £200 and the great British high street. *Fucking suicide, girlfriend!*

I knew I was a competent stylist. I loved the British high street and I had the confidence to accept a challenge but the format did seem pretty tilted against me. How could I even think about going up against Chanel, Dolce, Halston and Choo? These designers spend thousands of pounds sourcing the best materials in the world. They have the best pattern cutters, designers and creative minds in the business. *Pass me a bucket, I feel a little queer!*

I was also concerned the audience would think I was being a hypocrite since I'd made no secret of the fact that my wardrobe was bursting with designer clobber I'd collected over the years. I love designer clothes and I didn't want the fashion industry to think I was slagging them off, telling the public they shouldn't spend their hard earned cash on high-end luxury goods.

*   *   *

Colette convinced me I wouldn't be rubbishing designer clothes, instead, I would be championing the high street, giving viewers who didn't have the funds to splash out on labels ideas about how to look good without breaking the bank!

I listened, thought about it from that perspective and it made sense. On *How To Look Good Naked,* we championed real women, telling them that being size 18 was no better or worse than being a size 8. *Fashion Fix* could do the same, but with clothes. The message was 'Style, whatever your budget.'

The more I thought about it, the more excited I became. I knew that I would have to get over myself long enough to build a working relationship with Alexa but, who knew, maybe I would even learn a few things. I had a feeling this show could be huge. So I cross-stitched on the dotted line.

*   *   *

The production on the show began and it felt strange. I was working with a new production company, a brand new team and I was presenting a new show. I couldn't have felt more out of my comfort zone.

I enjoyed the Fashion Face-offs much more than

283

I'd expected. It was hard work and everything came from me but I got a real thrill from using my fashion nous again. The key was to give a high street item a twist, hide the details that made it look cheap, add details that made it seem more expensive and then accessorise to within an inch of its life.

I coined the phrase 'haberdashery chic' to describe what I did when I customised outfits. I'd get corsages, buttons, ribbons, braiding, trimmings, motifs—anything that would spruce up, for example, a dirt-cheap pair of gold shoes from New Look. I used belts as headbands, skirts as dresses, put tops on back to front and spray-painted handbags. I put beads on tasselled shoes, ripped sleeves off here and re-jigged hems there, puffed out with flouncy underskirts or cinched in with statement belts. Whatever the look—whether it was beachwear, summer brights, working girl, night on the town—I managed to get my looks together on the cheap and give them a designer flavour through their custom-made individuality. It was all great fun.

Originally, the customising of the outfits was going to be done off camera, but Colette loved watching how I did it and decided that it was great television. Now watching the styling magic is a signature of the show, but it nearly didn't make it on to the screen at all.

The production company had found four fashion mavens to go up against me: Marigay Mackee from Harrods (no shortage of labels there, I think you'll find), Erin Mullaney from Browns (yes, plenty of juicy designers in one of London's top boutiques), Lina Basma from Selfridges (the spiritual home of

284

fashionistas) and Brix Smith-Start from the Start boutique. All these ladies had to do was waft about, selecting the latest and most gorgeous designer dresses, with their acres of luxurious fabric, the finest shoes and the most outrageously expensive bags and jewellery, and *voilà*. While I was still sweating over a hot needle and a spray-starch can, they would be taking the weight of their Louboutins with a well-deserved martini.

When I wasn't doing that, I was racing about with celebrities. In the first series I met Geri Halliwell, Kelly Osbourne (who confessed she'd once spent $28,000 dollars on a coat—and she'd never worn it), Mischa Barton, Dannii Minogue, Lorraine Kelly (my gorgeous TV mum whose episode pulled in huge ratings as we rolled around on her bed), Lulu and Jamelia.

But the most exciting moment for me was meeting Joan Collins.

Joan was priceless. She agreed to do the show but we had to travel to Saint Tropez to film her. It was arranged that I'd meet her in the small town and, as her wardrobes were far away in London and New York, we'd go shopping together, so we could see her passion for couture and high-end brands in action.

The producers had arranged for us to meet at the big clock in the centre of town and from there we would hit the very expensive shops. On the day, in true Hollywood style, Joan was running late, which did not help my already frayed nerves. The heat was unbearable and I was dressed in my uniform of black jacket and skinnies—not the kind of clothes I recommend you wear while cavorting in the midday heat and cobbled streets of the south of France with TV legend Alexis Colby!

After what felt like years, a battered old people carrier rolled up (it was not dissimilar to an unlicensed minicab in Soho on a Friday night). The windows were tinted but I could just make out the most enormous white straw hat on top of a very heavily made-up Ms Joan Collins, who was sitting in the back seat. I opened the door with a very shaky hand, waited for Joan to alight, then greeted her with the obligatory double kiss, careful not to touch flesh. She lowered her head, lifted her sunglasses and said, 'Hello, darling, I knew you'd be wearing more make-up than me!'

With that she flicked her hair and strutted off, Percy (her husband/manager) in tow.

The afternoon was fabulous. We browsed casually in the local boutiques and chatted about her career in Hollywood, love life and, of course, her passion for style. She soon opened up to me and her stories were fascinating. It was as if she had always existed in the spotlight: she oozed glamour, sophistication and confidence.

As we roamed the streets of Saint Tropez, I was surprised by the lack of attention she attracted. This is Joan fucking Collins! I wanted to shout. How can you not want an autograph or picture? But it was as if she was a local, just out shopping for some bog roll before she went home to prepare lunch for good old Percy, who kept three metres away at all times and only spoke when he was instructed to. I desperately wanted people to fall apart in shock at the sight of Joan shopping but no one really did. The occasional 'Salut, Joan!' was shouted and a couple of Brits asked for a picture but that was pretty much it. How disappointing! I think my ego was more bruised than hers, as I so wanted to show off the fact I was Joan's new bitch, but I never got the opportunity.

About three hours into filming, I began to find my confidence: Joan was no longer the untouchable screen goddess I had built her up to be; she had become a telly friend. She chatted with me like we'd known each other the whole of our lives and at one point she actually looked me in the eyes. We shared a couple of jokes on camera and found a comfortable and steady rhythm. I was getting somewhere! Finally, we reached our final shop, Roberto Cavalli.

The crew was exhausted, I was exhausted, but Joan was still firing on all cylinders. The director, Ann Wilson, instructed me to wrap the interview up, so it was my last opportunity to ask Joan any final questions about her life as a style icon. We sat down in the store on a very camp purple pouffe and began the 'out-tro'.

'So, Joan, have you enjoyed today?'

'Yes, darling, it's been fabulous!'

'Have you learned anything from your Auntie Gok?'

'Darling, you have taught me nothing. Have I taught you anything?'

'Yes, Joan, you have taught me how to be a diva for the day, thank you so much!'

'You're welcome, Gok!'

We embraced as Ann shouted, 'Cut!'

Joan then turned to me and said, 'When will this be on the BBC?'

'Joan, this is for Channel 4. Do you even know who I am?'

The whole thing was an absolute scream and I

came away more a Joanie admirer than ever.

*   *   *

I began to realise that I was seriously exhausted. My feet had not touched the ground since I had begun filming the first series of *Naked*—I was now on my fourth show. I'd followed up my first book with another called *How to Dress*. I'd also designed a collection of underwear, endorsed glasses for SpecSavers and been to Australia on a promotional tour. I'd hosted awards shows, bought my first flat, been on every chat show in the UK, tried to maintain a social life and I was writing two fashion columns.

I was well and truly shattered. I wanted to tell Carol I was feeling the strain but I didn't because I was afraid she might think I needed to slow down. I couldn't do that—my job needed me. And the more work I was offered, the bigger the buzz I was getting. My addiction to overeating, undereating and always trying to please had now metamorphosed into a work addiction. As long as I was being called out to work at 7 a.m. and not getting home until midnight, I was being needed. I pushed myself physically and mentally and if at times it felt as though I was suffocating with pressure, at least I was in control. I ignored my body's cries of exhaustion and decided I would work as hard as I could to get the series finished and then speak to Carol about booking some time out.

Before long, we were nearing the end of production. I had managed to fight my insecurities and build a good on-screen bond with Alexa and I have to say, she taught me a lot about presenting in a studio.

The Fashion Face-offs were a huge success— soon to become everyone's favourite part of the show and the *Fashion Fix* signature—and I won every one! It was great to be able to show the viewers how to become their own stylists and not have to spend a fortune to look a million dollars. The very first face-off had the designers spending £13,000 against my £750. I still won . . . credit crunch couture, baby!

*   *   *

The production ran over by a couple of weeks and we were still filming when the first episode aired. I was nervous about what the critics might say.

The morning after the first broadcast, I walked into the studio, dumped my bags in my dressing room and headed straight for the newspapers.

Once again, I was gutted. We'd had a mixture of reviews and most of the critics who supported *Naked* loved the show, but a couple of the broadsheets were not in agreement. It didn't matter how many good reviews we got; as always, it was the bad ones that stuck in my side like a rusty old nail. One critic wrote something along the lines of, 'Has Gok had his moment?'

WHAT? I had only been on TV for two years and already they were wondering if my star was beginning to fade! Luckily the viewing figures had been very healthy and didn't reflect the doubts of some of the higher-brow critics.

I didn't want the bad reviews to bother me but I couldn't help it. It was so difficult to read negative stuff when we'd worked so hard to produce an entertaining and informative show with a bit of jeopardy, a bit of information and heaps of glamour, but we still couldn't please them. I was so tired and for a brief moment it didn't feel worth it.

My worrying began to knock me down but after several conversations with Carol and my family, I decided I had done as much as I could. I would just have to accept the fact that some people were going to love both shows, some just one and some none.

CHAPTER TWENTY-EIGHT

DRESSING MUM

The only time I have ever dressed a member of my family is when I invited Mum and Dad to an awards ceremony I was hosting. I'd spoken to Mum a few times about it and she had told me she was nervous about what to wear. I told her to buy something and I would send her the money as a treat.

As the awards got closer, I asked her if she had found something and she said no. Then it clicked: Mum wanted me to dress her but she was too proud to ask.

The weekend before the awards I cancelled my weekend plans and returned home to Leicester. I packed Mum and Dad up in the back of the car and off we drove to Marks & Spencer on a quest to dress Momma Wan.

The store was packed. I don't know how it had happened but everyone seemed to know we were coming. We entered the shop to what felt like applause. Hurrying Mum and Dad through the crowds, I figured we would be safer if we kept moving and spent as much time in the safety of the changing rooms as possible. I grabbed an armful of dresses and dragged Momma Wan into the fitting area, leaving Dad to stroll round the suits (Dad had decided it wasn't fair Mum was getting an outfit and he wasn't. Oh, how the roles had changed!).

Once in the fitting room, it was clear Mum

needed the help of some support underwear.

'Stay here while I go and get some big pants,' I told her, 'and cover yourself up, for crying out loud!'

I left her giggling in the changing room. On the shop floor, I made a beeline for the underwear section. Just as I got to the fascinators and handbags, a woman jumped out at me armed with a mobile phone and a pen and paper. Before she could ask me for a picture, I said, 'I am so sorry but I have left my mum in the changing room with just her bra and knickers on and I need to get back to her with some big pants . . .' As I smiled and went to walk past her, she grabbed my arm with a wrestler's grip and snarled at me, 'I don't care, I want a picture, you rude bastard!'

I could not believe it! How could anyone speak to a total stranger like that?

I stopped, spun on my Cuban heel and glared at her, saying, 'I told you, I am with my mother and she is far more important than your bloody picture, now let go of my arm!'

The woman was shocked by my response and it obviously pissed her off because she let go of her grip and said, 'You're nothing like what you are on TV! Well, you've just lost a viewer here, love!'

Now, I know I have a public job and I know that without the viewers I do not have a career. But come on—when my mum is standing in her bra and knickers in a changing room . . . Still, perhaps I was starting to feel the strain.

Dad chose the most expensive suit he could find, Mum wore the big pants and a gorgeous black cocktail dress and we all had a great night. The moral of this story is that mums need more than just big pants: they need loyal children who will always put them first.

Dear Mummy,

You are my friend. I don't know if you realise this but you are the first person I go to when I need advice. I may not always agree with you but you have the power to make my problems drift away. Your smile is the warmest place in my world and sometimes when I feel lonely, I close my eyes and imagine your smile. Over the years you've taught me how to love. I've never met anyone with so much love to give. Our family has always been an open door to anyone who needs help and that is down to you. I owe you so much for teaching me how to be kind to people around me. Do you remember when you and I picked up the Christmas tree in my Citroën 2CV, just weeks before Christmas, in the freezing cold? We rolled the roof back and squeezed the six-foot tree into the back of the car and we laughed all the way home. Whenever I'm sad, I listen out for that laugh. You will always be the centre of my world and without you it would not turn. I am proud to be your baby. You make my heart beat. I love you for a moment longer than eternity.

Babe x

As the first series of *Gok's Fashion Fix* reached the end of its broadcast, I was totally run down; most of my days were powered by nervous energy. Mum had started to get concerned about my health and our daily telephone calls were dominated with her telling me to take it easy. She advised me to tell the producers to give me a day off but, as I had done when I was sick at Central, I told her, 'I'm fine, please don't worry, really—I'm okay.'

Before I knew it, we were well into filming the new series of *How To Look Good Naked* and *Fashion Fix* had been commissioned for a second series. I couldn't tell the producers I was tired in case they thought I was either weak or a diva. Instead, I smiled as much as I could and kept my jumping around on camera to just knee height.

For the second series of *Gok's Fashion Fix*, we made some changes. Alexa was no longer my co-presenter and we brought in a whole new aspect to the show involving a member of the public who needed some help with finding out their body shape and what suited them best. *How To Look Good Naked* tackled body dysmorphia and issues of identity and confidence, with the women going on a serious emotional journey. Instead, *Fashion Fix* was unashamedly about fashion—the clothes, the shoes, the bags, the best shapes to wear and the latest trends. We came up with a new mantra for the show: 'Buy less and wear more'. I showed how, with some clever shopping and some body knowledge, it was possible to buy a capsule wardrobe of twenty-four mix and match pieces that could take any woman from work, to a meeting, to lunch with the girls, to a glamorous night out.

The celebrity aspect of the show had also subtly changed from the first series. Now I was taking label-addicted celebs and showing them how to shop from the high street. I'd dress them for a red-carpet event and dare them to wear my high-street outfit in front of the paparazzi. First up for the challenge was Janet Street Porter, who is one of the

294

most label-loving women I've ever met—she claims it's because of her height—but all credit to her, she wore my high-street outfit to an event and duly got snapped in it. I also riffled through the wardrobes of Cilla Black, Lorraine (making her second appearance), Lynda Bellingham, Alan Carr, Ben Shephard and Ruby Wax.

The Fashion Face-off had to stay, of course. Everyone had loved it in series one, and it had become part of the show's signature. But it wasn't working quite as well as we wanted. There wasn't enough at stake for it. Although I had a lot invested in the result, the ladies who had created the designer outfits in the first series didn't have quite as much riding on the outcome, as each fashionista only styled one outfit. Once they'd done their work, we didn't see them again. To introduce a bit more competition into proceedings, we decided that I would go head-to-head with only one buyer, Brix Smith-Start, although the same rules would apply—a high-street budget for me and unlimited designer spend for her.

Gok's Fashion Fix was high-octane fun that required lots of filming and lots of work with its fast pace and fun fashion elements. I loved doing it but by the end, I was even more worn out than ever.

It didn't, however, look as if I was going to get a break anytime soon, and I told myself I'd be mad to slacken off now, just when things were busier than they'd ever been.

There were some exciting challenges further down the line and I had to keep going; that was all there was to it . . .

CHAPTER TWENTY-NINE

THE WAKE-UP CALL

I was busier than ever in 2009. I didn't manage to get a rest as I continued with my filming commitments; as one show finished, I went straight into production with the next. I also signed a deal with Boots to produce my own line of body products, filmed *Celebrity Apprentice* with Comic Relief, filmed a comedy sketch for Children in Need, signed a deal with Dorothy Perkins to become their online style consultant, wrote another book, *Work Your Wardrobe* and continued my commitments with SpecSavers. There was also my underwear line and other corporate jobs.

In November I signed up to make a staggering twenty-one episodes of *How To Look Good Naked* and we started work soon afterwards.

During the first few weeks of filming, I found I was suffering from painful stomach aches. Thinking that stress was giving me indigestion, I started taking a daily dose of Zantac. What I didn't realise was that my body was telling me I needed to have some time off.

One day we filmed for a couple of hours but I knew something wasn't right. My stomach was hurting and I felt more exhausted than usual. By mid-afternoon, we'd finished filming but I was too tired to leave the studio and go home, even though my driver was sitting outside waiting for me. I felt dizzy and out of breath, and it was ages before I could gather up the strength to get out to the car.

On the way home, Steve, my driver, was concerned and told me I didn't look well: I was pale and my eyes were yellow and bloodshot. As soon as I got home, I fell into bed, thinking I was just exhausted. After an hour's sleep I woke up feeling nauseous and dizzy. I ran to the toilet and vomited about two pints of sticky black sick. I knew this wasn't right but I thought that if I went to a hospital, they'd tell me it was just something I ate and I would have wasted their valuable time. Instead I got back into bed and convinced myself I could sleep it off.

Within an hour I had vomited two more times, each time producing more of this sticky black mess. I called NHS Direct and described my symptoms. The nurse immediately told me to go straight to A & E, as she suspected I was losing blood internally.

Fortunately, my flatmate Gaynor was home. We have been friends for many years; in fact, she is my oldest mate—we met back in Leicester when we were both studying at Charles Keene. I still remember seeing Gaynor's frizzy hair bouncing round the dance studio as she stag-leaped into my life. Gaynor moved to London after I promised her a shitload of nights out, a chance to make more of her life and, of course, the coveted prize of looking after me—which she has always done with great finesse.

We went to the hospital and I was so tired and ill that I fell asleep in the waiting room before my examination and was woken up by someone asking for an autograph, which was a surreal moment.

As soon as I'd been seen by a doctor, I was admitted at once. They gave me tests and blood counts, and it turned out that my haemoglobin was dangerously low. The diagnosis was exhaustion and two stomach ulcers, which had been bleeding into my stomach. I'd lost a lot of blood while I'd been ignoring my symptoms and I was taken upstairs and had an immediate blood transfusion that night. They told me that they would be pumping me full of blood for the next five days.

In the event, I ended up in hospital for two weeks, and during my stay I had six blood transfusions, two iron transfusions and was told that if I had continued to ignore the problem then it could have been fatal.

The last five years had caught up with me: I hadn't been off camera for three years and I was, quite simply, fucked. But the problem went back further than this—my stomach lining was susceptible after my years of laxative abuse, which was how I ended up with ulcers. It really was the proverbial wake-up call.

The following day I was transferred to a private room at St Thomas's with its own little bathroom, which thrilled me because I'd never stayed private before and it felt rather swanky, I must say. In fact, it felt like a bit of a holiday camp compared to my punishing work schedule. My friends sent clothes for me, and Carol came rushing over to see if I was okay and to bring me anything I needed. Even Mum and Dad came hurtling down the M1 in the Wan bus armed with bags of sweets and love.

One afternoon, after I had been hooked up to yet another bag of blood, I was lying in my room alone, feeling shattered, when I suddenly heard the most extra-ordinarily massive and endless fart coming from the next room. I think it was the longest, loudest fart possible for a human being to make. Just as I was coming to terms with that one, another came roaring out of the next room again: enormous and impressive!

I clambered out of bed with my drips attached to each arm—one of saline and one of blood—grabbed the stands and wheeled them with me into the other room to tell off whoever it was. And there, in the room next to mine, was Sir Michael *bloody* Gambon.

'Dumbledore, you dirty bastard!' I said.

Sir Michael and I spent two weeks together and we had the best time ever. He was extremely funny and great company. He'd come to my room and we'd listen to Classic FM, then we'd go out and have fags together on the roof. We weren't really allowed to but we'd chat up the nurses to persuade them to let us out, and we'd stand there together in our PJs, our drips in our arms. It was like we were having a holiday romance in hospital together.

Gradually I began to feel better and life was rather pleasant. I had lots of visits from the people I loved. My beauty products had just been launched so all the samples came in for me to play with. I got so many bunches of flowers that I amused myself by making rosettes and headbands for all the nurses, decorating their caps and uniforms with corsages.

After my two weeks of convalescing in hospital, I came home feeling a lot better. The episode made me realise that I had to calm down a bit. I told myself I would never work that hard without a break again. How could it be worth it, if it killed me? *How To Look Good Knackered?*

CHAPTER THIRTY

CHANGING LIVES

Filming with Kelly Chamberlain was about to change my life. What made Kelly different to the other girls was that she'd had a mastectomy.

When it was first suggested it to me, my first instinct was to say, 'No'. I felt we were crossing a line into territory where we had no right to go. *How To Look Good Naked* isn't a religion, I told them, and it's not going to cure cancer. On the show we confronted basic body dysmorphia, but dealing with someone who had a disfigurement owing to a terrible disease . . . well, I felt it was wrong to try and fix something as serious as that.

After much discussion, the producers convinced me to do it. I agreed, on the basis that we would take filming one day at a time and if I ever felt uncomfortable with what we were doing, I would be able to stop.

I was apprehensive. I'd never met anyone with breast cancer or who had a mastectomy, although I had done some charity work for a magazine and interviewed a woman who'd told me a bit about the difficulties of buying clothes and bras after a mastectomy operation. She'd told me about the problem of getting clothes on and off because you can't lift your arms up, about what fabrics won't hurt the skin, and we talked about how to wear a head wrap to cover up the main side effect of cancer treatment: hair loss. So I'd had a tiny bit of experience, but nothing to prepare me for this hour-long show.

Kelly had been knocked so badly by her surgery that she didn't consider herself feminine or beautiful any more, and had put all of her wedding plans on hold.

As soon as I met her, I realised that although her issues were complex—I couldn't pretend she hadn't lost a breast or been badly scarred by her radiation treatment—she still responded to the same boosts as anyone else. During the course of the programme, she met other women who'd been through the same experience and come out the other side. She learned how to dress her new body and she blossomed as we progressed.

By the end, she was gorgeous, confident and ready to be a beautiful bride. For me, it was an epiphany. It reinforced how important the show could be. It was a safe place where women could go and it gave them a sense of community, whether suffering from breast cancer or body hatred. For the first time, we had been to a place where no other programme had dared to go, and it had proved inspiring. It had a powerful effect on our audience, too, and lots of good stuff came out of the show. Suddenly we were being quoted by breast cancer charities, and Kelly was asked to model for a bra company. I, also, found a lot of confidence through doing her show.

*   *   *

The production company went on to come up with the idea of *How To Look Good Naked—With A Difference* in which we would work with ladies who had disabilities. They'd lined up Clare, an amputee, Tracy, who was in a wheelchair, and Di, who was blind. My reaction was the same as it had been to Kelly's show. No way. I said I couldn't do it. I didn't want to pretend to be a messiah; I couldn't cure these ladies. I couldn't change them or make them well, and surely it was arrogant of me to act as though I could.

Once again, the producers talked me into it, with the same proviso. If I felt that the show wasn't working, we could stop it at any time.

I did a lot of preparation but found the whole thing very stressful and worried about it a lot. In fact, the day that we filmed the mirror moments with Clare and Tracy was the day that I fell ill and went into hospital.

After I came out, we went straight into filming the rest of the shows. It was unbelievable. It was the best decision we'd ever made and it made me fall back in love with the show all over again.

Di's show, in particular, affected me a great deal. It felt like the biggest challenge of all, and I admitted that I was scared—I didn't know what it was like to be blind or live in darkness.

When we filmed the mirror moment, I felt panic. I had never before tried to help someone who couldn't see what they looked like. Di was a fifty-four-year-old who had lost her sight as a young woman so she knew what colours were like, but she had last seen patterns, fabrics and tones in the seventies. She had no idea what she looked like and she described her condition as like being locked in a box.

When Di broke down sobbing, telling me how much she hated it, I put my arms round her and held her. Although I was terribly nervous, I tried to keep calm and I managed to say, 'Instead of me being so naive as to think I could just be your eyes for you and say to you, "Well, that looks gorgeous on you", why don't we try and create our own sight between the two of us?'

Di said, 'That would be fantastic' and I knew that somehow I'd found the right approach, although I was still unsure that we'd be able to do it. I designed Di a 'style bible' based on her body shape. It allowed her to feel different clothing shapes to enable her to work out which suited her body. Its front cover had a raised silhouette of her body shape, and when she opened the book she could take out magnetised cut-outs of the jackets, shirts, dresses and skirts that most suited her shape and put them over it, so that she could 'feel' her look. Lots of textured swatches and colours (for the friends that went shopping with her) would also help remind her of what she'd learned, and the journey we'd been on together.

The whole experience helped her win back some confidence in herself and once more I really felt the power of what we were doing. It was hugely affecting to see Di regain something she thought she could no longer have. In a way, she began to see again—not conventionally, but mentally. She could conjure colour and shape in her mind.

Di's show was more raw than any other. There were no big whoosh sounds, no bows and bangles. Everyone went on the journey with her, and at points in the show, you could suddenly imagine what it must be like to be blind. And for Di, it meant that, just for a moment, others could feel her darkness. I think that for her that that was the most powerful thing of all.

303

The shows changed my world completely. They were amazing. I walked away from them thinking that *How To Look Good Naked* was now an institution and that it had proven itself not only as formatted entertainment, but as a resource show. I'm told that the Royal National Institute of the Blind now use Di's show as a training tool, and that the style book is being introduced as an aid for the blind.

To make those shows was an enormous privilege and the response we got from the disabled community was incredible. We were inundated with thank yous. I hadn't realised that there were over two million wheelchair users in this country and they have no visual representation, apart from the sign on the disabled loo. We got Shannon, a wheelchair user, into an ad campaign for Debenhams—the first time that has ever happened.

How To Look Good Naked has come so far. It has become a show that deals with extremes. It has done so much politically and achieved a huge amount: it has been spoken about in the Houses of Parliament, campaigned for plus-sized models and petitioned for body confidence to be taught in schools (Ed Balls, the then Schools Secretary, agreed to implement the policy, but we'll have to see what the future holds now there is a new government). It has evolved with the support of the public who have wanted it to do more, to change and surprise them.

Most of all, *How To Look Good Naked* has let us into other communities—the larger-sized, the disabled, the old, the frightened, the unsure, the lonely—and for a time we all feel a part of something positive. It brings us all together. It is an incredibly clever and important show, and I'm so lucky to be at the helm of it.

Had I not starved myself and suffered loneliness and body hatred, I would never have the kind of empathy I do with the people who allow us to tell their stories. *Naked* makes us feel less alone and I can't think of any other programme that does that in quite the same way. I owe so much to *Naked*, more than just giving me a job, fame and some cash. *Naked* has given me the strength to face my own body demons. I am confident my own body dysmorphia is kept at bay because of the show's empowering message.

Proper Fish and Chips

INGREDIENTS

1 telephone number of Mum and Dad's
  chippy
6 cans of Stella
Box of letters from your family

METHOD

Call Mum and Dad and let them know you are at the Watford Junction service station and that you'll be home in 30 minutes. Ask them to fire up the deep fat fryers. Drive the remaining 20 miles home. When you get back to Mum and Dad's house, park up, leave all your bags in the car and forget about them until later. Enter the house, kicking off your shoes. Wait for Mum to bring the fish and chips home, armed with a massive smile and a bear hug. Gorge on the salty chips and crispy fish until you feel sick. Lie back on the sofa, open a can of beer and carefully go through all the wonderful letters your family has sent you over the years. Enjoy. Rejoice. Feel full of food and love.

CHAPTER THIRTY-ONE

THE VIEW FROM HERE

In 2008, I made a documentary called *Too Fat, Too Young* in which I met young people struggling with obesity. I also re-visited my own past—the Beaumont Leys estate, Babington Community College, even Charles Keene, where I watched a video of myself, huge and unmissable, bounding about on stage.

It was both immensely painful—more than I'd expected—and positive. It made me realise how much my past contributed to who I am today, and to my success. I suffered the worst kind of bullying as a child. It was whispered, discreet and far more personal than a public display of humiliation; it was hidden pokes and pinches that couldn't be told.

The truth is that that lost, insignificant fat boy will never leave me. I am sure the bullies had no idea that when they poked, pinched and called me names it would stay with me forever. After they had left me to cry, alone and unloved, they didn't consider what damage they had done. But today I thank them. For without the jibes and hate, I wouldn't be the person I am today.

I'm still painfully sensitive to criticism and ridicule even though I've taught myself to live it down. I still worry about gangs and walking down the street alone. I still worry about not being liked. That might seem ridiculous but sometimes, even now, I find it hard to believe that I'm successful, despite all the evidence to the contrary. When I'm watching TV or listening to the radio and they mention this Gok Wan person, it feels as if he isn't real. It feels like they're talking about a fantasy version of me, the television creation.

I'm not just that person—I hope I'm more than that. I think that person is great, and I'm very proud of him and what he has achieved. But off screen, I'm just me—a normal boy, who has friends, goes shopping, goes partying, eats and drinks sometimes a bit too much, but come on, I'm a council estate boy who drank cider on the swings at fifteen! Even if it doesn't make sense to other people, I like watching football and drinking a can of lager as much as I love hitting the shops with my girls. I can't be anything different from what I am.

Sometimes all the fame and celebrity feels as though it's just on loan. That it isn't really mine. And it might all go away one day. If it does, I'll still be proud of how far I've travelled and what I've done. The reality is, I know I could have easily ended up at the bottom of the pile, daydreaming my life away, but I decided a long time ago I wanted more from life than to just get by.

I never set out to be a celebrity. I wanted to be an actor so that I could hide and be anyone else but me. All I ever wanted was to be happy in my skin and with myself, and I think I've almost achieved that. I've accepted that my scared, vulnerable, bullied self will always exist alongside my confident, successful, outgoing self—and I think I'm happy with that. In fact, without both elements, I wouldn't be as good at my job.

*   *   *

308

People who know about my past always want to know how I became thin. Now you know I did it in one of the worst ways possible. I am not ashamed I starved myself because I have learned to deal with my regrets. But I will never forgive myself for scaring my family.

Am I cured? I'm not sure. In many ways, I am better. I've accepted my complex relationship with food and learned to live with it. But anorexia is insidious. It never goes away and it has come back to visit me several times over the years, when I've felt low, out of control, lacking in confidence and a failure. I've managed to beat it each time but it's always lurking, waiting to pounce on me and pull me back into its grip.

Sometimes, just before I go to sleep, a thought floats into my mind . . . *Tomorrow, I'll start my diet* . . . and that's the danger signal. That alerts me to be on my guard. The truth is, many battles are over but the war is not yet won. I don't know if it ever will be. But with the strength I have found over the years I am now able to fight it.

The whole area of food and my weight is difficult for me because I am a person who has changed my body and yet I ask women to accept themselves the way they are. I will always struggle with the fact that this is a contradiction. But no matter what my own problems have been, I firmly believe that you've got to embrace who you are as a person. You do not need to lose weight because you look in a magazine and see a woman who is airbrushed, re-touched, underweight and on a catwalk. And I know that because I've been on both sides of the fence. There's no point in losing weight and becoming addicted to the gym if you don't understand the person you are. You can never be happy that way. Accepting who and how you are and resolving to make the most of that person is the key. I truly believe that.

Today, I've found my stride. I know what I'm good at, I've grown in confidence and I'm beginning to be the person I've always wanted to be. I'm pleased with my relationships, and I've never felt that way before. The last ten years have been amazing and I couldn't have done it without the sources of strength in my life. My friends are crucial. While it's true that these days I do get invited to some glitzy affairs and big celebrity bashes, I'm still the guy who likes to hang out with his friends, and I couldn't live without the love and support of my best mates (you know who you are). Evening drinks by the river, chatting for hours and eating dim sum in Soho are some of the things I live for. Thank you.

I am now thirty-five. I have friends for life I will always love, respect, depend on and, more importantly, trust. You are my sight when life has blinded me and you are my touch when I am numb. Thank you for allowing me to be the person I have become.

My other great source of strength is, of course, my agent, Carol. I could go on for chapters about how much I owe her, but she wouldn't like that. Carol has looked after me so well over the last ten years. She's my protector, my personal Rottweiler and my guardian angel. She manages my career, negotiates my deals, keeps the media at bay and is always looking out for me. She is the first person I talk to when I'm panicked about work and she can always reason with me and sort things out. She knows me so well and I trust her completely. I talk to her about everything, we argue all the time, but she always talks me round because I know she truly cares about me and I have such respect for her judgement.

All I want to know is where we are going next on this exciting journey of ours . . . ! *Lilililililililili!*

*   *   *

This brings me to my greatest source of strength—my beloved family. Once, on holiday in Singapore, I missed my family so much that I had four small tattoos, little stick figures to represent each one, done on the inside of my right arm, each expressing a facet of their character. In a strange way it allows me to be forever young.

On the right is Kwok-Lyn, my amazing brother, who shares my sense of humour, accepts me exactly as I am and is my oldest friend. He is my safe place. I know that life has only just begun, but I am not afraid of what it may ask of me because I know Kwok-Lyn will always be there to shield me when I am scared. I'm so proud of what he has achieved, and I adore his family, Lisa and their beautiful daughters—there is space reserved for my nieces Maya and Lola in my family tattoo, ready for when they're older.

Next to him is Oilen, my sister . . . well, my love for her is overpowering at times. I care so much about what she thinks. In 2008, *The Times* asked Oilen and me to do a piece called 'Relative Values', and after much discussion we agreed. The journalist asked about growing up on the estate, being mixed race, fat and of course about my being gay. It was strange listening to Oilen speak about me, but also moving. She called me kind and caring, and said how worried she'd been about me when I went through my hardest times. She said: 'He's like a spot of glue—he's the physical link that binds us all together.'

It was like I'd been waiting for those words my whole life. I'm proud of Oilen, her work, her cleverness, her spirit, and proud to be her baby brother. Our bond is unique.

*   *   *

Then there are my parents. Dad on the far left, and Mum on his right. Writing this book has reminded me what we have all been through and how much I owe them. Mum is the most non-judgemental person in the world. She never says you are wrong, her door is always open and she will always listen and advise, but only if you want it: if not, she will simply listen. In my eyes she has the gift of love. She is the centre of my world.

Being able to give something back to my parents has meant so much to me. Dad is nearly seventy now, and he and Mum were still working six days a week in the chippy. At last, I've been able to make a huge difference to their lives—I've been able to pay off their mortgage, so they can finally retire. They are still totally in love and only happy when they are together, and it's now time they celebrate their love without distraction.

What I have—all of it—is down to my parents, to my family and their support. They have been with me through thick and thin. I'm so happy that I can do this for them after everything they've done for me.

Dear Daddy,

I never realised that one day you would be the one person I would find it hardest to tell 'I love you'. It's not because I love you any less than when I relied on you as a child, it's perhaps because I am afraid one day you will not hear me. You and I are one. I think, behave, shout and laugh like you. I know one day I'll have your toothless smile. You have always called me 'Babe' and that name has protected me. When my life is tough and I feel out of control, I know I have somewhere to hide and leave my stress behind me. That place is in your heart. Thank you. I will always vividly remember picking blackberries with you on the rally. It didn't matter we lived on the estate; you managed to find me somewhere safe to play. Daddy, I know it was hard for you to find time for your family because the restaurant needed you as much as we did, but I need you to know it's okay. You did what you had to do to make a life for us; we never wanted for anything, and it was your hard work that did that. I missed you but I understand. I so fondly remember you

313

kicking the ball into the sky so high, it seemed to get lost in the clouds. In my eyes, my dad is the best footballer in the world. I remember going to work with you aged six, dressed in my tuxedo, my hair slicked to one side with handfuls of your Brylcreem. It felt amazing to look like you.

There is something I've never told you. When I was young I would sometimes go into your and Mum's bedroom, close the door and open your jewellery box. I would sit on the stool facing the big round mirror, put on your rings and pretend I was you. I would watch myself in the mirror, hold my hands to my face and imagine myself as you when I grew up. It was the safest place in the world. I know I've not been the perfect son and I know sometimes you've looked at my life and been concerned about my choices but I want to thank you for always allowing me to make my mistakes. It's that support which makes you the best dad in the world. Daddy, you will always be my hero. I love you.

ACKNOWLEDGEMENTS

Firstly, so many thanks must go to my family . . . without you, I wouldn't have a story to tell. Your undying support and guidance has allowed me to have a life I am not only proud of but also one I now wouldn't change. You are my everything; my first thought in the morning and my last thought at night. I could not exist without you and writing this book has reconfirmed just how much you mean to me. I will love you forever and longer, and even longer than that. Thank you.

My friends . . . I regard our friendships as our greatest successes. I would not have all I have today without each and every one of you. We have partied for hours, laughed for days, loved for years and I know we will be friends forever. Thank you.

Carol . . . what can I say? Who would have thought we would have got this far? You have shown me friendship and support without compromise. Thank God I found you. Maybe it was destiny . . . maybe it was fate . . . Whatever brought us together, I am grateful it did, Bubala! Thank you.

Sue Murphy and all at Channel 4 . . . Thank you for believing in me even when I didn't. Your vision and nurturing have made me the most confident and happy I have ever been. You have given me a home and a place where I can exist in harmony. Thank you.

Ebury . . . As you know I was unsure whether I would ever get to this stage. When we first met, I doubted whether I had the courage, skill or story to write this book: thank you for convincing me otherwise. This has been such a wonderful journey of self-discovery that has allowed me to put so many of my demons to rest. Thank you.

Kirsty . . . well . . . thank you. I could not have done this had you not been involved. I know you have felt my pain and cried my tears and I am so grateful you did. You have not only shaped my paragraphs, corrected my spelling and made sense of my confusion, you have edited your way into my heart forever.

ALL THE PRODUCTION CREWS I HAVE EVER WORKED WITH . . . Thank you, for your knowledge, dedication, loyalty and support. Without every single one of you I would not have had the opportunities and experiences that have made my life so rich and full. Thank you.

My viewers . . . Your continued support and loyalty have not only kept me going when I thought I couldn't, you have also played a major role in repairing the confidence of a lonely, fat and insecure boy from Leicester. Had you not tuned in and believed in me, then who knows where I would be today?

I love you all so very much.
Kowkhyn/Babe/Gok/Auntie Gok
x

CHIVERS
LARGE PRINT
−direct−

If you have enjoyed this Large Print book
and would like to build up your own
collection of Large Print books, please
contact

Chivers Large Print Direct

Chivers Large Print Direct offers you
a full service:

• Prompt mail order service

• Easy-to-read type

• The very best authors

• Special low prices

For further details either call
Customer Services on (01225) 336552
or write to us at Chivers Large Print Direct,
FREEPOST, Bath BA1 3ZZ

Telephone Orders:
FREEPHONE 08081 72 74 75